HOPE
IS
CHANCEY

HOPE
IS
CHANCEY

9

KAY DEW SHOSTAK

Kay Dew Shostak

August South
PUBLISHING

To Dee Dee —
There is always
Hope!
Love, Kay

ISBN: 978-1-7350991-3-2

SOUTHERN FICTION: Women's Fiction / Southern Fiction / Railroad / Bed & Breakfast / Mountains / Georgia / Family Fiction/ Small Town Fiction

Text Layout and Cover Design by Roseanna White Designs
Cover Images from www.Shutterstock.com

Author photo by Susan Eason with www.EasonGallery.com

Published by August South Publishing. You may contact the publisher at:
AugustSouthPublisher@gmail.com

Dedicated to Linney E. Dew
The best Daddy ever

CHARACTER LIST

Jackson and Carolina Jessup – Moved to Chancey one year ago. Operate Crossings, a bed-and-breakfast for railfans in their home. They have three children: Will, 22; Savannah, 16; Bryan, 13. Will married Anna after the move and they have a new daughter, Frances. Carolina also runs the bookstore side of Blooming Books.

Jackson's family – Mother Etta lives at the beach in South Carolina. Father Hank is married to Shelby and lives in Kentucky. Two brothers, Emerson and Colt. Emerson is the oldest, and he and his wife have three daughters and live in Virginia. Colt is the youngest, is single, and moved to Chancey with his girlfriend Phoenix.

Carolina's family – Parents Goldie and Jack live in Tennessee. Carolina is an only child.

Missus Bedwell – Lifelong resident of Chancey. Recently widowed.

Peter Bedwell, 45 - lives two doors down from his mother.

Laney and Shaw Conner – Both from Chancey. Shaw owns an automotive dealership. Laney partners with Carolina in the B&B. They have three children: twins Angie and Jenna, 17; Cayden, 8 months.

Susan and Griffin Lyles – Susan is sister to Laney and manages the Lake Park. Griffin and Susan are currently separated. They have three children: Leslie, 19; Susie Mae, 15; Grant, 13. Laney and Susan's mother is Gladys Troutman.

Gertie Samson – She has one child: Patty, 28, married to Andy Taylor. Gertie was raised in Chancey and returned after her daughter, Patty, settled there. She owns a lot of property in town. She lives in the house she, Patty, and Andy run their businesses out of.

Ruby Harden – Owns and runs Ruby's Café on the town square. Lifelong Chancey resident.

Libby Stone – Works with Ruby at the café and is married to Bill Stone. Daughter is Cathy.

Cathy Stone Cross – Libby and Bill's daughter is married to Stephen Cross, a teacher at the high school. They have a young son, Forrest.

Kendrick family – Moved to town for father Kyle to open new Dollar Store where he hired Anna Jessup as Assistant Manager. Wife Kimmy and their four children live in Chancey. Kyle's daughter, Zoe, from a previous marriage lives with Kimmy and cares for the younger three children.

Shannon Chilton – Operates florist part of Blooming Books. Lifelong Chancey resident. She's 30 and recently ended a relationship with Peter Bedwell.

Bonnie Cuneo – Works in Blooming Books. Retired teacher who lives in Laurel Cove with husband, Cal.

Alex Carrera – Opening new restaurant on Main Street called AC's. He and his girlfriend, Angie Conner, live above it.

Happy New Year, and welcome to Crossings!

Or should I say, "Happy New Year! Welcome to Crossings B&B"?

Jackson here, and I'm thinking we should call our house, not just the B&B, Crossings. Sounds good, doesn't it? Although we're not exactly at a real railroad crossing like people might imagine. Hmm, I never thought about that. We've got the railroad bridge, and the driveway is a crossing. This is new, having time to really think about things here. Not being on the road feels like a whole new life, being here day in and day out. I'm not saying it's been easy all the time. This place is more like a busy railroad station than a simple crossing. I'm glad my office is downstairs so I'm out of the fray.

In just the month I've been working down there, we've had my ex-almost-sister-in-law living in the Orange Blossom Special room, which set my brother Colt off. Luckily, Phoenix is now living in her own home down in town. Not so luckily, she hired us, Colt and me, to finish the remodel. Also no longer living here are the Bainbridges, a brother-and-sister team of gossips and hoarders who filled up my basement with their boxes of stuff while their house was fumigated. Good riddance to them and their junk!

Still with us is Silas Pendersen. Kind of strange having a movie star living here, but he seems like a good enough guy. I guess he's officially courting Susan Lyles. Of course, seems like real old-fashioned courting shouldn't start until her divorce is final, but then what do I know about stuff like that? Carolina thinks there's still a chance for Susan to get back to-

gether with Griffin, but he seems pretty happy up in his golf club mansion. He's offered to teach me how to golf now that I'm home more, and I think you can see the railroad from a big part of the course up there, so I might think about it. Especially since Bryan is still enjoying being a caddy there.

I thought I'd get more time with the kids now that I'm home, but they don't seem to be here much. Savannah is a senior, so I expected her to be gone a lot, but Bryan is never here either. Will is the one I'm seeing more of since he's left his job at the dealership and is working with me and Colt in the new business. Of course he's also pretty busy being a new dad. Baby Francie is only a couple weeks old, but she sure is fun. I don't feel old enough to be a grandpa, but then I guess no one asked me.

I'm glad I had the extra time to write this down, catch you up on things. All right, I haven't mentioned the mayor's race yet, have I? Honestly that's the real reason I'm writing this. Missus and Laney both wanted to write this note to y'all, but they can't keep their begging for votes to a reasonable level. They are both like runaway trains with this election, which is only a few weeks away now, thank goodness! Everyone kept wanting someone else to jump in the race, but you know, no one else did. I'm thinking it takes special folks to want that badly to be in charge of things—and not many are that special, if you know what I mean...

Now I know there's lots more going on in Chancey, but I can't recall what you might want to know. Guess I should've had Carolina write me some notes. If you want to know about what trains were running back twenty years ago or how to build a railroad *bridge, I'm your guy, but all that other stuff? Not so much.*

So have a good one and see you at the open house later. Maybe I'll have my welcome figured out by then.

Jackson

Chapter 1

"Ricky's been more help than you this morning. Get off the couch." I prod my daughter, who is curled up on one end of the couch, turned completely away from the pregame show on the television. "Kickoff is at noon and folks will be getting here soon."

Savannah rolls over. "I did everything you wanted yesterday. This is too early to have a party."

"I obviously don't make the bowl game schedule." I fall down on the other end of the couch and mute the television. The silence feels almost as good as the soft cushions. "Having a New Year's Day open house to watch football sounded good last week for the whole minute and a half I took to think about it."

She mumbles, "Whose idea was this anyway?"

"Your dad's. He's turning into a social butterfly since he's been home so much." Jackson had pretty much been on the road for a year and half, since he took the job with the railroad and we moved from the suburbs of Atlanta to Chancey. He was overseeing a project in South Georgia, which is wrapping up. Last month he started working from home, and then just before Christmas he asked to go part-time so he could start a construction/remodeling business with his brother Colt. He used to complain when we had weekend activities here, even though Crossings B&B was originally his idea. Now, however, he's all, "The more, the merrier!"

I push Savannah's legs toward the edge of the couch. "Get up. You need to do a quick check on the bathrooms to make sure they're ready for company."

"Morning, Savannah. Carolina. I'm going for a quick run," our resident movie star, Silas Pendersen, greets us as he jogs into the living room. He starred in a made-for-TV movie filmed in Chancey in the fall and hasn't left. He thinks he fell in love with my friend Susan Lyles. She's still married, but that isn't keeping her from wearing the engagement ring Silas gave her right before Christmas. He stretches his arms as he heads to the front door. "What time does your party begin?"

I get up. "Soon. The Georgia game kicks off at noon. Then there are games all day, though I figure most people will want to be here for the beginning of that game specifically."

He looks at the clock above the television. "I'll probably miss the beginning, but I'll be back not too long after that." He waves and then jogs out, closing the big, wooden door behind him.

I pull on Savannah's arm until she also stands, and I push her toward the B&B hall and bathroom. I do another check of the kitchen, where chili is heating up in the Crock-Pot. I'll move it onto the dining room table later, where all the bowls, plates, crackers, and drinks are set up. Our guests are bringing desserts to share, so half the table is empty for them. I can't believe how hard I found entertaining when we moved here. Of course maybe it was so hard because I fought everything about this place tooth and nail. In my defense, the folks in Chancey *were* pretty pushy.

"Hello! We're here!" Laney calls from the front door.

Speaking of pushy...

Red and black greet me as I step into the living room. Laney, Shaw, and baby Cayden are standing there, all wearing Georgia-red button-up shirts and black jeans. Well, Laney is wear-

14

ing a straight black skirt and boots. "We left our coats in the car since it's so warm. Figured it would save you space." She looks around. "Are we the first to arrive?"

"Yes, you beat Missus. I know that's all you care about."

Shaw plops down in one of the wing chairs next to the fireplace, in perfect alignment for seeing the television. "I'm here early to get the best seat in the house." He arches up and reaches into his back pocket, pulling out a silver flask. "I'm all ready for the game." His grin crumbles when Laney drops his son into his lap.

"Here's *his* bottle. I have to talk to Carolina for a minute." She grabs my arm and propels me into the kitchen.

Over my shoulder I tell Shaw, "Jackson is out back getting the fire pit ready. I'll tell him you're here, but I know he'll be inside in time for the kickoff."

Shaw hollers back, "Don't bother him. I've got my boy, both our bottles, and the remote control. I'm good!"

"What time did you get home?" Laney asks as she bustles around to the French doors to look out back. "You were still out there dancing when we left. Can't believe our babysitter had to be home by one. What happened to the good old days when grandmothers stayed home on New Year's Eve to watch their grandkids and let the young folk have a fun night out?"

"Speaking as a grandmother now myself, grandmas just wanna have fun. It was close to two by the time we got home, and of course, since I'd been thinking about all this today and everything from last night, I barely slept. My chili smells good, though. I'm using F.M.'s recipe." I stir the Crock-Pot and wait.

My friend turns around, her eyes on fire. Her dark hair is still big, even in her new, shorter style, and her lipstick matches her shirt perfectly. Her purple-blue eyes, though, are her most striking feature, especially when she's got them made up like she does today. She managed to hold off on the false lashes while she was "simplifying" in the fall, but now they are back with a vengeance, complete with layered shadow and thick eye-liner. "Well? Was he?"

"Was he who? Grab the cord so I can take this into the dining room." I lift the Crock-Pot and carefully head to the dining room table. She grabs the cord and follows me.

"Peter!" she demands.

"Yes?" comes a deep voice from the living room. "You need something, Laney?" Peter asks as he steps inside the door. He has on a long, dark gray overcoat. Around his neck is a crimson scarf with the Harvard H sticking out on the end. He's carrying a bottle of champagne and steps to the side to let his fiancée enter. She's carrying a tray of éclairs topped with a decadent, glossy chocolate frosting.

"Happy New Year!" Delaney says as she comes inside. "The chocolate was still wet, so I couldn't put any wrap on them. Where should I sit these?"

Shaw peers up over the edge of the silver platter. "Right here by me would be perfect!"

Delaney laughs and bends down to offer him one. "Help yourself."

"Thank you. Those look delicious," I say. "You can sit them on the dining room table. Did you make them?"

Peter speaks up. "Yes, she did. Queen of the ball in the evening, master of the kitchen in the morning. What can't this woman do?"

Delaney flushes and smiles as she moves toward me and Laney. "I enjoy baking, that's all."

Laney's eyes are narrowed, but I can see the tray is tempting her. I cave and grab an éclair. "These are so light. And that chocolate..." I take a bite and swoon. "Now you've spoiled me for donut shop éclairs!"

Delaney smiles, then looks down to unbutton her coat. She's wearing a long, camel-hair coat and, underneath, jeans with a black sweater. Up close I can see she's tired, but she takes a deep breath and smiles at me. "Thank you, and thank you for coming last night."

"Thank you for inviting us." I reach for her coat, but Laney grabs it first.

"Let me take it. I'm sure Carolina has other things to do. We appreciated being invited last night too. Such a big crowd. So many different people!"

Delaney frowns a bit. "My parents like to entertain. They love having a big crowd. I can take my coat. Peter, want me to take yours?"

Peter lays it on the couch without missing a beat of his conversation with Shaw. He consequently misses the evil look Laney gives him as she rushes over to scoop up his coat. "Here, Delaney, I'll show you where we're putting them." She puts out an arm to guide Delaney, then turns back to me. "Where are you putting the coats?"

"On the bed in the Southern Crescent room." I watch the two women head toward the B&B wing. The New Year's Eve gala to celebrate the engagement of Delaney LaMotte and Peter Bedwell was the fanciest party I'd ever been to. It was at a Southern mansion turned event venue down toward Atlanta. There was a retired senator and other notables, but the less notable people caused the most interest. The most interest and the most questions.

Questions Laney is hopefully getting answers to on her way to put away coats.

There's not a better person for the job.

CHAPTER 2

"What are you doing hiding over here?" I say to Colt, who is sitting on the living room stairs, just above the landing. "Can you even see the TV?"

"Some. Just seems kind of crowded over there." He nods in the direction of the living room, and he's right. It is crowded.

I sit on the stair below the landing, where the TV can't be seen at all, but it feels good to sit down. Besides, Georgia has the game well in hand. There's another bowl game on another station, but the preponderance of black and red here means we won't be turning the channel until this one is over. "Did you have some chili?"

"Not yet." My brother-in-law stares in the direction of the television, but that's not what he's watching. Phoenix stands next to the fireplace, although it's not lit today since the weather's been so unseasonably warm.

I doubt Colt has been any farther than these steps since he came in the front door. He wasn't at the engagement party last night. He said it wasn't his kind of thing, but I wonder if that would've been true if he still had Phoenix on his arm. She was there. Oh, she was most definitely there.

Today she's wearing a plain blue shirt and jeans with her hair in a ponytail. Last night she was all flame. Her skin-tight dress was the color and sheen of fire. Her red hair was down and sleek. She is tall without heels, but last night she had on sky-high pumps. There's just something about a woman who comes to a fancy party alone. Like the villain in a James Bond movie.

I'm not exactly saying she's a villain. I mean, we don't really know that. Yet.

"Come with me." I pull on Colt's arm, and we stand together. "You need to eat." I don't let him go until we are in the kitchen and I have found a beer to put in his hand. Spotting Jackson out back, I open the door and push him out that way. "Go out there. I'll bring you a bowl of chili in a minute." Following him onto the deck I take a deep breath. It smells so fresh out here. Some of the kids have a football game going on down the hill, on a flat patch just past my dead garden. It actually looks best this time of year, when it looks like everyone else's garden instead of a weed-filled square of choked vegetables. But this year... this year it'll be better. I mean, maybe...

"Here you are!" Susan comes up behind me carrying an extra-large bottle of water. "How did you pull all this together today? I'm dying." She collapses into one of the deck chairs. "Y'all didn't leave until we did last night."

"What's with you showing up last night with Griffin?"

She lifts a shoulder clad in red. Her turtleneck has a cute G on the neck. Cute, but on me it would be bent in half. You need a long, thin neck to carry that off, and Susan has a long, thin neck, along with a long, thin body. She seemed so country when I first met her, but now... now she's polished, grown-up. Except when it comes to her and Silas making out like teenagers. Yep, she's still wearing his engagement ring. I nod at it. "Seriously. What's Griffin think about that?"

"He didn't say. We went together because Delaney's father is on the board of Mountain Energy, and since we both work for Mountain Energy, we thought it was a good idea. Besides, Silas didn't want to go." A frown crosses her face.

"Why not?"

She shakes her head. "He said he's done with big parties like that. He's ready to just be at home when he's not on a shoot."

I cross my arms and pull them tight against me. "I don't know what you think you're doing. Your kids have to be confused. I mean, everyone else is!"

Closing her eyes, she lays her head back against the cushion. "I didn't come here to be lectured. My head hurts and I'm tired."

"Fine. I'm going to get Colt some chili." I move past her, but she grabs my hand and pulls me back a step.

"Speaking of Colt..." She looks around until she spots him on the lawn. "So, has anyone figured out what happened with Phoenix last night?"

"No, and I'm about ready to just ask her."

That wakes Susan up. "You wouldn't!"

"Probably not. But there has to be some explanation for the police looking for her and her leaving like that." I stretch to look in the back doors, where she's still in the living room. "She doesn't act like anything's wrong."

Susan drops my hand, lays her head back again, and recloses her eyes. "Well, if you find out, you know where I am."

She's just a bit too laid back for my taste now. She used to be all energy and ideas. She made me look put together. Now she's like, well, like a cat. A cat that's been into the cream. A lazy, satisfied cat just so happy with herself.

Now I wonder who else is that happy this morning: Silas or Griffin?

I made batches of chili a couple of other days this past week, so I take one of those bowls out of the fridge and pop it into the microwave. I'll heat it, then add it to the lowering level in the Crock-Pot. While it's heating I peruse the table and see that it looks fine, well-stocked with crackers, jalapeños, shredded cheese, several dips and salsas, and tortilla chips. The best thing about arriving in Chancey totally inept at throwing parties is that everyone helps out. They fill empty garnish containers, search for more cups, carry out full bags of trash, all without me asking. There's a talent to attracting control freaks who will take care of things for you. Let's just say I'm very talented in attracting control freaks—and I've learned how to make it work for me.

Looking at the table and kitchen, I'm also keeping an eye out for Laney. I haven't had a chance to talk to her since she went down the B&B hall with Delaney to put away her and Peter's coats. Part of her getting answers, the important part, is telling me. I scoop up a Styrofoam bowl of chili for Colt, sprinkle some cheese on it, and stick a spoon in. Grabbing a handful of saltines, I look once more around the room. We took down the Christmas tree to give us more space for the party Other than that all the Christmas decorations are still in place. I'm ready for them to be gone, back in hiding for another year.

But I don't see Laney.

The deck is more crowded than it was when I went inside. We're lucky it's such a nice day and folks can be outside; there are really a lot of people here, a nice mix of newcomers, Chancey folk, and some from Laurel Cove. Add to that all the kids running around, and it's getting pretty hectic. But it's the last big shindig of the holidays. I'm ready for a nice, quiet January spent playing with my new granddaughter. That little family is staying home today, and I miss them. Okay, I miss Francie. Will and Anna have become just her ride to Grammy's.

"Here you go," I say, handing the bowl to my brother-in-law.

"Where's mine?" the mayor asks.

"Inside on the table, Jed. Wait—you're no longer mayor, right? As of today?"

The big man with the red hair, round face, and wide grin nods. "Yep! Just call me Principal Taylor. Been over at the high school getting my office all set up."

Between bites Colt asks, "So, who's mayor until the election?"

Jed shrugs. "Nobody really. Council takes care of things most of the time anyway."

I laugh. "Don't tell Laney or Missus that. I think they're ready to be handed a crown, a scepter, and absolute power. Yet I haven't heard either one of them put forth a platform or even a single concrete idea."

Jed plunges his hands into his pant pockets. He's wearing a baggy pair of old jeans and a long-sleeve button-up shirt with a fleece vest over it. "Yeah, I know they think it's a glamour job with a lot of power, but it's really not. As for them not having a platform, I don't think they've even considered that. It's just a popularity contest for those two. Glad I'm out of it." He looks over at Colt again. "That chili looks mighty good. Can I get anyone else anything?"

"Couple more crackers," Colt mumbles, his mouth full. Jed nods at him and lifts his eyebrows at me as he turns.

"No, thanks. I'm headed back inside myself in a minute." As Jed ambles off, it dawns on me that even if he wasn't there last night, Colt might know more about Phoenix and the police than anyone else. "So, you and Phoenix still not talking much?"

He shakes his head, concentrating on chewing, then grumbles, "Beats all, don't it? I bring her here and she dumps me. Opens a business, rents a house, then hires me to fix it up for her? I get mad, and then I get confused about how it all happened, and then I forget to be mad. Besides…" He puts another spoonful in his mouth, and I wait. "Besides, Mom tried to warn me. Everybody tried to warn me." He tips his head and looks straight at me. "You think she used me?"

Oh! I'm supposed to be asking questions, not answering them. "Phoenix? Use you? Why, I don't know. She is kind of, well, different. Maybe you need someone not quite so, uh, glamourous?" What? How could anyone think the ex-Vegas showgirl who stole a local judge from his long-time wife, then left him to hightail it out of town with the championship high school football coach would use people? Go ahead and roll your eyes. I would be if said football coach wasn't standing right in front of me.

He nods and thinks. "I thought you were going to say 'obvious.' Mom always said she was obvious. I just never thought about what that meant. What do you think it means?"

My voice squeaks. "Obvious?" I look around for some distraction. "Oh, I don't know. Just kind of that she lays it all out there. You know..." I snap back to look at him. No time like the present. "Has she ever been in trouble with the police?"

Now it's his turn to look for a distraction. His mouth is closed tightly and frowning as he scans the backyard. Then he squeezes out, "Not recently."

"But she has been? Could they be looking for her now for anything?"

"There's Jed. I need those crackers." And he's gone just like that.

That was not about crackers.

CHAPTER 3

"Missus wasn't here." The thought pops out of my mouth the same moment it enters my head. I straighten up from where I'm relaxing on the couch. Jackson is on the other end, remote in hand, staring at another bowl game. The only light is from the fireplace, and we are blessedly alone.

My husband doesn't look at me as he says, "I know. Asked Peter and he said she had things to do."

Now, should I be more interested in the fact that Jackson missed Missus and I didn't or that she had something more important to do than come to our party? She and Laney have preened and campaigned at every holiday event since the parade. There were too many voters here for her to miss this and still be alive. "That's all he said?"

"Yeah."

I wait for more, but Jackson just turns up the volume a notch or two. Laying my head back again, I can't believe I didn't miss Missus. Not until this very moment. I mean, there was a lot going on, especially when Georgia tried to give the game away toward the end. Everyone crowded into the living room and the dining room, where we'd plugged in the television from our bedroom. After willing Georgia to win, everyone was exhausted, and folks began leaving. I chatted with Betty Taylor about no longer being Chancey's first lady. She's ecstatic and had no problem unburdening herself of the role. She didn't have many nice things to say about our town. She reminded me of a certain newcomer a couple of years back named Carolina Jessup. All that negativity isn't very attractive, is it? Phoenix avoided me, so I never got to talk to her, and Colt left before the game got close. Peter claimed everyone's attention, something he's getting a little too used to, I think, when he announced he's opening up a law office on the square. He went into detail on the remodeling he's planning to hire an Atlanta firm to do. Felt a bit like he was trying to say Colt and Jackson are too small-time to work for him.

Delaney stayed glued to his side, and I'm having more and more trouble seeing the independent, successful photographer she first appeared to be. She's perfecting that tilted-head, looking-upward stance of a dutiful politician's wife. It's not very attractive, but you don't get in much trouble that way.

I lift my phone off the end table and turn it back on. I was tired of talking to people when I sat down; plus I planned to doze a bit. A couple of thank-you texts pop up, and I answer those, but there's still nothing from Laney. Every time I cornered her at the party, she shook her head at me and whispered, "Later." Well, darn it, it's later!

I text her: "Want to talk?" Then I go to Facebook to find our party splashed all over my newsfeed. That's why there were so many people here. I am not one of those hosts who likes to rub folks' noses in their not being invited, but I know some people can't wait to do that very thing, so we just invited everyone we could think of. Maybe I'll become more used to throwing parties and become more blasé about hurting people's feelings, but I sure hope not.

Missus has liked all the pictures and even commented on some of them, but when folks respond that they missed her, she either says nothing or responds with a smiley face emoji. Then I see she's posted a picture of some luggage in front of a long staircase. Looks like the staircase in the new wing she and F.M. built for Anna and Will. "Oh no! Listen to this!" I jerk toward Jackson. "Missus posted this a bit ago: 'I had a nice, quiet afternoon to move out of the bedroom I shared with my beloved husband, F.M., for over fifty years. My son wants it for his new bride. Although, has a wedding date even been set?'"

Jackson mutes the TV. "What? She put that out there for everyone?"

"Yes! Oh my word. Missus has declared war."

"Are you going to respond to it?"

"Looks like everyone is scared to. I mean, if you say anything bad about Peter, she could change her mind and then nail you for that later. Mention the wedding that everybody is already talking about not having a date? Mention F.M.? There are only two likes, and those are people I don't know. I bet everyone is like me—no idea what to do." I look back at the phone. "Some-body's typing... No way! It's Peter and he says, 'Mother, you know I hired professional movers to help you in the morning. Let me know if you want me to cancel them. By the way, you missed a wonderful party.'"

Jackson and I stare at each other. He shakes his head, then turns back to the game and unmutes it.

The idea of Missus and the new Peter teaming up was dis-concerting. However, a full-out war has me even more unset-tled. Missus meeting her match is scary enough—but them living together? Delaney might want to reexamine her options.

We do have rooms open.

My phone rings. "It's Laney," I say as I get off the couch and head toward the B&B hall. It's empty because Silas, our only guest, went out with some folks from the party. "Hey," I barely get to say before she unloads.

"She's going for the sympathy vote! Poor, poor Missus. Her son is kicking her out of her bedroom. And can you believe her invoking F.M.'s name like that? We all know he'd probably vote for me anyway. He knew how power hungry she could be. I wouldn't put it past her that this is something she and Peter have worked up together. They are still thick as thieves, believe you me!" She pauses. "Well? Aren't you going to say anything?"

"I'm just getting settled into the window seat of the Orange Blossom Special room. Jackson is watching a game, so I came in here to talk. Besides, I couldn't get a word in edgewise with you. Who knows what's up with Missus? I didn't even realize she wasn't here today until just a bit ago. I do agree, though, that there's every chance she's not really mad at Peter. I think that's why no one is saying anything. Too scared." I put her on speaker so I can scroll through Facebook, catching up on things while we talk.

"Yeah, I bet that's it. So about Delaney." She's thinking, so I let her think while I see if Delaney has a Facebook page. She finally says, "About Delaney, well, I like her. I don't want to like her, but she seems pretty decent. Pretty normal. What I can't figure out is why she wants to get tangled up with the Bedwells."

"Maybe she's actually in love with Peter."

"Puh-leese. Have you ever seen two people less in love? No, I guess I don't mean *less* in love because I can name at least two couples who actively despise each other. Maybe it's more like 'less interested.' I mean, she seems interested in him—not in love, but interested. He acts like she's something he's bought. You know, 'Here's my new car. Isn't it lovely? Don't you wish you had one?'"

"Laney!" I burst out laughing. "You're too much." I sigh. "Too much, but right. That's exactly how it feels. Which is sad. He honestly seemed to *feel* more for Shannon."

"Wait. We're getting too far ahead of ourselves. Back to the engagement party. Where was Peter? Do you think he was really with Phoenix?"

"I want to say no, but that's sure what it sounds like." When it came time to make the formal engagement toast, Delaney, her parents, and Missus were gathered at the front of the room near the band. Yes, a full band. I told you it was fancy. Peter was nowhere to be found; then he came strolling in the front doors. For half a minute he looked startled at his enthusiastic greeting and his future father-in-law loudly calling him to the front. Then he held up his car keys and said, "Car alarm was going off. Must be a short in the electrical system." Then he jogged forward. However, while everyone's attention was on the toast, Laney—ever vigilant—saw Phoenix come in the same front doors. "I don't know what to think except that I miss the old Peter."

"This *is* the old Peter," Laney says. "He was always just a bit above everyone else in town. He didn't have the angry chip on his shoulder like he does now, but he still did as he pleased. Even up to leaving town. Yes, Missus drove him away, but it was just as much F.M.'s goodness that bothered him. F.M. would drag him around to apologize when he misbehaved. Peter would apologize, but you never got the feeling he'd learned anything." She clicks her tongue. "And when he came back and was playing the ghost, it wasn't his dad who knew he was doing it."

"Oh, that's right. I hadn't thought about that." I shoot up a little prayer of thanks that I didn't get any closer to Peter than I did. I came real close to ruining my marriage, and I had no idea who Peter really was. Or at least had the potential to be.

"Maybe he could've changed, but I think he missed that train," Laney says, basically reading my mind. "So, anything on what the police wanted with Phoenix?"

"Colt acted weird when I asked him."

"Colt will fess up when he finds out his girl has already moved on."

"We don't know that."

"Maybe you don't." She yawns. "I've got to go. Cayden's been waking up in the middle of the night here lately. I know why you're supposed to have kids when you're young."

I laugh. "Just being with Francie a few hours reminds me of—" I cut off what I was saying because I hear a loud laugh. A woman's laugh. "Someone's here. I guess I better go see what's going on. You have a good night."

Through another yawn she says the same to me, and we hang up. I hadn't turned on a light when I came back here, so I walk through the darkness, out into the hallway, listening. That's Shannon, I'm pretty sure.

"There she is!" Jackson announces, but his eyes do not look as enthusiastic.

Shannon rushes toward me. "You said it was an open house to watch the bowl games. I guess everyone else came earlier? Silly us." She flings back toward the man she's left standing near the front door. "Danny, I want you to meet my good friend and shop partner, Carolina Jessup."

I meet him in the middle of the room, and we shake hands. He's keeping one eye on the TV. "Nice to meet you, Ms. Jessup. This game is coming down right to the end."

Jackson says, "That it is. Have a seat." Danny steps back and sits in the chair Shaw commandeered this afternoon.

"Can I get you something to drink?" I ask, but Shannon shakes her head.

"No, we're not staying. I just wanted you to be first to know." She beams at me, then looks back at Danny, who is still watching the television. She frowns at him, then turns to me. "We couldn't be here earlier because, well, we got married!"

Jackson glances at me, then stands and steps over to Shannon to hug her. "Congratulations!" As he releases her he stares at me and my lack of manners. I'm frozen in place. Jackson meanders over to Danny, who is still seated, and offers him a hand. Without really looking at him, Shannon's new husband shakes Jackson's hand. Again Jackson turns to me, this time furrowing his brow to get me to move. "Carolina?"

Sure. Yes. I should offer congratulations. I should hug Shannon, shake Danny's hand, and see if we have champagne. That is absolutely what I'm going to do. Right now.

And I do.

Because what I'm thinking... what I'm thinking can wait. It can wait about nine months—maybe more like seven months now.

CHAPTER 4

When Jackson used to be on the road all week, I made sure to not schedule myself to work on the weekends at Blooming Books, the combination bookstore/flower shop I share with Shannon. Now I enjoy being in the shop for at least a little while on Saturdays, our busiest day. Although I'm not sure how busy we'll be on the second day of the year, Gertie Samson's moonshine cave in the basement of Andy's Place has pulled some tourists in from neighboring towns. Towns with more to see, more places to stay, more places to eat. Just more.

This past Christmas was the first time Chancey has tried to, as a whole, lure folks here for the holiday. The Christmas parade and Santa's workshop went well, but there weren't crowds for either. Mostly locals, and you know, I'm kind of fine with that. With more people working from home, we're getting people moving into the area for the lower cost of living and a quieter lifestyle, and as long as they come shop for books and flowers, we'll be okay.

Bonnie opened the store this morning, so it's almost eleven before I head down the hill. It's another warm day—well, warm for winter in the mountains. As I cross the railroad tracks near the square coming into town, it looks busy. Cars are parked around the square and along the line of shops across from it. As I get closer, I can see why. The decorations are coming down.

Those newcomers I mentioned are go-getters. They jumped all over Chancey's rededication to Christmas. Missus got the ball rolling, but Athena Markum and her friends picked up the ball and ran with it. Our signature color, originally for Christmas but now apparently for every day, is Missus Blue. It's pretty, but every day? It's a dusty, medium blue, which Missus wore a lot of as a child. (And does even more now that it's named after her.)

Anyway, the miles of blue ribbons are being rolled up, dried magnolia leaves are being shoved in garbage bags, and metal spools are filling with ropes of tiny white lights and extension cords.

Oh, now that is sad. The square will be dark again. I'm going to miss the lights. I always take our Christmas lights down at home a little at a time so it's not all over at once. But nope, the magnolia wreaths and lights that hung on the old lamp posts are also gone. These energetic thirtysomethings are like locusts—nothing is spared. However, I'm not complaining out loud. I don't want to have to do it.

I park behind our building since all the spots are taken out front. The back door is unlocked, as it usually is during the day, and I walk in. "Hey, y'all. Did you see the square? It's like Christmas never even happened." I can complain here. These people all agree with me. "I wasn't ready for it all to be taken down!"

"Oh," Bonnie says. Bonnie, who is on top of a ladder removing the Victorian angel from the top of our Christmas tree. The sweet tree, which was flocked with fake snow and bedecked in ribbons and lace like an old English fairy tale, but is naked now. "Happy New Year?" she adds somewhat sheepishly.

Our high school part-timer, Susan's daughter, Susie Mae, is sweeping up any remnants of the cotton batting that served as snow in our village scene. I didn't even get to see the little lit

32

houses and church with the real stained-glass windows one last time. It's all gone. Susie Mae frowns. "It is sad, a little bit."

"Well, who knew you two were going to get all sad? I thought it was a good day to get back to normal," Bonnie explains from her vantage point above a stripped tree that can only be described as pitiful. I walk over to the tree and reach up to take the angel from her so she can climb down the ladder using both hands.

"I guess it is a good day for that," I say. "I just wasn't ready. No, it's good to get started on the new year. Clean slate and all that." Holding the regal angel, I look around the big space. Bonnie's magic turned our shop into a Victorian dream based on Charles Dickens's *A Christmas Carol*. "Even the quotes are gone?" She'd hand-lettered quotes from the book, blown them up, outlined them in gold and black, and filled the walls and shelves of the shop with them. "I was thinking we could leave the ones not specifically about Christmas up."

Bonnie arrives back at ground level. "Sure. They were just so dusty. I can bring them back after I take them home and wipe them off, I suppose, although they look a little worse for wear at this point."

"You're probably right. No. It's good to have it all down." Wrinkling my nose I see what she means about the dust. "I always forget about how dirty everything is when all the decorations we've been cleaning around are taken down."

Bonnie points at the packed cartons I'd walked past coming in the back door. "Cal is coming to pick those up later. He's made room in our garage and built new shelves for Mother's decorations. It was good to see them used again."

Bonnie's mother died ten years ago, but they'd not had a good relationship, so Bonnie had shoved everything in a storage unit and left it there until this year. Bonnie and her husband, Cal, went through it all and brought the beautiful Victorian decorations here.

I pat her back. "They were perfect. Thank you for doing all this. Both the decorating and un-decorating." I unbutton my corduroy jacket and shrug it off. "Have we had any customers?"

Bonnie follows me toward the coatrack. "A few. Listen, uh, can we talk for a minute?"

That gets Susie Mae's attention, and she looks at me. Her naturally wide eyes grow even wider. She's one of those teenagers who is always listening, always paying attention. Probably why her blog, *Taking Chances in Chancey*, is so popular. "Sure. Let's step outside. It's nice in the sunshine." I'm afraid I know what Bonnie has to say, and there's no need for everyone to read in the blog about her leaving Blooming Books before I can try and talk her out of it.

Bonnie's interior decorator dreams were rekindled when she was hired to bring Patty and Andy's new house up to date with green glass, tangerine pillows and rugs, and white tulips everywhere. It was phenomenal. I was afraid its success meant she'd be leaving the bookstore, so I hated every bit of it. (Although it was truly amazing.)

Outside the bright sunshine is full of voices from the square. Our sidewalk is busy, but we walk to the corner outside what used to be Peter's Bistro. It's undergoing renovations to become AC's, Chancey's first real restaurant.

"Carolina," Bonnie begins before we reach the corner, "I am sorry about taking the decorations down before checking with you."

"No worries. You know that if you waited on me to be ready to do things, nothing would ever get done. That's why you cannot leave me." I reach out to lay a hand on her arm. "Please say you're not opening your own design company. Unless"—I pull a very pitiful face—"unless you really, really want to."

She smiles, but only half a smile. Bonnie is a retired teacher, so she's very good at not being played by pitiful faces. "Oh, but I do want to. I've spent an inordinate amount of time over the holidays deciding how to go about opening my own design business. It's a dream I've carried around for a long while, and it's high time I made it happen."

"Oh, don't put it like that. I like you. I want you to have your dreams come true, but I want you here with me." Yes, I know I'm begging, and yes, that has always been part of my plan. "What will I do without you?"

"I was hoping you'd say that." Bonnie turns so her face isn't in the sun.

I turn, too, searching that face. "Wait, what? Hoping I'd say what?"

"That you don't want me to leave. That you want me to stay. So here's what I'm thinking."

"Hey, Mrs. Jessup, Mrs. Cuneo. How about some gourmet hot chocolate?" Angie Conner pushes through the doors of the bistro, or AC's, as I've got to get used to calling it. She has two mugs in her hands. "It's so good. Just a touch of chili powder, which doesn't make it spicy, just warmer. I don't have the whipped cream machine ready, but it's still really good."

This conversation with Bonnie is important, but not so important that I'm turning down gourmet hot chocolate. Although I bet I'd even pause it for a packet of Swiss Miss with those pebbles of fake marshmallow and lukewarm water. I'm not that picky when it comes to chocolate.

"Thanks," we both say as we accept our mugs.

Angie beams. "You can take the mugs back to your store with you. I'll pick them up later. Gotta go!" Angie's hair is still dyed black, but her goth makeup looks dramatic instead of cartoonish like it used to. It looks like a choice instead of a declaration of war, which it was when we first moved here. She's turning eighteen next week and announced she was moving in with her boyfriend above the restaurant just before Christmas. Laney and Shaw are still deciding what to do since apparently their daughter didn't listen to them when they forbade her from moving in with Alex.

Kids. What are ya gonna do? You can't live with them, and well, that's about it.

Bonnie and I take tiny sips, judging the temperature of the drinks. "Oh, this is so good," Bonnie says. "So what I'm thinking is that since—"

"Miss Bonnie!" Susie Mae yells from the shop. "Your husband is at the back door. He's loading up the boxes. Do you want me to tell him anything?"

"Tell him I'll be there in a minute," she says loudly. Bonnie doesn't yell, and I can see she's not happy about raising her voice out in public. "Bother!" she exclaims. "Here comes Missus, headed straight for us." She turns to me and leans closer to speed-talk. "I want to open my design business in the back of Blooming Books. I've measured and thought about what I need, and I can work around still managing the bookstore." Switching her mug to her other hand, she grabs my elbow. "Let's go inside and I can show you."

We hustle toward the shop but don't beat Missus, who waits at the door for one of us to open it for her. "Carolina. Bonnie. Are you hawking books on the sidewalk now?"

I pull open the door for Her Majesty. "If that bothers you, then yes, we are. You can't upset me this morning. I just got fantastic news." Missus enters the door while I put an arm around Bonnie's shoulders and squeeze.

Bonnie blushes and also moves inside, straight to the back where her husband waits.

"Hello, Cal," I call to him, then turn to Missus, who is waiting beside our sitting area. She's so full of energy I don't even think about offering her a seat. She's wearing a winter-white coat with blue trim. "Beautiful coat. Is it new?"

"Do not try to distract me, Carolina."

"Okay. You have my full attention." I cross my arms and

wait. She also has Susie Mae's full attention from where she's dusting the bookshelves, so I hope this isn't confidential.

"You need to host a bridal shower for Delaney. I'll pay for everything. It will be top notch. Date, place, menu..." She waves a hand covered in gray suede as she closes her eyes and shakes her head quickly.

"Me? I'm not figuring all that out."

Her eyes snap open. "Of course you're not. I will tell you everything you need to know, but etiquette rules that as the groom's mother I must be behind the scenes."

"I highly doubt etiquette says you should be behind the scenes. I'm pretty sure it says you shouldn't be involved at all." Of course this is a bluff. I have no idea what etiquette says.

"As if I'd leave something this important to you." She rolls her eyes. "No need to feel insulted. I don't know *anyone* I would let do this. The LaMottes' standards are extremely high, and we will rise to them. Do you hear me, Carolina? We will rise to them!"

A look of doubt crosses her face, but she pushes past me toward the door. "I have a campaign to run. Come to dinner tonight and we'll talk more. You can bring Jackson." She leaves the bell ringing in her wake, and after the door settles closed, the shop is quiet.

Susie Mae steps out from behind the bookshelf, her phone in hand. "I know I'm not supposed to be recording people anymore without them knowing, but..."

I shrug. "Good idea. Might come in handy at the murder trial."

Chapter 5

"You didn't say what time," I shout at Missus's back as she marches down the sidewalk. I darted to the door to catch her, but I'm not chasing her. She doesn't look back, just holds up her phone.

"Crazy woman," I mumble, walking back inside and behind the counter where my phone is. Sure enough, I have a text from her saying, "Dinner at five o'clock." Good. I have plans at seven. I shoot Jackson a quick text about dinner as I walk back to where Bonnie and Cal are talking.

Cal is an older man who matches Bonnie well. They both are very efficient and buttoned-up. They give me a kind of old school, upper-class feeling. "So I hear we have a new venture afoot! Good to see you, Cal."

"Good to see you, Carolina. Bonnie told you her idea?" He doesn't look enthusiastic, but I can't tell if that's his normal expression or if Bonnie's being met with resistance.

"Yes. Sounds like it's a good plan for both of us."

Bonnie turns from where she holds a tape measure against the wall. "Here, underneath the stairs is plenty of room for some shelves. My desk will go there and—"

"I'll leave you ladies to it. I'm going to try and get a couple of holes in while this weather holds." Cal turns and leaves through the back door. Bonnie and I stare after him.

"He's not a fan of my new venture. I suppose you can tell?" Bonnie glares at the door as it shuts, then turns to me. "I *am* doing this. Cal will come around or he won't, but it doesn't really matter. He'll be on the golf course anyway."

"I'll help however I can. There is plenty of room back here, isn't there?"

"Maybe some more lighting like the movie crew had in here would help," Bonnie says, looking around. Her eyes stray to the back door, and she sighs. "I wish Cal would be more excited. I've followed him and his job around our whole married life." She whips around to me. "Don't get me wrong. It's been a very good life, and I wouldn't change it. I loved teaching and raising the kids, but decorating was always my dream." She takes a deep breath and smiles at me. "And we're going to make it come true. I have no desires to do anything but a job at a time. Small jobs would be so great and…" She shivers and hugs herself. "I'm just so excited!"

Laughing, I hug her. "Me too. Also I'm glad you're still going to be here. With Jackson at home I'm good being here more. Very good with it." I say with a wink at her. "We'll make it all work out. Why don't I get Jackson and Colt to give us some ideas on lighting and shelves?"

"Would you? That would be wonderful, but I think we better get back up front. Looks like Susie Mae has her hands full."

"Grammy's here with lunch," I announce as I push into the cabin. Anna had said to come on in when I got here. I'd run by Bobby Jack's and brought barbecue sandwiches for the three of us even though it's already almost two o'clock.

"Hey," Will greets me as he strides across to the door. "Those smell good. I'll take them. I know you need your hands free."

Anna is seated on their bed, which takes up one corner of the cabin. She smiles up at me, then looks down at the bundle beside her. "She's just been changed and is ready to play. She knew you were coming."

Leaning over, I hug Anna. "How are you? Exhausting, isn't it?"

She squints up at me. "In some ways it's better than I thought it would be. I mean, I just never knew how much I'd like her."

I bend over the bundle of sweetness, and my fingers tingle, wanting to pick Francie up. "Should I leave her? She seems happy."

Anna laughs. "Oh, pick her up. You're practically vibrating. She's happy most of the time, so go ahead. I'm going to eat, so you can sit here or at the table. Wherever you want."

As my daughter-in-law stands and slowly walks to the table, I slide my hands under the pink-and-white blanket and lift my granddaughter to me. She has brown hair and is just so tiny. She's looking at me, studying me, and then she wiggles and pulls her little fist up to her mouth. I cuddle her and walk around the bed to the window. Her eyes widen at the outside light, then close, but they open quickly. It's a soft day, and as her eyes adjust she keeps them open longer. I've never seen a baby that doesn't love looking outside. My Francie is no different.

"These are delicious, Mom. Thanks," Will says as Francie and I make our way over to the table in the kitchen area where they are eating.

"I figured you were tired of all the home-cooked food I hear everyone's been bringing you."

"Everyone's been so nice. Our Sunday School class putting together that food chart has been amazing. We have so many leftovers… You should take some," Anna says. "But you're right. It's mostly casseroles, so these are perfect."

A frown crosses Francie's face when she hears her mother

talking, and I can't help but grin. "She heard you talking. She's just brilliant, I'm telling you."

Anna laughs. "Now you sound like your son. Like I was saying earlier, I thought I'd love her. You know, like love because she's my baby. But I really think she's fun. I didn't think I'd like her this much. I thought she'd be such a"—Anna scrunches her face—"not a burden exactly, but more of a chore than fun." She rolls her eyes at herself and takes a big bite of sandwich. "Just ignore me. It's probably lack of sleep."

Will gets up. "Can I get you something to drink, Mom? Water, tea? We've got jugs of sweet and unsweet tea someone brought."

"Sure, some tea would be great. I got y'all a new job this morning."

"Colt and Dad?" my tall, lanky son asks as he puts ice in a glass.

"Yep. Bonnie's going to open a little decorating business in the back of Blooming Books."

Anna nods as she chews, then, swallowing, she says, "She did an amazing job on Patty's house. Not my taste, and I'm not sure it's Patty's, but Gertie was paying, so…"

"Exactly. Thanks," I say as I take the glass from Will. Francie is wiggling a bit more, so I bounce my other arm. "You know, when Colt and your dad started this venture, I thought there wouldn't be enough business. Now I'm concerned about you three having time to do your real jobs."

Will and Anna's eyes dart to each other. Anna shrugs, then picks up a potato wedge and takes a bite, clearly leaving Will to do the talking. He clears his throat. "Funny you should say that. We, well, I've been thinking about taking this semester off from school. What with the baby and Anna going back to work in February, it just seems like it would be best if I took some time to get us settled."

I bounce as I walk back toward the window, cooing at Francie and taking a couple of deep breaths. At the window I laugh. "Hate to break it to you, but things don't really settle down once you have a baby." Then I turn. "But I completely understand what you're saying. What would that do to your schedule for graduating?"

He's seated back at the table. "It'd definitely put a wrench in it all—"

Anna interrupts him. "If anything this is the best time *to* go back. I'm on maternity leave until mid-February. You'd have almost half the semester done by then. Your mom is right. It's not going to get any easier later!"

She finishes her statement with a look in my direction, like we're on the same side. "Oh, no," I say. "This is y'all's decision." Francie squawks just once, but it's as good an excuse as any to stop this conversation. "I think she's getting hungry."

Will jumps up from the table and comes to me. "Here, I'll take her." He grabs the thick, crocheted blanket I gave them at their shower, and as he takes his daughter, he wraps it around her. "I think she needs a breath of fresh air. Mom, you didn't even eat."

I touch Francie's little face, burrowed against her daddy's shoulder. "I ate my potato wedges on the drive. Your daddy and I are going to Missus's for dinner at five, so I'm going to leave my sandwich here for y'all."

Will pulls away, and with his long strides, he's at the front door in two steps. "We'll just be a minute."

He leaves and Anna sighs. "I don't want him to stop school."

I take his seat at the table across from her. "I gathered that."

"He would be such a good teacher, and he likes school. He hated selling cars, and I don't want him to ever have to resort to that again." She squeezes out more ketchup to dip her wedges into. "Maybe the remodeling will take off, but maybe it won't. I don't like not having options." Her frown deepens as she runs a piece of potato through the ketchup.

"My son may be a bit too much like his mother. I'm not a good decision maker. I tend to be fine with the status quo. A little too fine sometimes."

"And I like that about you, and him! But honestly..." She sees the surprise on my face, which I didn't remove fast enough. Her mouth pops open, closes, then opens again for her to say, "Sorry."

Okay, I have to laugh. "No, it's just most of the time when you admit something negative about yourself, folks deny it for a bit before they just straight-up acknowledge it!"

"I really am sorry, but we've just been going round and round, and I really think that's his main problem. He's enjoying this. He's completely happy like this with the three of us, but it's not real life. People bringing us food, the weather being warm so the fire is nice, not necessary. Francie being an infant in a cradle next to our bed." She flings out an arm toward the bed and cradle. "We can't live here forever!"

"You're right. I hadn't thought of all that. It's just so sweet here with the three of you, and, well, do you have enough firewood? See, I hadn't even thought of that."

"Peter had a truckload delivered, so I think we're good."

"That was nice of him. Have you seen much of him and Delaney?"

Anna shakes her head. "He's busy opening his new office. I guess I didn't realize he actually had a law degree. Delaney seems nice, doesn't she?"

"Very nice. Your grandmother informed me I'm throwing her a bridal shower. That's why we're having dinner with her tonight. To be told the details."

She laughs. "Grandmissus's favorite kind of meal."

I pat her hand. "Listen. Bring Francie to the house tomorrow so you and Will can have a day out. Spend some time talking, planning for the future. Not just the future around the corner, but five years out. Will may not be great at making decisions, but he's pretty good at planning. He likes to have a plan."

"That's true. It's supposed to be another pretty day. Maybe we can do a picnic or something outside. Oh, I'm excited now."

The front door opens. "She is done with me. Done walking around. Done with everything but her mama!" Francie is not happy. Anna and I stand.

"This is my exit cue." I gather my purse and jacket, then lean over to kiss my grandbaby and give Anna a little hug. "We will see you tomorrow."

"Tomorrow?" Will asks.

"Anna will explain. Love y'all." I give him a hug and then scurry out to give them some privacy. With the closed door against my back, I pause. "Lord bless them," I say, then chuckle. "They sure are going to need it!"

Chapter 6

"Look! I brought Delaney!" I announce as I walk in the side door off Laney's big, wrap-around porch. I pull Delaney into the bright light off the dark porch, and the wide-eyed looks that greet us tell me they didn't get my hurried texts.

The hostess straightens up from where she'd been leaning on her granite island in the middle of her huge farmhouse kitchen. "Welcome. Let me just get another margarita glass." She gives me some wicked side-eye as she walks past.

I ignore her and nudge Delaney ahead of me, farther into the kitchen. "You can put your pocketbook and coat here on this chair. Sorry we're a bit late. I tried texting y'all."

Susan raises her hands. "We've all sworn off phones for the evening. No kids, or men, or—"

Delaney interjects, "Mother-in-laws-to-be?"

There's a quick pause, and then, when there's a burst of laughter, I know I made the right decision.

Beau leans off her wooden stool, holding her hand out. "Beau Bennett. We met at something or other."

Delaney unwraps her scarf. "Oh, I remember *you*! I mean, I am a photographer, and you're a model. You are so photogenic." She laughs. "I went home and googled you, and I have to say, you could still model for Victoria's Secret to this day!"

Beau smooths her hair back as she resettles onto the stool. "I like you. I like you a lot."

Susan rolls her eyes. "Worst part is she's had four kids since then."

Lifting her drink, Beau says, "Another reason to celebrate: I've decided I'm done having babies." She winks at me. "Told Carolina I was wavering a bit back when the movie crew was in town, but that ship has sailed, and I'm having my tubes tied. Laney, where are their drinks so they can toast with me?"

"I had to open a new thing of salt. I rimmed both glasses, hope that's okay." Laney, her gold-and-purple caftan swirling as she hands us our margaritas, stops to look into her unexpected guest's eyes. "I'm so glad Carolina invited you. Make yourself at home. After all, our names are practically the same!"

"Hey, that's true," Susan agrees. "Okay, here's to Beau closing the baby factory and Delaney getting to know us better."

After we clink glasses and I take a sip, I ask, "Are we staying in here? Last time we were out on the porch, and it was so nice. I wish it was warm again."

"I have us in the den. Shaw is upstairs with Cayden. Jenna and Angie are out."

Susan stands and starts walking toward the den. "Where's my lovely niece Jenna?" Lowering her voice she says in an aside to me, "We all know where Angie is."

"I heard that. You're my sister. You're supposed to have my back." Caftan swirling even more, Laney floats past us to get to the den first. The lights are turned low, there's a fire lit, and candles sparkle around the room. The den is small and off to the side of the kitchen. There's a big living room at the back of the house with lots of windows and decking, which leads right out to the pool. It's the house Shaw was raised in, but he and Laney gutted it and remodeled several years ago. Its wide-open, clean look is appealing as always. White walls, shiny wood floors, and lots of windows make up the palette for Laney's simple decorating. As over the top she is in her own style, she's just that sparing with her home. She told me she focuses on comfort, and as I settle into one of the two high-back chairs, each with its own little footstool, I relax for the first time tonight. Delaney sits next to Susan on the loveseat beside the fire.

"Your house is so beautiful," Delaney says as she leans forward, her elbows on her knees. She's wearing brown, low-heeled boots, cream knit leggings, and a brown-plaid flannel shirtwaist dress with a wide leather belt. Her hair is pulled back in pewter barrettes on either side of her face. "This margarita is delicious too."

It gets quiet, and we can faintly hear a television from upstairs and Shaw talking to Cayden. I take another sip, a long one, then speak up. "Okay. So here's the deal with dinner at Missus's tonight."

Smiles appear and Beau says, "Finally!"

"Jackson and I drove separately since I was coming straight here. I got there first, and there were no lights on. None. It wasn't dark yet, but still, it felt weird. We rang the bell, and after a long wait, Missus finally opened the door. She took us into the kitchen, where she had salads from Zaxby's for us."

Only Delaney isn't staring at me with her brow furrowed and mouth half open. She's settled back in the corner of the loveseat concentrating on her drink.

Beau blurts, "No, she didn't!"

"Sure did. She said it was a working dinner, what did we expect?"

Susan asks, "Then why did she say to bring Jackson?"

"Exactly what Jackson asked. She said it was because she didn't think I'd leave him on a Saturday night, but I think she just wanted a witness to how she's being treated."

We all take small glances at Delaney, but she's not taking her focus off her glass, so I continue. "Anyway, we sat at the kitchen table, which, it's a perfectly nice kitchen, but it still felt weird. Especially at night. The big lights are so harsh, it felt like we were being filmed in a studio or something. She didn't need me, or anyone, there, of course. She went over her plans in detail, asking for no input from either of us. Sorry, Delaney, if you didn't already know about your shower." I grimace at her. "Anyway, we ate our salads, and then Jackson stood up and said he was going home."

"That's when we came in," Delaney says as she sets her empty glass on the table beside her. "Peter and I had been out to dinner. A dinner I invited Missus to, but she said she had plans with friends. We could hear voices in the kitchen but couldn't figure out who would be in there."

I grin. "I thought Peter was going to have a stroke when he pushed open that swinging door and saw us. He was beside himself!"

Beau twists in her chair and folds a jean-covered leg underneath her. "What about? That you were there or eating in the kitchen? What?"

Delaney shrugs and shakes her head, so I take a shot. "I think all of it. But he did say he couldn't believe we were eating take-out salads in the kitchen. Then Missus started explaining what we were doing, and he realized his mother is pawning the shower off on me. No offense, Delaney, I'd love to do a shower for you, just not one Missus plans. He also said he couldn't believe that this was why she wouldn't go to dinner with them and she was acting so injured. Honestly, he was mad about everything, and they started shouting at each other. Shouting! I was stunned, but not for long. Jackson was already standing, and he grabbed my arm and pulled me up. He pushed me ahead of him, and then when we got to the kitchen door where Delaney was, I, well, I grabbed her. Told her to come with me."

My impromptu guest looks up and swallows. "I wouldn't have left them like that, but, well, Peter's been saying I need to get to know people and I'm so tired of them fighting all the time." She looks so ashamed that we all fall quiet for a few minutes.

Then Laney stands up. "I have a chocolate flourless cake that will go wonderfully with another round of margaritas or coffee. One of you get the drink orders, I'll bring in cake for everyone, and then we can enjoy that while I tell y'all just exactly what is going on in the Bedwell house." She plants one hand on her hip and squints down at Delaney. Pointing a finger her direction, she promises, "You are going to be *so* glad you are here tonight."

Chapter 7

We all opted for decaf coffee with our cake. Settled back in the den, Laney picks up her cup, holds it in front of her with two hands, and declares, "It's a good, old-fashioned power struggle."

Susan rolls her eyes. "Duh? We all know that."

"But do you know why?" Laney lifts her chin and surveys the room. "Delaney, do you know about the will? F.M.'s will?"

Delaney shakes her head, licks her lips, and looks nervous. Then she holds out a hand, palm facing Laney. "Do I *want* to know about the will? I really do love Peter. I really do."

I notice Beau's eyes narrow at Delaney's declaration.

Susan pulls her eyes from Delaney to her sister. "Tread lightly, sis."

Laney shakes off her concern. "If you love him you need to know what's going on. If you don't want to know, then I won't force you to listen."

Delaney blinks and reaches for her coffee. "Go ahead. I'm fine." She studies her coffee like she studied her drink earlier. She's pulled into herself.

I speak up. "Come on. I thought this was just a girls' night. Fun, drinks, chocolate cake... do we really need all the drama?" I'm dying to know what Laney knows, but I can find out later.

Delaney laughs. "Sorry, but we are talking about Missus and Peter. Of course there is going to be drama, and I guess I better get used to it." Taking a breath she looks brightly at Laney. "So, about the will?"

Laney winks at her. "It's not that bad, and it will help you understand what's going on. Okay, here's what I found out. Don't ask how, just remember when you vote that I do always get to the bottom of things. Anyway, Peter has always had his hand on a good bit of money, but F.M. lamented him having it and kept things in check just by being the good man that he was. Peter truly did want to please his father."

"I miss F.M.," I say, and the others nod.

Delaney says, "My parents and I came to the funeral here. That's when Peter and I got back in contact."

Laney agrees. "It's also when Missus and your father got back in touch."

"They did?" Delaney is puzzled, and it shows. "What do you mean? In touch about what?"

Laney lowers her eyes to gaze at the ring on Delaney's hand.

The woman grabs her hand up to her chest. "Our engagement?"

"Both Missus and your father decided they'd left the future in their children's hands long enough."

Interjecting, I doubt Laney. "Missus was fine with Shannon and Peter. Shannon was a rock for the family during all that time."

She scowls at my doubt. "Missus might have been fine with Shannon if she honestly thought Peter would be. Peter was never, ever going to be happy with Shannon Chilton. Missus is a snob, but"—she looks at Delaney—"sorry, but Peter? Peter is an even bigger snob."

Looking around the circle I see agreement, even when I look at Delaney. "Really? I mean, that's not the Peter I know."

Susan reminds me. "But you've known him a year; we've known him all our lives. Delaney, you don't look shocked."

"I'm not." She pulls her hair around to lay on her shoulder, and she plays with it as she stares at the fire. "I don't know that I'd call him a snob, more that he's interested in tradition and standards. Our families go way back, and we did date in college. Maybe he could've been happy with Shannon, but she dumped him, remember?" She pauses, then takes in a breath and sits straighter. "But what does this have to do with the will?"

Laney chews on her bottom lip, then folds her arms. "In his will, F.M. gave Missus a monthly stipend and put control of everything into Peter's hands."

"What? How could he do that? Wasn't everything jointly held between the two of them? Husband and wife?" Susan asks. Delaney has settled back into her chair, watching the rest of us.

"Nope," Laney says with a sigh. "Mrs. Baldwin, the town treasurer before me? She told me a long time ago how that's really how Missus and F.M. got together. That whole rigmarole about the beauty pageant was true kind of, but mostly Missus's father, the judge, owed a lot of money to folks. F.M. bought it all up and took the hand of his daughter in the deal."

I shake my head. "No, that can't be true. F.M. was so humble and down to earth."

"True, but he knew better than to let Missus have control of things. I checked into it years ago. Everything was in his name."

Susan asks, "The Bedwell house?"

Laney nods. "Everything."

Delaney stretches. "The cake was delicious. Thank you." She stands up. "Here, let me take everyone's plates to the kitchen." She collects plates, although we hand them up reluctantly as we want to continue the conversation.

She leaves the room, and Beau cocks an eyebrow at Laney. "Do you think she already knew that?"

Laney pushes up out of her chair. "Not sure. But she knows it now, and that's all I was concerned about. I like her, and I didn't like her being blind in this situation." She's left the room by the time the rest of us are up and collecting our coffee cups.

Susan leans her head toward me and Beau. "Anyone else think my sister is being just a bit too altruistic? Does she really care about Delaney?"

"Yes, I do think she cares about Delaney," I say, but then I add, "She also cares about having an ally in the enemy camp. After all, the title of mayor is on the line, and we know how Laney feels about titles."

Beau laughs. "Remind me, does that title come with a crown?"

Chapter 8

Jackson whispers because he's holding our sleeping grand-daughter. "Strangest in all of this to me is Laney keeping it a secret for so long."

"She said it was official business and she felt it was her duty to not say anything."

He scoffs. "She felt it was her duty to wait until it could help her the most."

"There is that. Isn't this the sweetest thing God ever made?" We're on our couch, and even though we have her carrying seat and a sweet cradle upstairs, Francie is taking her nap in Jackson's arms with the two of us watching. Will and Anna brought her over here as soon as we got home from early church. Francie cried a good bit, as we might've tried a little too hard to get her settled. Savannah and Bryan were here also, and we were all a tad excited.

The crying got rid of her aunt and uncle, but Grammy and Grandad thought it was cute crying. So sweet, not like crying at all. More like a bird chirping. Of course the dirty diaper proba-bly helped speed her aunt and uncle on. But seriously, it wasn't even like real poop. It was cute poop!

When I look up, I see Grandad is asleep too. I put my head back, but the thoughts just whirl and whirl. On the drive home last night Delaney didn't say much except that she really does love Peter. That she's loved him since college. I tried to get more out of her about their dating, but she changed the subject. And I let her. I was tired.

Last night was so fun. We swore we wouldn't wait so long to get together again. Delaney fit with the rest of the group; we're all about the same age, but it's strange how different we are.

I'm not from here, married with three kids and a grandchild. Susan is from here and is kind of divorced with three kids. Laney is from here, married with three kids, one only six months old. Beau has four kids, no husband, and isn't looking for one. She says she's no longer looking for any men since she's decided she doesn't want more kids. No one asked what that means exactly for her love life. Delaney, I found out, is my age, forty-six, and she has never been married. We've all had an assortment of jobs, but have all lived most of our lives in the South.

I'm glad I invited Delaney. She fits in well. I did notice when I dropped her off at Missus's house last night she didn't even go inside. She got in her car and drove away. Luckily she drove off to the south and didn't see me in my car, tucked in behind some bushes across the park, watching.

"Can I talk to you?" Silas sticks his head in the door of the Orange Blossom Special room, where I've retreated with my phone.

"Sure. I'm just in here to keep from waking Jackson and Francie up."

"I saw them. Also saw the picture you put up of them on Facebook, so I knew you were around somewhere." He comes around the bed and angles the chair toward the window seat, where I'm snuggled up.

55

"Next weekend the B&B rooms are full," I say, "and I love sitting in here looking down to the river." The bare tree limbs give an even better view of the water and the hills on the other side. Clouds are building, and we're supposed to get some snow flurries tonight. Our warm spell is quickly coming to an end.

"It is a nice view. Maybe next time I come I should ask for this room."

"Next time? Are you leaving?"

He stares out the window another minute, then looks at me as he scoots back into his chair. "Do you think I should stay in Chancey?"

"Me? What does it have to do with what I think?" I lay my phone down after I click it off so he can't see my texts with Susan.

"Okay, do you think Susan thinks I should stay?"

"Maybe you should ask Susan that."

His immediate look of disdain is followed by a smile. "You know, I have asked her. I've asked her about a million times." As he jerks his head to the side, his hair falls onto his forehead just like it does when he's on screen. I forget how good-looking he is since I'm around him so much, and he's such a nice guy. A nice guy head over heels for my friend. He's working his jaw, and he's turned farther away from me. I look down at my lap to avoid watching him try not to cry.

His voice is husky even after he clears his throat a couple of times. "She's unlike anyone I've ever known. So honest and fun, but I can't avoid the fact that she's got a life that doesn't include me." He shrugs and looks at me. "Maybe that's some of the attraction?"

"What do you mean?"

Leaning forward he rests his elbows on his knees. "I've been thinking that when I say she's unlike anyone I've ever known, that is way too true. I don't know if you know this, but I was a child actor. I've lived in Hollywood my whole life." He sits back and runs his hands through his hair. "What if it's just that she's, I don't know, normal?"

I laugh out loud, and soon he can't help but join me. "Well, I wouldn't tell her that!"

"Well, duh. I'm not stupid. I mean there's a, you know, an attraction. A big one."

"Yes, we've all seen that."

He sits back and actually blushes.

"But, Silas, don't discount that. Even Laney was telling Susan a real attraction shouldn't be ignored."

"You talk about us? The three of you!" His eyes are wide.

"Well, yeah, I mean, some." I cock an eyebrow at him. "That's normal, in case you don't know. They are sisters after all."

We sit quietly, and a smile creeps up on his face. "I know that is part of the normal I like—her family. Heck, even this whole town." He looks around. "Don't think I thought places like this really existed. Look at this; this could be a scene in any number of TV movies I've done."

The room is my favorite, and I warm, thinking of it being in a movie. The white comforter with the old Florida map quilt, the silk orange-leaf-and-blossom garland across the top of the circular dresser mirror, the filmy, white sheers in the windows. Even the pillows in shades of orange and green cushioning me and decorating the bed. "And I don't even have the music on in here."

Silas grins. "I've become addicted to that song." He holds up his phone. "I even downloaded the Johnny Cash version. I have to say I've learned a lot about railroads staying here."

"Welcome to my life. So, what exactly are you thinking about you and Susan?" I might as well ask what I want to know. He wanted to talk.

Staring at me, he nods as if in thought, then abruptly stands. "You're right." He starts tucking his shirt into his jeans. "It's more about this town and being 'normal' than anything else.

It's time I quit playing around. She doesn't really want to marry me." He's halfway to the door when he says again, "You're right."

"Wait, I didn't say that. Silas, stop!"

He turns around, but only for a second. "Appreciate the talk. Gotta go." He's in the living room by the time I unwrap from the blanket and get to the end of the hall. I start to yell his name again, but see that Jackson and Francie are still asleep. However, the door slams behind him, and they both awake with a start.

I agree, Francie. Crying's the only option.

Susan's going to kill me.

CHAPTER 9

"Thanks for coming down here so early," Susan says in greeting as I slide into the booth at Ruby's. "I have to be in the main office by nine, ready for a meeting."

"No problem. Kids were both still sleeping. Can't believe there's only two more days of Christmas break left. Jackson was headed downstairs to work. I don't know how this part-time thing is going to work exactly, but he seems excited."

She grimaces. "Financially y'all going to be okay?"

"I guess. We still have all our insurance, and he's getting about two thirds of his salary. They have a ton of remodeling jobs, but whether that'll be profitable remains to be seen." I stretch a hand out across the table. "Listen. About Silas…"

She pats my hand. "Don't worry. I know you didn't really tell him what to do." She blinks a couple of times and takes a deep breath. "He's so sweet, and I already miss him, but it's for the best." Stretching out her empty left hand, she studies it. "I shouldn't have taken his ring, but it was like a fairy tale. And I really did feel a lot for him. It was, it was intoxicating."

"Plus, he is *fairly* good-looking."

She looks up and matches my grin. "Extremely good-looking." She sits back and surveys Ruby's. "It's good to be getting back to normal, isn't it? I love when school gets out and things can relax, but I also like when it's back and we have a schedule. Plus, it's good to be past the holidays."

I pick up my empty cup. "Where's Libby?"

"She poured me a cup when I first got here, but that's the last I saw of her." We both stretch, looking back toward the kitchen area. Susan slides out. "I don't see her or Ruby. I'll go check."

I turn around in my seat and watch her walk back to the quiet kitchen. It's early, so there's only a couple of other occupied tables. Those folks all have coffee and muffins, I notice. At the opening in the counter, Susan stops and turns to look at me, raising her hands in question. I shrug back at her, so after another pause she pushes past the swinging half door and walks back into Ruby's usually bustling domain. She turns and looks at me again. By this time the other patrons have realized something isn't right, and one man gets up to follow Susan.

"What's going on? Where's Libby? Where's Ruby?" he asks.

Then the back door blows open and Libby rushes in. "Oh my. Susan? What are you doing back here? I'm coming. I'm coming." She grabs the coffee pot off the burner. "Shoo! Go on back to your table. Mr. Prescott, you ready for a refill too? Everybody go sit down." She corrals the two inquiring minds back toward their tables and refills coffee cups, saving ours for last.

"Oh, Carolina! I didn't even see you come in. Y'all ready for muffins? We have the last of the Christmas flavors, plus a new corn muffin with bits of ham in it. What can I get you?" She stares at us as if daring us to ask what's going on. Where's Laney when you need her? She's never silenced by a mere stare.

Susan says, "I'll take anything with cinnamon," then focuses on me with a look that says it's my turn to stick my neck out. She did go behind Ruby's counter after all.

"I'll try the corn-and-ham muffin. Where's Ruby?"

Libby's lips press together. Her eyes well, then blink furiously, as she chokes out, "She's out back."

"Is she okay?" I ask.

"No. Not really. Jewel's moving today."

"Oh, today?" Susan laments. "Poor thing. It's gotta be so hard, her only child moving so far away. Is she out in the cold?"

Libby nods. "Sitting in her car. She don't want folks to see her crying."

I move to slip out of the booth. "I'll go sit with her."

Libby blocks me. "Oh no. Never. She would have a fit. She's real proud like. But, well, ya could…" She looks around. "You could give me a hand if you're not busy."

"Okay, I guess…"

Susan shakes her head. "I can't. I have to get to work. Matter of fact, I probably need to take my muffin to go at this point."

Libby sits the coffee pot in front of me. "Just fill up folks' cups, and I'll take care of the kitchen." Then she's gone, scurrying back behind the counter as the bell over the door keeps ringing, and I realize there are already a couple of tables waiting for coffee.

"Guess I better get to work," I say, scooting off the seat.

"Wait," Susan says, holding out her cup. "Top me off. I'll go get my muffin and pay at the back counter." She winks at me. "Looks like you're going to be too busy to talk much more anyway."

Chapter 10

"People can be downright rude!" I say, slamming into the house around noon. "These people are our neighbors and friends, and they acted like spoiled brats."

My opinions go unheeded because there's no one to hear them. Pausing, I listen, but there are no noises from upstairs, no running shower or music. The kitchen is empty, and when I open the basement door, there's no voice or computer keys clacking. The house sounds, and feels, empty.

It does strike me how quickly I've gotten used to the house never being empty anymore. A look out the front window tells me Savannah's car is gone, but Jackson's truck is still here, so I check out the backyard and see Jackson walking up the back hill.

"Hey," I call, stepping onto the deck. "What are you doing out here?"

"Just took a walk to clear my head. Been on the phone all morning. Where've you been? Thought Susan had to go to work early."

I meet him in the yard. "She did. I ended up waitressing at Ruby's. Today is Jewel's moving day, so Ruby spent much of the morning out in her car crying."

"And you got to play waitress?" He kisses me as he grins. "Sounds fun."

"Anything but. People can be so rude. So demanding. People we know!" We walk back up the deck steps. "Now I smell like food and coffee."

"I know. You smell awesome. They should bottle this." He pulls me close and nuzzles me while I laugh.

"Stop. Where are the kids?"

"Susie Mae picked Bryan up just a while ago to go up to Grant's. I got to see the new car she got for Christmas. Andy called to see if Savannah could come in to work for a couple of hours, so she stumbled out of here half asleep shortly after you left."

We enter the warm kitchen. "Oh, it feels good in here," I say.

"So, how was Susan? Upset about Silas?"

"Not really. We didn't get to talk too much. She did say she shouldn't have taken his ring. She misses him, but it seems like she never thought it was a real engagement." I close the just-opened refrigerator and lean against the door, my forehead pressed to it. "I'm really kind of disappointed in her. She seemed like such a stand-up, no-nonsense person when we moved here."

He pats me on the back as he walks past. "Well, things change. I've got a call starting, which will take most of the afternoon. Remember, we need to eat early since the chamber of commerce meeting is at six thirty."

That gets me to lift my head away from the fridge door. "Wait. You're going to the meeting?"

He stops, basement door open. "Sure. We're a new business. Colt's coming up with a name this afternoon." After a grin and lift of his eyebrows, he jogs down the stairs, calling, "So if we can eat around five thirty, that should work."

I walk over to close, not slam, the basement door. I mean, that wasn't exactly a slam, was it? Dinner again? What's with these people and eating every day? This time I open both the refrigerator and freezer doors and actually concentrate. I pull out two frozen pork loins, the kind packaged with seasonings. Okay, one is garlic and black pepper. The other is teriyaki. Close enough. I set them out to thaw and decide I'll think about side dishes later. When my phone rings I take it as a sign to leave the kitchen completely.

"Hey, Laney."

"Hey. Did you know Silas left? I mean, of course you know. He was staying there. So, when did he leave? Is he coming back? Wait, he didn't move back in with my sister, did he? I'm going to wring her neck! I'm trying to be patient and not say what needs to be said, but this time—"

"Calm down," I finally get in. "You'll be happy to hear they are done." I plop into the chair next to the front window.

"Done? Like, done done? Oh, happy day!" Then she immediately lowers her voice to a sad level. "But how is Susan? I mean, I'm assuming he broke up with her. She's never been able to tell anyone no on anything. Is she upset? Should I call her?"

"She didn't seem too upset. It's like she always knew it wasn't a real engagement."

"Of course it wasn't a real engagement! Crying out loud. How many times did I tell you, tell everybody, that! Okay, now, what should I wear to the chamber of commerce meeting tonight?"

"What? Why would you be coming?" This meeting is getting out of hand.

"Hello? I'm going to be the mayor of this town. Of course I need to be there. I have some fabulous ideas to help our businesses. I've never been to one of these. Does everyone wear what they work in or more professional clothing? I have a very sharp pinstripe suit I'm dying to wear if it still fits. Makes me look so serious. I even bought some glasses. Of course they're just clear, but they really say that I'm all business. Get it? All business? For the chamber of commerce meeting?"

64

"Are you on Retta's agenda? She's pretty strict about what we discuss."

"Retta Bainbridge? Honey, we're thick as thieves. She's even helping with my campaign."

"Let me guess. She hates Missus." That's really not that much of a guess. Missus has rubbed most everyone in town the wrong way, unless they're new to town. Somehow she's got the new, younger folks in her pocket.

"Hates her with a passion. But then, who doesn't, right? This election is a cakewalk. So, you do think the pinstriped suit?"

"I have no idea. Wear whatever you want. Hey, I've got to go." I lean forward and study the small, gray car pulling across the railroad tracks. We wouldn't have guests arriving on a Monday, would we? Then I remember who I'm on the phone with. "There's a car pulling in. We don't have any guests arriving today, do we?"

"Today? Monday? No. Not until late Wednesday evening. You know, when I'm mayor, you'll have to take over more of the scheduling duties at the B&B."

"But I don't want to do that." I stand and watch as the car door opens.

"Don't whine, Carolina. Besides, if you need extra money it's easier than waiting tables at Ruby's. You know you're not all that good with the public early in the morning, so I wouldn't get used to what Ruby's paying you. Gotta go get ready for the meeting. See ya soon!"

I pull my phone away and stare at it. She thinks I'm waitressing at Ruby's for pay now? And the queen of insults thinks *I'm* not good with people in the morning? I stomp to the front door. She really should be nicer to me. After all, her opponent in her already-won mayoral race is walking up my sidewalk.

"Hi, Missus. New car?"

She automatically tips her chin up as if I've challenged her.

"Yes. The environment should be a concern for all of us, Carolina."

"Oh, the election."

She prances past me. "Some of my constituents are alarmed that my opponent's husband makes a living selling huge, pollution-belching SUVs."

Closing the door I chuckle. "So you traded your big, old Cadillac in for something more environmentally friendly. I get it."

She sits on one end of the couch, tugs her gray suede gloves off, and waits for me to sit.

I pause beside the couch. "Can I get you something to drink? Water? Tea?"

"No, thank you. Please sit down. You make me nervous lurching over me like that."

"I'm not lurching. I'm walking. Now I'm sitting. Tell me how I'm doing that wrong."

She actually studies me, then shrugs. "I've come to ask for your help."

"No." I shake my head and sit back in my chair. "I've already told you and Laney that I will not get involved. I support you both."

Her eyes fly open, and she brings one ungloved hand to her throat. "Oh my. Nothing like that. I'd like your help organizing the first ever Chancey Book Festival."

"Book festival?" I can't help it. I'm leaning forward. "We don't have a book festival."

"But we should, don't you agree?"

"Possibly. But..." I lean back. "Remember your dessert festival or whatever it was we did back in the fall? Sounded like a good idea, but all that rain? All those leftover desserts?"

She waves her hand. "Weather happens. Besides, if you'll recall, Southern Desserts was your idea. I am sure you'll run it better this year. This book festival idea is something the North Georgia Tourism Council is putting forward for smaller towns like ours to promote literacy throughout the region. The date is the first weekend in March, and the idea is for book lovers to go from town to town, hearing speakers and buying books."

"Oh! Like those World's Longest Yard Sales. There's one in Tennessee that goes across the whole state."

"Of course there is." She closes her eyes and takes a deep breath. With a pained smile she opens her eyes. "If that is how you choose to see it, then so be it. As owner of our bookshop you would need to take a leading role, working with other book lovers across the area, deciding on speakers and guest authors, setting up readings. How does all that sound?"

I can't help but frown. However, try as I might, I can't find a flaw in this scheme. "Wonderful. It actually sounds wonderful."

She stands and begins pulling on her gloves. "That's what I thought. This will be my first event to oversee as mayor. We will make sure it is the envy of every other town, correct?"

It sounded like a question, but it wasn't. Not really. She's already halfway to the front door. As usual, she waits beside it for me to open it. I tug on the door, letting in a chilly breeze.

She shivers. "There's that cold front the meteorologists have been warning us about. Wear a warm coat tonight, Carolina." On the porch she turns around. "However, do not be concerned about a presentation on the book festival for the chamber this month. I will handle it. Perhaps I will ask for a few remarks from you." She eyes my outfit of jeans and a sweatshirt, which saw service as a waitress uniform all morning and has the stains to prove it. "Try to look at least somewhat professional. Inspires confidence, you understand." She shivers again and hurries down the steps toward her new small car.

You think anyone would notice if I don't show up tonight?

CHAPTER 11

A big, black hearse sits in front of Blooming Books and causes a sinking feeling to appear in my stomach as I round the corner. I parked around back to avoid the crowds tonight at the chamber meeting—and to possibly slip out if things go wrong. But if we're starting with a hearse, how much more wrong can things go?

Retta meets me at the door, waving her hands and telling me to back up. "Out of the way, Carolina! We need to get through!"

"Why? What's going on?" I assumed this was regular Chancey craziness, but maybe there really is an emergency. I hold the heavy door open for her to go back inside the store, still flapping her arms and yelling instructions. Two young men hurry out the door. One is dressed in a black suit; the other looks like he's on the grave-digging side of the business. The one in the suit gives me an appropriate nod; the other huffs by, ignoring me, but then growls, "Hold that door," when I start to go inside and let it close.

They open the back doors of the hearse and reach in. What in the world are they doing? Then they both pull back and start my way, each with arms full of folding chairs.

Lord help us! I hold the door, let them pass, then follow. "I guess you're expecting a crowd?" I ask Retta. Our fearless leader is decked out in a long, draped black cover of lightweight

68

material over a silver-sequined shirt. Solid sequins. She has on wide-legged black pants and black flats with silver-sequined designs on the toe. Her hair is styled big and tall like she's going to a party. Well, a party in the South. What do you bet this is her chance to get double duty out of her New Year's Eve outfit—worn every New Year's since 1988?

She's got Bonnie and Shannon arranging chairs first in one direction, then another. I hang up my coat slowly so as to not have to deal with chairs. My coworkers cut their eyes at me, rolling them a bit, but then Bonnie is all sweetness and light, asking Retta if everything looks okay. Bonnie's wearing a pretty orange suit jacket over a pair of dark brown pants and a print blouse. That's not what she had on this morning when I stopped in.

Shannon steps over beside me. "Bonnie apparently wants to get in the chamber with her new business. I mean, why else be that nice to Retta?"

"Oh, and that explains the sharp outfit." I look down at myself, then take the opportunity to study Shannon. "Guess neither of us are worried about impressing Retta Bainbridge." Shannon has on a tent dress. I try to remember if she's always worn this type of dress. It is her signature color, purple, but it's awfully flowing and big. The white turtleneck underneath it is smooshed up around her short neck, and that makes me tug on my own mock turtleneck.

Shannon bustles around me to go behind the counter. "Have you talked to Gertie?"

"Not in a couple days. Why?"

A door slams, the door to Patty and Andy's apartment upstairs. Shannon's head jerks to look in that direction. Mine does, too, at first, but then my gaze lingers on Shannon when I notice her grin. She shouts, "Hey, babe."

Sure enough, it's Danny Kinnock loping down the staircase. He's tall and almost lanky. He has a happy face with a small nose and brown eyes. His hair is also brown and flops on his forehead in an attractive way. He looks just like I would expect a guy all the girls in high school wanted, but who hasn't actually decided to grow up, to look, which is exactly how his ex-wife and her mother described him when they came to see Shannon and me last fall. The meeting was not nearly as scary as it sounds, since they were more than happy to finally get rid of him.

Danny winks at Retta as he passes her, and she giggles. He smiles at me as he stops in front of the counter and leans on it in front of his wife, his face only a few inches from her large bosom. "It'll be great." He finally raises his eyes to her face and gives her a look I know he perfected in junior high. She reacts accordingly, a giggle and a dipping of her chin. Although that makes her turtleneck even more unattractive.

Okay. I'll play the mean, middle-aged lunchroom supervisor breaking things up. "What's great?"

He rolls over onto one elbow and looks up at me. "Our new place. Upstairs."

Shannon's giggle sounds more nervous. "Yeah, we're moving in upstairs. Gertie said it's okay."

I don't see why she's nervous. It actually makes sense. "Okay. Sounds like a good idea to me. I better see if Retta needs any help." I turn away and make a face only Bonnie can see. I don't like Danny Kinnock. I don't like how Shannon acts around Danny Kinnock. I only hope I don't have to see a lot of Danny Kinnock.

Bonnie chuckles as I walk up to her. "So, you're not a fan of our newest addition?"

"He seems kind of smarmy. I don't know. I just liked who Peter and Shannon were when they were together. Now Peter has become the devil, and Shannon has turned into an unpopular seventh-grader. I'm not sure which I hate more."

"Speaking of Peter and Shannon..." She leans closer to me

and lowers her voice. "When did Shannon start wearing tent dresses?"

I take a step back and clear my throat, but a quick look at Bonnie tells me she's only fishing. She doesn't actually know anything like I do about Shannon putting off buying a pregnancy test right after she broke up with Peter. "Well, it is purple," is all I can think to say, but then the front-door bell jangles and a noisy group spills inside. "Time for the meeting."

She shakes her head and quirks her mouth at me. "Okay." She frowns. "Think Retta will let me in the chamber even though I've not officially opened my business?"

"Looking like that?" I wave at her outfit. "Of course. You make us all look good!"

CHAPTER 12

"They're a tad too salty for me," Laney announces from her seat on the end of the front row. She showed up late, loudly complaining of having to walk so far in heels because of the lack of downtown parking. We had all turned to listen to her complaining because it beat listening to Retta drone on and on, nearly breaking her arm patting herself on her back.

The crack in our fearless chamber president's voice early in the meeting said she could just cry. Well, it wasn't just her voice; she actually said it. "Just lay right down in the middle of the street and cry!" were Retta's exact words as she ruminated on about how she had brought the Chancey Chamber of Commerce back to life. So when Business Barbie in the pinstripe suit and heels came in the door, we all turned to listen. Laney complained about the lack of leadership in our town until she saw there wasn't a seat saved for her on the front row; then she stopped complaining long enough to tell Jackson to drag her an empty chair up and place it on the end of the front row. She finally sat down and quit complaining but looked around the room, throwing waves, winks, and kisses.

Her wrinkled nose and large, concerned eyes are now trained on her daughter, who is glaring at her. Angie and Alex brought samples representing their new menu, and the rest of us are enjoying them. Laney is probably enjoying them too, but she knows there's only one bed in that apartment above the restaurant, so, yeah, that's influencing her taste buds. Laney's concerned look turns to a glare as her daughter stalks over to her. The Conner women stare at each other; then Angie grabs the crab cake from her mother's hand and throws the offending bite over our heads. It smacks the back wall, and Angie sniffs at her mother. "There. I fixed it." She looks around as she walks back to the front. No one else complains.

"They are delicious." Missus sighs. "I would love another one, but I do have to watch my figure. I do not want to have to resort to wearing pinstripes to make me appear slender."

Angie smiles her gracious hostess smile as she hands a crab bite on a dark blue napkin to Missus. "Oh, Missus, *you* never have to worry about that!"

The gasp from Laney causes Retta to bang her hand several times on the table in front of her. "Alex, please continue your presentation so we can move on. No one informed me you were bringing samples." She shrugs apologetically in Laney's direction as she talks.

Alex is almost as good-looking as his uncle from New York, who is hands down the best-looking man I've ever seen. His blue-black hair, dark complexion, and sexy smile are all mimicked in Alex, but Alex hasn't got the age that brings it all together. Still, he's very attractive and a good speaker. Chancey's going to have its first real restaurant, and I try not to look excited because Laney's watching us all. I really hate that Angie threw that crab appetizer, not because we have to clean it up, but because it's one more hurdle to getting her and her mother back on good terms so we'll be allowed to go to the restaurant opening.

"Lunch will be casual and served from eleven until two every day. Then dinner service will begin at five, but only Tuesday through Saturday. We're planning some special events for Sunday evenings. We hope to be announcing the opening day for

AC's soon." Alex heads back to his seat, then stops. "Oh, and thank you for letting us join the chamber." He nods to Retta and smiles at the rest of us. Angie is in the back picking up the crab cake pieces. I get up to help her as Retta begins talking again.

"Here, let me throw that away." I reach out an open napkin to her, and she puts the pieces in it. "They were delicious," I whisper. "Don't worry about your mom. She'll come around."

Angie's faded, black-dyed hair is pulled back in a low bun. She's thin like her aunt Susan, and she's wearing a white shirt with black pants just like Alex. "I don't know if I even care anymore," she says in a soft, sad voice.

I pull her into a one-armed hug. "Of course you do, honey. It's hard to let our kids grow up. And you are only eighteen." She jerks away from me, but I lean toward her, trying to look in her eyes. "I know. Eighteen feels old, but when it's our kids it just doesn't. She doesn't want you to get hurt. That's all."

"She doesn't want me to hurt her reputation." Her face tightens up. "Like I could!"

"Shh, not so loud. You and Alex did a great job tonight. Y'all are still happy?"

Her face melts. "Yeah. I mean, I'm happy. I hope he's happy." She turns to look up where he's seated. He's leaned back, busy on his phone. Totally checked out of the meeting. "Peter told us to come tonight and bring some samples. I don't have any idea what this actually is."

"How are things going with Peter being your partner?"

"Good, I guess. He and Alex and Alex's uncle talk; I'm more into the decorating, and you know school starts back on Wednesday." She motions at the napkin in my hand. "Thanks. Sorry for throwing that."

"No problem. Guess we better get back to the meeting."

She smiles and heads toward her empty seat, across which Alex has sprawled. How long the good-looking, twenty-five-

74

year-old New Yorker will be happy in a tiny town in North Georgia is anyone's guess. Sure, he's getting to run a restaurant, and he and Angie seem to make a good team, but really? For all her attitude and gumption, she's still just a high school kid fighting with her mom in her hometown.

"Carolina will explain," Missus says as I walk back into earshot. She turns to me. "No, not from back there. Come to the front and tell us your plans."

My plans? "I assume we're talking about the book festival?" Missus is no longer looking at me, but Laney more than makes up for it as she's staring a hole into me. I give her a shrug and a smile, then walk up front. "It's across the areas of North Georgia outside of the Atlanta area and the collar counties." I'd done some reading up on the book festival's overall plan this afternoon after Missus left our house. "The North Georgia Tourism Council is sponsoring it and will coordinate the speakers and special events. It's the first weekend of March, and well, that's all I know so far." I scoot back to my place and collapse in my chair just as I hear Retta call Colt's name.

"Thank you," my brother-in-law says as he stands. Preparing to hear him speak makes me nervous. Colt's not one for big speeches or big crowds unless there's a football involved. "I appreciate all this," he says, "and well, I'm glad to be here. Um, guess you want to know the name of our company, right?" Retta nods. "What I came up with is Colt & Company. You know, not the word 'and,' but that sign that means 'and.' Right now it's me, my brother Jackson…" He motions for Jackson to stand, and he does halfway before sinking back into the folding chair beside me. "And my nephew Will is helping some too. He's not here, as we told him to stay home with Anna and baby Francie." He looks around the room. "Anything else?"

Peter stands up. He's not said a word so far. He didn't even say anything when the two businesses he's backing, AC's and Phoenix's new juice bar, made their presentations. But he sure seems like he's about to say something now. "I have a question: How do you propose to do all the work you're contracted for when you and Mr. Jessup both have full-time jobs? Have you not perhaps bitten off more than you can chew?"

Peter has on a dark suit and a bright red tie, and as he walks from his chair around to face Colt, he looks like a lawyer addressing the jury. Colt shifts around from foot to foot, looking like a guilty witness.

"Uh, we think we have it handled." He takes a breath and tries a little laugh. "We're surprised as much as you are, Peter. It's exciting, so many projects going on at once here." His laugh fades, and he looks straight at his questioner. "And we definitely appreciate the support you've given us, Peter. Hiring us for several of your projects."

Peter's right eyebrow jumps. "Several? Try all. All of my projects." I'm surprised by this news, but Jackson and Colt don't object. You'd think being together twenty-four seven would mean I'd know what's going on with my husband, but obviously not. Peter smirks at me like he knows I'm in the dark, and then he continues. "I decided to give your business an important shot of confidence: AC's, the lovely Phoenix's juice bar, her home, which of course she's leasing from me, and my own law office, which I hope to have use of sooner rather than later." He inhales, then releases his breath slowly while looking around the room. "It appears as if you and your family hold our town in limbo."

Colt frowns, then looks down. Oh no. This was what I was afraid of. His shoulders slump, and he waggles his head like he's confused before he collapses back into his seat.

However, Jackson stands up. "Of course, Peter. Exactly as we hoped when we began this business. Chancey is in good hands with us. Very good hands." After a pause, he folds his arms and cocks his head. "Whether other new businesses can say that remains to be seen. Right, Peter?"

Peter scowls but then quickly laughs. "Right. Of course. Good hands." He goes back to his seat, but as he begins to sit, he realizes Jackson is still standing and watching him, so he doesn't sit down and Jackson doesn't sit down. Finally, Retta stands and, fluttering her hands, says, "Let's move on. Everyone sit down."

I reach up and jerk on Jackson's arm. "Sit down, John Wayne."

He slowly eases into his chair, then puts an arm around me and squeezes.

Ya just never know who's going to show up at a small town meeting.

Chapter 13

All thoughts of taking John Wayne home and having my way with him galloped right out of my head when, right in the middle of new business, Ruby popped her head in the door. "Buttermilk pie is ready when y'all get this fool meeting over with. C'mon, Retta, enough already!"

Needless to say, there was no more new business to discuss.

Half the crowd left at once. As we're cleaning up, Bonnie grins. "This feels like a dream come true. Bonnie's Designs is a real thing. I'm a real business!"

Holding out two folded chairs for Colt to add to those stacked against the wall, I nod at her. "I'll buy you a piece of pie to celebrate. I'll buy two, one for you to take home to Cal."

"You don't have to do that. Besides, I'm going on home. It's dark, and I hate driving all those curvy roads in Laurel Cove at night."

"I don't blame you," Peter says, coming up behind her, pulling her elbow to turn her, and then reaching for her hand to shake. "Congratulations on your new business. Can I get on your appointment schedule for a consultation? My office should be completed..." He looks up and raises his voice. "Um, Jackson, when will my office be completed? Since you say everything is under control."

Even with his back to us, I can see Jackson stiffen. After only a beat he continues stacking the chairs folks are bringing him. He says loudly, "We've written so many contracts I can't pull the exact dates from my memory right at this moment. I'll call you with that information first thing in the morning."

Colt speaks up, walking our direction. "Here it is. I have a copy of your contract on my phone. Looks like right around the second week of February is when we agreed to have your renovations completed, Mr. Bedwell. However, Mrs. Cuneo is welcome to come see the space anytime. Might be easier to get her involved before we do some of the finishing touches, right?"

Bonnie steps forward and nods enthusiastically. "Oh yes. What a good thought, Mr. Jessup. Name the day, Mr. Bedwell, and I'm at your service."

Mr. Bedwell preens. I turn to the side and gag. He clears his throat like he's speaking before Congress. "Why yes, that is a good idea. Tomorrow morning we will all meet upstairs in my new office."

Colt holds up a hand. "That's not going to work for me." He cocks an eyebrow. "That other job thing? Teachers have a workday tomorrow."

Peter's face hardens. "Just what I was afraid of…"

"No problem," Jackson interjects. "No problem at all for me to be there. What time, Mr. Bedwell? Name it."

"Nine a.m. sharp. Does that work for you?" he questions Bonnie with a stern look.

"Absolutely," she answers. "Now I really must be leaving."

While all this was happening, the rest of the crowd moved on. The chairs are stacked to the side for pickup in the morning. Colt and Jackson are moving the table back where it belongs in the bookstore. Peter is closing up his black leather satchel, and I walk Bonnie to the back door, which I lock after her. Walking up beside the counter I notice Phoenix is standing off to the side, halfway behind the coatrack. "Hey. You going over for some pie?" I ask.

She smiles, but only one side of her mouth participates. Her hair is long and sleek tonight, and she's wearing a trench coat, belted tight, accentuating her figure. "I don't believe I like buttermilk, so no. No, thank you." She looks over my shoulder at Peter. Her eyes follow him on his way to the door. "Excuse me," she says, brushing past me. The door hardly begins closing before she's out of it and walking next to him.

Grabbing my coat I give them some time to get down the block. Then I step to the door and open it. They're easy to spot as they stride down the sidewalk past Ruby's, where light spills all the way out to the street. I take a few steps in that direction to see where they go. The door to Phoenix's studio does eventually open, but I can't tell if they both entered.

"You ready to lock up?" Jackson asks from the door.

"Sure. My purse is still under the counter." We get the keys and lock up, and then I head to Ruby's with a Jessup man on either side of me. "So, what did you two think of your first chamber meeting?"

Colt speaks up. "Fine. Uh, did Phoenix leave with Peter?"

I shrug. "Leave with? I don't know if it was intentional like that," I lie.

Jackson squeezes my waist where his hand rests. He knows I was watching them. Then a sigh escapes my Jessup. "Dude. Forget her. She's moved on."

We're quiet until we get to Ruby's front door. The place is not full, but it looks like most of those in the meeting are here. Colt holds the door for me and Jackson to walk through, and he follows us, then stops.

"I think I'll go see if Phoenix is in her studio. I'm not sure she's ever had buttermilk pie, but I think she'd like it." He's gone before I can turn around and stop him.

Missus is calling my name from a booth about halfway back,

so I turn in her direction. However, I don't move that way until I'm sure Laney isn't here. Seated with Missus is Delaney. "I don't remember seeing you at the meeting," I say as I walk to their table. Jackson stopped at a front table where Kyle Kendrick, area manager of the Dollar Store, and a man who owns a used electronics shop out by the highway are seated.

Delaney shakes her head, her mouth closed around a bite of pie. She moans and leans back. "This is amazing. You have to get a piece."

Missus scowls at Delaney, then at me, before saying, "All right. Get me a piece too."

Delaney gives me a quick wink, and I hurry to the back counter. "Hey, Ruby." I lower my voice. "How are you?"

Ruby is one of those people who looks like she's always been old. Thin, lots of wrinkles, stiff, gray hair, brown splotches on her arms and face. Tonight, though, she really looks old. It's something about her eyes.

She nods at me, then motions to the opening in the counter. "Come on back here a minute, would ya?"

She heads farther back, and I follow her until we are next to the ovens. She talks to me with her head hanging. "I want to say thanks to you, Carolina, for stepping in to help this morning. I don't rightly know what happened, but when Jewel texted they'd crossed the state line I just felt like a part of my heart tore right off. How could my girl live in a different state? My grandbabies?" She sighs and then looks up, and I see her eyes are dry but lifeless. That's what's making her look genuinely old.

I grab her and hug her. Weird thing is, she lets me. "Ruby, you know Chancey will be just fine if you move to be with your family. We'll miss you an awful lot, but you need to be happy."

"Right. You're right, but you know what? It's time for Jewel to have a little space all her own. She's a grown woman, and, well, I need to let her spread her wings. I can't say how long I'll give her this space," she finally says with a chuckle, "but I'm

81

staying put for right now. Maybe work on myself some. See what new tricks this old world can teach me." She laughs again, and there's a bit of light in her eyes. She whips her dish towel at me. "Now get on the other side of that counter! You know I don't allow nobody back here! Skedaddle!"

I laugh as I skedaddle, although I do grab two saucers of pie on my way. Libby holds up the coffee pot as I pass her. "I filled your cup already."

"Thanks. It was fun working with you this morning, but your job is harder than I imagined!" She smiles and ducks back behind the counter as I continue to our table.

"Took you long enough," Missus complains. Delaney has slid over to the wall, so I sit next to her. Missus takes just a tiny bit of the rich, yellow pie onto her fork. "I'm only having a bite. Did you leave Peter at your shop? Where is he?"

If I'd known she was going to ask about Peter, I would've hurried and filled my mouth. I shrug and quickly fix that empty mouth thing.

Surprisingly Delaney answers her. "He's excited about reopening his law practice, so he was going straight home after his meeting to study up on some old case law."

Missus doesn't believe her. I don't believe her. Heck, I don't think even Delaney believes herself. But, well, the pie is good, the coffee hot, so I'm not challenging her. "I'm excited about the book festival. Did Missus tell you?" I ask as I turn to my seatmate.

"A little. So each town does their own festival, but they're also joined together?"

"That's what it sounds like. The tourism council will be advertising and promoting each festival and coordinating speakers. This way we can get some authors that would only do events in or near Atlanta. I want to come up with a theme for ours. You know, something catchy."

"Oh, that'll be fun," Delaney says. "I'd be happy to help. When is it exactly?"

"First weekend in March," Missus and I say at the same time.

"Jinx," I shout, but Missus just gives me an arched eyebrow and says, "By that time I'll be fully comfortable in my new position of mayor and also able to help you in any way possible. Since this will be my first event as mayor, there can be no problems." As she looks down to lift her coffee cup, I sneak an eye roll at Delaney. I also motion to Missus's pie plate, which is empty. Of course mine is too, so I'm definitely not judging—just noticing.

Delaney smiles at us both as she sticks her left hand out for her engagement ring to sparkle at us. "And by the first weekend in March I'll be back and settled. Ready to plunge into Chancey life!"

Missus frowns. "Back from where? I was not aware you had travel plans."

Delaney gives us both sweet, innocent looks, then announces, "Back from my honeymoon! Peter and I are getting married Valentine's Day weekend."

My mouth pops open, as does Missus's. However, while mine is silent, words come spouting out of hers. "What? Peter didn't tell me."

Delaney laughs. "Of course he didn't. He doesn't know yet."

Chapter 14

"My feet were killing me! What is it my feet don't understand? All I did was have a baby, not a foot transplant. I am not buying all new shoes!"

Laney quiets down a bit on her end of the phone. I texted her to call me any time after seven this morning so I could fill her in on last night at Ruby's. Before I can get a word in, she adds another excuse. "Besides, there is no buttermilk pie that can hold a candle to my meemaw's."

"Well, you should've come barefoot. And I'd really like to taste your meemaw's pie."

"She's passed now, and Mother never did get the hang of it. But back to it: What did Delaney mean Peter didn't know yet?"

"Just that. He told her to take care of everything, and so she apparently did. She was real tickled with herself too. It did throw Missus for a loop, so that was fun to watch."

"What did Missus say? You're right, I should've come barefoot."

"At first she was flabbergasted and kept stuttering that"—I imitate Missus's highly offended voice—"Peter had to be consulted and Peter didn't mean to be left out and Peter should be here now." My words fade. I haven't mentioned Peter leaving with Phoenix last night. Now that I think about it, Delaney did agree with Missus that Peter should have been there.

Laney lets the pause linger for a moment. "Okay. So, where was Peter? You know, don't you?"

"Not exactly. But it doesn't matter now."

"Whatever. You can tell me about that later, but Valentine's Day is just over a month away. Did Delaney say what the rush is for?" She pauses, then asks, "Does someone have a bun in the oven?"

"What! Why do you say that?" Then I realize she's talking about Delaney, and I laugh. "Of course not. She's our age."

"Duh!" Laney says. "And why don't my shoes fit? I just had a baby. At my age. I know for a fact Peter would love to have an heir."

"What are you talking about? Did he say that?"

"He's a man. He doesn't have to say it. A man with an inheritance and no kids to leave it to. He's always been big on the whole tradition thing."

"Delaney said the same thing about him the other day. He's big on tradition."

Laney shushes me. "Shoot. Cayden's awake. He was up at four a.m., and I hoped he'd sleep in this morning. Well, I better go. Thanks for filling me in. A Valentine's wedding! I have the cutest red shoes, so my feet better figure their problem out fast!"

She hangs up, and I can't help but chuckle at Laney and her feet as I snuggle deeper into my afghan. It's almost eight. The house is warm and quiet. Jackson is down in his basement office working before he has to go meet with Bonnie and Peter. Bryan spent the night up at Grant's, and Savannah is still asleep. She was out late last night. She and her friends were making the most of the last night of winter break with a bonfire at one of her friend's family's farms. She told Andy she wasn't coming in extra today so he shouldn't call her.

My phone rings, and I think Cayden must've gone back to sleep, but then I see it's Colt calling. "Hi, Colt. How are you?"

"Hey. I've only got a minute. I'm at school for the teacher's workday, and first session is starting. So, uh, is it true Peter's getting married Valentine's weekend?"

"Looks like it."

He's quiet. I wait for more but finally decide he needs a prod. "Why?"

"Just wondering." Then he goes quiet again.

"Did you find Phoenix last night? You never came to Ruby's."

"I found her."

Man, this is worse than trying to get information out of my kids. "So, was she at her store?"

There's more silence. Then he blurts, "I've got to go," and hangs up.

I wonder what that was about. Did he find her and end up staying at the store with her? Did he find her alone with Peter? If she wasn't with Peter, why would Colt be asking about Peter getting married? I need more coffee, so I get up, and as I do, I say out loud, "Poor Colt."

"Why poor Colt?" I hear the question above and behind me, where Savannah is coming down the stairs.

"I didn't hear you get up. I thought you were sleeping in?"

She's wearing her flannel Christmas pajamas, and her hair looks like she just rolled out of bed. "I was, but I'm going to go look at some houses with Ricky."

"Oh, really? Why?" I don't like the way that sounds, but I tamp down my alarm as I do my best to nonchalantly stroll into the kitchen.

"He asked me to. Can you pour me a cup too?"

I pour my coffee and then fill a cup halfway up for her. She looks over my shoulder. "Fill it all the way up. I've decided it's not real coffee if it's half milk."

"Oh, aren't we feeling grown up today." I chuckle, but she doesn't join me. I turn, and she's leaning with one hip against the counter. She reaches out for her coffee and takes a sip. Her face shows just how much she misses the milk.

"Maybe just put a touch of milk in it," I suggest as I sit down at the kitchen table.

"Maybe," she says, opening the refrigerator. She pours in a dollop of milk, then comes to the table. She takes her seat, one leg folded up underneath her. She holds her coffee with both hands and pulls it to her chest for warmth. "And you know, you're right."

I hate to mess with that, but I don't know what she's talking about. "Right about what?"

"About me feeling grown-up. I had fun last night, but everyone seemed so childish."

I do not, *do not*, roll my eyes. "Really? How?"

"You know. Usual stuff." She shifts in her chair, pulling her leg out from under her and sitting up straight. "Maybe I'm just seeing things more through Ricky's eyes now."

"Could be. Sounds like Ricky's really liking the real estate business."

"Oh yeah." She nods, and her words are louder, more animated. "He says it's great to be really doing something, not just learning about stuff you're never going to use."

The basement door opens. "You mean stuff like I'm using right now downstairs?" Jackson asks. "The stuff that pays for this house and your car and, well, everything?" He almost, but not quite, slams the door. "So, what now? You going to drop out of college before you've even finished high school?" he demands, standing at the end of the table, hands on his hips. His morning must not being going well if he's loaded for bear this early. Plus, while we get the gist of what he's saying, it's not making a lot of sense.

Her eyes narrow. "I didn't say that!"

He throws his hands up in the air and walks to the sink.

She stands. "I did not say that—exactly. But I am looking

at all my options. I mean, not quitting high school of course. But just because you and Mom went straight to college doesn't mean I have to!" She storms out of the room and stomps up the stairs.

Jackson jerks a water bottle out of the refrigerator, and he does slam *that* door. "I'm going to town," he growls as he wrestles his jacket off the coatrack. Then he's gone too.

Living with John Wayne may be overrated.

CHAPTER 15

"Thanks for coming in early, Susie Mae." I hang up my coat and look around the empty store. "Where's Shannon?"

Her blue eyes and grin widen further, and she points upstairs.

I whisper, "She hasn't left you down here alone all morning, has she?"

Susie Mae shakes her head. "Not exactly. I'm to text her if anyone comes in. She and Danny are getting moved in up there, I guess."

"Danny's here too?" I can't help but wrinkle my nose when I say his name.

The seventeen-year-old laughs. "I thought you liked everybody."

"I don't *not* like him. Exactly." I sweep past her to the counter area. "Has Bonnie been around? I know she had a meeting with Peter and Jackson this morning."

"Nope. Can I run up to Ruby's and see if she has a muffin left? I'm starving."

"Of course. See, Shannon should've been here so you could go out earlier."

Susie darts to the front door. "She asked, but I wasn't hungry then. You want one?"

"No, thanks." But before I can tell her to put on a coat, she's gone. Well, it's not like she'll die from exposure out there on the sidewalk.

I put my purse under the counter and look over things. The store is so quiet, much like the house was this morning once Savannah left. That's why I called Susie Mae to come in for me. It's rare these days to get any quiet time in our house, so I took advantage of it. Enjoyed coffee and a book in the morning sunshine. I even lit a lemon vanilla candle and put on some instrumental music. I like that New Age floaty stuff this time of year. Feels very clean and sparse. Searching my phone's music app, I connect to the Bluetooth and have music playing in the store while I light a couple of candles Bonnie has put around the space.

"Oh, you're here," Shannon says, causing me to jump.

"Oh my goodness! I didn't hear you coming down. Susie Mae went to get a muffin." I dig out my feather duster from behind the shelf, where I left it yesterday. "You getting settled in upstairs?"

Shannon stands in front of her floral cooler, studying its contents. "We are. I think it needs some fixing up, but Danny's fine with the way it is." She giggles. "He says he just wants to get started on our married life."

I meander in her direction. "How is married life?"

A frown crosses her face, but she shakes it off and smiles at me. "It's good. All I ever dreamed of."

Checking outside to see if Susie Mae will be blowing in the door any time soon, I step closer to her. "So, how are you feeling?"

"Good, I guess." She chews on her bottom lip and then leans forward to put her forehead against the glass of the cooler door. "What am I going to do?"

"You're pregnant, aren't you?"

She twists her head to look at me, one side of her face still smushed against the glass. "I think so."

"Shannon." I sigh and put my arm around her shoulders. "You have to find out for sure."

She jerks upright, sloughing off my arm. "No. No, I don't. I have work to do." She pulls open the cooler door, forcing me to step back.

"Did you hear about Peter's wedding?"

That causes a moment's hesitation, but just a tiny one, and then she's got both hands full of arrangements and is bustling away from me. "What about it?" she asks over her shoulder.

"They set a date."

"Good." Setting everything on the table she turns toward me, her face hard as stone. "Reckon they need a florist?"

"Probably, but I figure you'll be too busy. I mean, isn't Valentine's Day one of your busiest times?"

Someone should shout "avalanche" because the stone of her face completely slides off. "Valentine's Day? *This* Valentine's Day?"

"Yep. Next month."

"Hey, hon, what are you thinking for lunch?" Danny calls as he bounds down the stairs, jumping the last couple and landing flat-footed on our cement floor. "Oh, hey, Miss Jessup."

Now I know, especially for some of my northern friends, being called "miss" or "ma'am" makes them feel old. I've always liked it, as it seems polite and sweet. Until now.

"My name is Carolina," I snap.

His brown eyes go sad. He flutters his eyelashes as he folds his arms across his chest and hangs his head.

Oh, for crying out loud. I've hurt the baby's feelings. Shannon shoots me a fierce look, and I acknowledge that I was rude. "Sorry, Danny. I'm just in a bad mood, I guess. Why don't the two of you go to lunch? I'll handle things here, and Susie Mae will be back soon. Bonnie too." I smile—no, really—I smile, then move behind the counter.

"What d'ya think, babe?" Danny asks Shannon. Standing

with his hands tucked in his back pockets, he looks sideways at her, giving her a flirty grin.

Shannon reaches up to him, hands on the sides of his face, and pulls his lips to hers. "Why don't you go get us something and bring it back here? I have an arrangement that has to be done before lunch." She snuggles into him. "We can have a private lunch upstairs."

"Sure," he says as he pulls away, his hands having never left his back pockets.

Quickly I duck my head like I'm looking under the counter. I hear keys rattle and look back up to see him striding away toward the back door as he talks to his wife. "I've still got your keys. Think I'll run out to the blacktop and get some chili dogs. Easier than going to your folks' house and getting your mom to make us some sandwiches."

Shannon scurries after him. "Don't be hassling my mother to make sandwiches," she says, then realizes how loud she is. They speak more quietly for a moment as I try to ignore them. Then Shannon comes bustling to the counter. "Can you hand me my purse?" She grabs it and takes it back to where Danny waits.

All I can hear of their conversation is Danny's solution—"Just give me the twenty"—and then the back door closes. Shannon takes her time coming back up front.

I move over to find my feather duster again, and she goes behind the counter to put her purse back. She leans on the counter and looks out the front windows.

"You know, he's right. A chili dog will be good."

Susie Mae came in with extra muffins only a few minutes later. However, they were leftover "healthy" ones from Ruby's, so they went straight in the trash. She explained, "I got the last good one, and it had stuck in the pan, so I got it for free. Had some kind of meat in it, but it was good."

A group of ladies followed her in the door, and the door rarely stayed closed for five minutes at a time after that. Bonnie arrived full of energy and ideas, both about decorating Peter's office and selling books. Shannon talked to customers while arranging floral orders, and before we knew it, it was time to close. On weekdays we close at five, and almost magically the traffic stopped at four forty-five.

"What was that? I don't know when we've been that busy on a weekday." I exhale as Susie Mae collapses on the couch and Bonnie leans on her elbows from behind the counter. Shannon is seated on a stool at her worktable, scrolling through her phone.

"Here it is," she says. "Couple folks mentioned it, but I didn't have time to look. North Georgia Tourism Council has an ad up about the book festival. We're near the top of their listing. How did we rate that?"

I grab my phone and pull up the site. "Wait, those pics are of us—I mean, Blooming Books." I walk over to sit beside Susie Mae, and Bonnie leans over our shoulders.

"Those are here?" Susie Mae exclaims. "I mean, I know they are, but…" She looks around. "Guess it really does look that cool."

"Ohh," Shannon says. "Magnify one of them."

"D. LaMotte Photography." I hand my phone over to Bonnie so she can take a closer look. "I didn't know Delaney took those. It was sometime before the decorations were taken down."

Bonnie holds out my phone to me. "It's hard to believe, but it does look that nice in here. Even without the decorations. The books and flowers. Everything."

Susie Mae stands up. "Well, I sure will miss being here tomorrow. I have to go back to school."

I grab her arm. "Can you come in after school?"

She shakes her head. "No, I'm joining the yearbook staff. I like publishing *Taking Chances in Chancey*, but figured I'd like to see how it works with real paper and pictures. My counselor thought it'd be a good idea if I want to go into journalism in college."

"That is a great idea," I say, with Bonnie and Shannon agreeing. Susie Mae smiles and shrugs as she pulls her backpack out from beneath the counter. "I gotta go." She throws the words over her shoulder with her backpack, and she's out the front door.

Bonnie shudders. "These children not wearing coats make me freeze just looking at them." She rubs her arms, then looks at me, then Shannon. "Maybe this isn't the best time for me to start my business. Looking at those pictures and with the book festival coming up, I have a feeling today was just the beginning."

"Nonsense!" I climb up off the low couch. "We just need to hire some more help. A mom whose kids are back in school or a college student needing extra money." I pick up books that have been left on the table to be reshelved. "Or do you have any friends up in Laurel Cove that might be interested?"

Bonnie thinks while she gathers books left in odd places by customers who decided they didn't want them. I always wonder what changed their mind. Did they find something better? Realize they already own it?

"I know!" Shannon says as she slams down her scissors onto her worktable, making the flowers in the bucket beside her tremble. "Danny! Danny needs a job, and since he'll be living upstairs he'll always be available. It's perfect!"

Bonnie says nothing. I say nothing. I finally walk out of the shelves to look at my partner. "Danny? *Your* Danny?" Shannon holds up a finger at me because she's on the phone, but I try anyway. "No. Shannon, don't call—"

"Hey, babe, good news: I found you a job!"

Turning around I find Bonnie leaning back against the flower cooler, her eyes closed and mouth moving.

I assume she's praying.

Chapter 16

"I feel like I should just reopen the commissary we had in the bookshop during the movie." Lamenting my woes over speakerphone to Susan helps a little, but it doesn't help with the real problem at all.

My family all want to eat, but they are too busy to be in the same place anywhere near the same time. Scratch that. They are all downtown, which is what led to my reopening the commissary thought.

"How's the work at Phoenix's house going? Didn't Peter get most of that done when he and Shannon were living there?" Susan asks.

"Apparently not. He talked a good game but didn't do any of it." I crimp foil around the edge of my casserole dish. "I'm headed there right now, so I'll let you know."

"Stop by when you're done. I'm sitting here kicking myself for sending Silas packing. You haven't heard anything from him, have you?"

"Why would I hear anything from Silas Pendersen?"

Susan pauses. "He was staying up there. Y'all were friends."

"Not really. Listen, I've got to go. I'll let you know when they're done eating, and maybe I will stop by."

"Yes. Do come by. I'm lonely. Talk to you soon."

She hangs up, and I throw a bag of tortilla chips into my

big canvas bag, where they land on top of the Mexican casserole that was supposed to be tacos. Taco Tuesday sounded like a good idea until I found out no one was coming home for dinner. Jackson and Bryan are working on Phoenix's house, and Savannah is working late doing inventory at Andy's Place. I decided to put all the taco fixings in a dish, sprinkle cheese over top, and bake it a little. They can dig into it with the chips. I throw a couple of waters and sodas into a small cooler, and after collecting my purse and coat, I head outside.

It's a very calm night with temps hovering near fifty. Of course it was dark by the time I got home from the shop, which makes it feel colder. I load up the car in a couple of trips and then head down the hill to town. Between the holidays, Jackson working from home, and Francie's arrival, things have been too chaotic for my tastes. I like routine. I like easy. Hauling a meal to the jobsite is not easy, so we're going to have to figure something else out since it looks like the construction business is going to take off and actually be a success.

Parking on the street in front of Phoenix's house, I remember how excited Peter seemed when he bought it. He'd decided to stand on his own two feet. Anna was new to town, and she lived there with her uncle for a while. Then Shannon moved in, and it really did seem like his home. Given everything that's happened since, I'm not sure how we let ourselves fall for that. Or maybe I'm the only one who fell for it.

The house is still small, dark, and sad-looking. Only a couple of doors down, the Bedwell family home shines in the dark. It's big, with lights in almost every window. Looks like they've added some exterior lights, soft ones under the eaves, and more in the yard, some looking like flames. Did I miss that when the Christmas lights were up, or are they new? Or have they been there forever and I never noticed? Who knows?

Then there's Andy's Place, which actually belongs to Gertie. It's as big as Missus's house, but looks like a retail establishment with its share of neon. Either way, both buildings make this small house look like a poor relation. Heading up the concrete stairs from the sidewalk into the front yard, I see how very little Peter has done with it. He admitted to the whole town he'd been playing around at fixing this place, and it's clear to see he's right. This was all playacting to see if he could be one of us. Once again I'm struck by how little I knew him.

"Hey, Mom. What did you bring?" Bryan holds the screen door for me to pass inside.

"Taco dip. Go grab the cooler from the back seat. It's on the driver's side."

The screen door slaps behind him, and I move into the quiet living room. Jackson hollers down the stairs, "We'll be right down."

There's no sign of Phoenix, so I take my time looking around and try to remember the last time I was here. Peter and Shannon had a party, and things don't look that different now than they did then. Matter of fact, they don't look different at all. This is all the same furniture. But then again, what would Peter do with it? He can't move it into his mother's house. It's already full. Plus, I guess Phoenix didn't exactly come with furniture. I knew all the remodeling was being done upstairs, but I expected the downstairs to look at least a little different.

I sit the casserole on the kitchen island. It's one big room on this level: kitchen to the back, living room to the front. As I open the bag of chips, the guys come down the stairs and Bryan strides in the front door.

"Hey, hon," Jackson says as he hugs me and gives me a quick kiss. "Thanks for doing this. We're starving, but if we keep at it we can knock it out tonight. Just come back for some finishing touches."

Colt washes his hands behind me. "Yeah, thanks. Really need to get this done."

The terseness in his voice causes me to raise my eyebrows

at Jackson. He shrugs, then nods backward, toward the stairs. "Will's on the phone with Anna. He'll be right down."

"Okay. Dig in. Plenty for y'all. Savannah just texted that Gertie sprang for pizza for everyone doing inventory, so there's no need to save her any." They all gather round the dish, taking turns shoving their hands into the bag of tortilla chips. "Guys, there are plates."

"It's more fun this way," Bryan says. "Mom, you ought to see how good I've gotten at hammering. It's all my muscles from weight training."

Jackson laughs, and Will joins him as he comes up to us. "Hey, Mom. Anna says hi."

"How's Francie? And Anna, of course."

He takes a deep breath and lets it out, contentment rolling off him. "They're great. Just great."

Colt gives his nephew a dirty look, which only I can see. Poor Colt, working here in Phoenix's home where he is only welcomed as a worker, not a friend. Definitely not a lover.

Brian goes back to discussing his muscles. "Ain't that right, Coach? I've been doing a lot of weight training, haven't I?"

Colt grumbles something and then shoves a loaded chip into his mouth. He gets up, walks to the fridge, and opens it. "Anyone else want a beer?"

Jackson and I exchange another look. Will says, "No, thanks," then adds, "Should we be going into a client's refrigerator like that?"

Now a husband and father—still clueless. I give him that mom look, and Jackson smacks his arm. Even Bryan shakes his head at his big brother. Colt opens his beer, and as he turns toward us, he takes a long swig, then pauses and takes another. "Let's just say this client is an exception. God knows I've bought her enough drinks. About time she repays the favor."

I scoop out some of the dip onto a plate, put chips beside it, and take it over to where Colt is leaning against the counter. "Here. You need to eat."

"Thanks." Then his voice softens, and he shakes his head as he drops it so his chin nearly sits on his chest. "I still miss her. Don't think she misses me."

He takes another drink, and then I reach for, and take, the beer out of his hand. "Eat some first." He doesn't argue, just turns to the plate and starts scooping. I lean closer to him. "You have to take care of yourself. She's not what you thought she was. Happens to most of us."

He mumbles as he eats, and it's just the two of us in the conversation, our backs to the others. "Not to you and Jackson. Or even Will."

I laugh and pat his back. "You don't remember your brother being married to Shelby for that short time back in college? I can tell you about my wayward past another time." I sneak a look at Will, who is talking with Bryan at the end of the counter. I whisper, "And remember who was in your apartment before you moved in? Anna and Kyle Kendricks?"

"Oh yeah," he says, and as his stomach fills, the hard edges on his face ease. I can see his thoughts balancing out. The only way to maintain a pity party is to ignore the woes of the rest of the world. We often just need that slight perspective shift, but so often we avoid anyone who might provide it.

Bryan has eaten a lot—fast. "Want to show me your hammering handiwork?" I ask.

He leaps off the stool beside the island in answer. "Come on!"

I wink at Jackson as I pass and am happy to see Colt bring his plate and beer over next to his brother and nephew. The stairs are tight, not grand like those in Missus's home. At the top they end in a hallway with four doors leading off it. Directly in front of me is a door half opened. I stick my hand in and flip the light switch to discover that it's a small room full of boxes.

Looks like this is where Phoenix is sleeping while the master is remodeled. This, I believe, was Anna's room when she stayed here. I remember her talking about painting her room lilac. It's a small, nondescript room with two windows, no closet, a twin bed, and all those boxes.

"In here, Mom," Bryan calls, so I flip the lights off and turn down the narrow hall. I see a bathroom, which looks very plain, but not in a stage of remodel. At the end of the hall, there are two doors. One opens to the same side as the bathroom I just passed, and the other faces the front of the house. Obviously they once opened into separate rooms, but no longer. It's a large master suite. The bedroom to the side is now partially a bathroom. It shares a wall with the hallway bath. This bathroom has a sliding door, which opens it up to the huge master bedroom. Three windows along the front of the house have been replaced, and the new ones go from floor to ceiling. The ceilings up here are not high, but the tall windows makes the room appear much larger.

"See, here's what I was doing," Bryan calls, and I turn around to find him in a closet. A huge closet with so many shelves. "I did this wall here," he says with a tug on the edge of the wall. It separates the closet into two sections.

"Very impressive. This whole closet is very impressive. I bet Phoenix really likes it."

"Yeah, she was here earlier."

"She was? Where did she go?"

He continues tugging on the wall as if to check his hammering skills for real. "I don't know. She used to be nicer, don't you think?"

"Maybe. Or maybe we just like your uncle Colt so much that we hate that he's not happy because she broke up with him."

"Yeah, maybe." He picks up his hammer. "I finished all my work, so I'm going home with you. Need to read some history."

"Okay." I grab him with one arm. "I'm real proud of you

working with your dad and uncle like this. They really appreciate your help too."

He grins big and ducks under my arm, heading out of the closet and room. He says back at me, "Well, I'm glad to be learning all this stuff. I don't want to be a peckerwood like Uncle Colt says Peter is and have to call real men in to do my work."

I open my mouth to tell him not to talk like that as I follow him down the hall, when I hear Peter's voice from below. "Oh, is that what Uncle Colt says?"

Bryan stops in his tracks and looks at me. He cringes and waits for me to catch up. I shove him a bit and whisper, "Go on down. Can't stop now. Apologize too."

He starts down the stairs, saying with a bit of a laugh, "Sorry, Peter."

As we hit the lower steps and see the room, we find Peter and Phoenix beside the front door, staring at Colt as he strides toward them, saying, "Yeah, that's what I say."

"Okay, guys. I think you three should go upstairs and finish, and I'll clean up the kitchen. Bryan says he's going home with me." I rush in front of Colt, redirect him upstairs, and motion for Will and Jackson to follow him while instructing Bryan to get everything ready for the car. "Hi, guys," I say, turning a bright face to the newcomers. "Upstairs looks great! Good use of all that space. Phoenix, you're going to love it! Jackson says they'll be pretty much through tonight."

Phoenix smirks at me, then strides past me as she takes off her long, winter-white coat. "They can't be done early enough for me. It's so cumbersome having laborers in the house. Peter, can I get you a drink?"

I stare at him and say under my breath, "Please don't antagonize Colt. Just leave."

He looks at me like he doesn't know who I am, then lifts his head. "I'd love a drink." Looking back at me he smiles and adds, "My usual."

"Peter!" I hiss.

He scoffs, then leans closer and lowers his voice. "No worries about your poor brother-in-law, Carolina. I don't fight with the help."

He walks past me toward the kitchen. Bryan has collected everything, and with his head down he steps to the side and lets Peter pass. I just grit my teeth and open the front door. Behind me I hear my youngest, which makes me look back.

"Mr. Peter? Did you play football when you were in high school?" He's squinting back toward the kitchen.

Peter shrugs at him. "No."

Bryan grins and nods. "Okay. Just wondering. See y'all later." He turns and moves out the front door. I follow him, then rush around him to get to the van and get it opened.

"Thanks for carrying everything." I start the engine, and we pull away from the curb. "Why did you ask Peter about playing football?"

His grin is easy to see in the dashboard lights. "He's acting like a bully lately, and I just wanted to mess with him."

"Mess with him? What are you talking about?"

"You know. You ask them a question that doesn't mean anything, but they don't know that, so then they think you know something they don't know." He chuckles. "Bullies can't stand that." He disappears into texting for a moment, then asks, "Can Zoe come over? We'll study together."

"Sure. I can pick her up." His thumbs flying, he's gone again. But he's left a smile on my side of the van.

CHAPTER 17

"Sorry about last night," I say to Susan as I scoot into my side of the booth at Ruby's. "Bryan needed to come home, and then Zoe came over to study."

"No worries. Your coffee's hot. We saw you coming, so Libby just filled your cup. Speaking of Zoe, how are the Kendricks?"

"Good, I think. Zoe's a lot happier and doesn't have to babysit all the time. Kimmy is still working at the newspaper and even doing some writing on the side for magazines, Zoe said last night. They're still in therapy and pretty open about it, which sounds like a good thing. You know, helps keep you accountable."

"Susie Mae says everyone thinks Bryan and Zoe are a couple except they don't know it."

I laugh with her. "Yeah, she told me the same thing yesterday. Bryan is totally smitten, and I think he's decided to just wait on Zoe to be smitten too." I sigh and sit back. "I'm so glad school is back in. A little order out of the holiday chaos is much needed at our house."

Susan also sighs, but hers is more sad than relieved. "I miss the holidays already."

"Not me!" Libby declares as she sits a plate on our table. "Forrest being back in school proves there's a loving God in charge! That boy about wore me out."

"Cathy busy with her lingerie business, I guess?" I ask.

"Busy as a one-armed paper hanger!" Libby laughs loudly. "Yes, Cathy is going great guns with her business, and you'd think Forrest's daddy would have helped out, seeing as he's a teacher and had time off, but noooo. He's doing some tutoring stuff up at that fancy private school in Laurel Cove."

"Stephen Cross is teaching at Darien Academy? That's where Grant goes." Stephen Cross is not our favorite teacher, so Susan looks concerned.

Libby slumps, her forearm resting on her jutting hip bone. "Not exactly teaching. Some kind of SAT prep thing. They paid him right good for it, so I guess it was worth it. He and Cathy want to buy a house." She rolls her eyes and shifts her hips for the other one to jut out. "Those two beat all I ever saw. Muffins there are, um…" Her eyes focus on the muffins, but don't come up with anything. She shouts, "Ruby, what muffins did I give them?"

Ruby yells back, "From here they look to be brown. How in tarnation would I know what you gave them?"

Libby doesn't have a mean bone in her body, but there is evil in her eyes. Her jaw stiffens and she growls, "Ruby says they're brown." She gives both of us a quick look, then moves on to the next table.

Reaching for my brown muffin I whisper, "This place is getting dangerous. I bet I need some butter for this, but I'm not asking."

Susan laughs. "Ruby'll figure things out. She's hit some rough patches in the past. Mostly revolving around Jewel, and this time will be the same. If we survive it." She watches me take a small bite. "So. What is it?"

"Oh, it's amazing. It's, uh, sweet, but oh, I'm not good with flavors."

Susan tries hers. "Maybe orange? No."

"Lime," Ruby says as she comes out to our table, then motions for Susan to scoot over so she can join us. "Lime and brown sugar. Jewel has a lime tree in her new yard there in Florida, and it's plum covered with them. Did you know citrus is harvested now? Like in the winter?"

"You used limes from Jewel's yard?" I ask.

"Don't be silly. It just gave me the idea. But something green or light-colored felt too springy, so I tried brown sugar and even some cocoa powder. You like them?"

"They are really good. So different," I say. "How are you doing? Jewel getting settled in?"

"Yeah, they love it there. I'm doing okay. Libby's getting on my nerves something fierce."

Susan's eyes go wide and she presses her lips shut, but I'm not that smart, and not ready to throw the older waitress under the bus. "She sure was a big help to you the other day when you weren't feeling good." I stare at her so she knows everyone knows she wasn't just not feeling good.

"Do you think I don't know that? That's part of what makes it so hard. Libby!" she shouts, startling Susan and me.

"What?" Libby spits back. I didn't realize she could actually sound like that.

"They need coffee refills and butter, and the muffins are lime and brown sugar. Ones in the oven are lime and, uh, I don't remember. But I'll let you know." She pauses, clears her throat, and says just as loudly, "Thank you."

Libby gives me her happy grin over her boss's head. "Why, you're welcome. You want some coffee, Ruby? I'll watch the oven for you. Sit and visit for a minute."

"No. Thank you, but no." She pushes out of the booth and shuffles behind the counter.

I watch her slowly move along. "She just seems old now, you know?"

Susan nods. "I do. She and Missus both have lost their spark, and things just don't feel the same in Chancey."

"At least we know why you've lost your spark. Still not heard from Silas?"

"No, and I've decided that's a good thing."

"Really? I agree, but what got you to that conclusion?"

Libby approaches our table with her fresh pot of coffee. "Sorry about that earlier. Other muffins are lime-and-carrot served with cream cheese on the side." She shrugs as she pours. "Who knows what that'll taste like? Anyway, there's your butter. Y'all forgive Ruby. She'll be back to normal soon." Lowering her voice she bends toward us. "I'm working on something." Then with a wink she's gone, both of us staring after her.

We meet eyes and pause. "As I was saying," Susan continues, "Silas is gone, and while he was a good thing for a while, I learned a lot about myself and what I want."

"Good." I lift my cup for a sip of Ruby's fresh, hot coffee. "So, what is it you want?"

"Griffin. I want Griffin. I'm getting my husband back."

Chapter 18

Being careful to be quiet, I let myself in the front door of Blooming Books. It's only a quarter until nine, and we don't open until ten. Susan made her declaration of reclaiming Griffin, but that was all. I had time, but she wanted to get to work. So now I'm here early and alone, which is how I want to keep it. I'm not even sure if Danny and Shannon have moved in upstairs, but if they have I want them to stay up there for now.

Danny is starting out here this morning, and I'm sick about it. He's a nice enough guy, I think, but he's just a bit too good-looking. I've always had a mistrust of really good-looking people. Honestly, that's some of my issue with Savannah, I think. I never imagined my daughter would be one of those pretty, popular kids, but I'm kinda used to that now. I think.

I turn on some lights and light the candles near the front window. Bonnie has once again decorated our window, and it's so cozy. Flannel pillows and throws draped around books all with winter themes. Mugs of fake hot chocolate, piles of marshmallows (stale by now) are accented with sedate, woodsy flower arrangements that lean toward comfort more than the big, bright holiday arrangements do. Shannon provided Bonnie with pots of green plants to tuck around the window and store as she says that's what a lot of folks want this time of year, something actually living.

There are stacks of books to be put back on the shelves as we were too tired to straighten everything last night. As I pick up the first stack, I hear steps upstairs. So they did move in. I'm going to give Danny a chance. It's not his fault that Shannon and Peter have so totally screwed everything up. Of course, I'm the only who knows how completely screwed up things are.

"Carolina?" Shannon calls down the stairs.

"Yep. I'm here."

"Okay. We'll be down in a bit. No hurry, right?" She chuckles, and I can't help but roll my eyes. However, I'm not through the first stack of books before Danny comes loping down the stairs. Smile in place I step out to greet him.

"Good morning! So y'all got moved in upstairs?"

He comes to a sudden stop. "Miss Carolina! You about gave me a heart attack! I didn't realize you were down here." He half turns toward the stairs and looks up.

I hear the creaky plumbing that says Shannon is getting in the shower. He looks around, brown eyes wide like he's surprised not only to find me here, but to find himself here. "Forgot something," he blurts, and he hurries to the back and then dashes up the stairs, his long legs taking them two and three at a time.

"Okay. That was just weird," I say to myself and go back to reshelving books. I do not, repeat, do not check the cash register drawer or the petty cash.

"Good morning!" I call out as Bonnie comes struggling in the back door. "Here, let me help you."

"Thanks. If you'll take these, then I can get the fabric samples." I take the crate to her new space and then go back to hold the heavy door open.

"Look at you! Fabric samples and everything. You sure that's all?"

"Yep. All for now. The less I move in, the less I have to move when Jackson builds my shelves." She unloads her armful onto the crate I carried in and then pulls off her coat. "Have you been here long?"

"A while." I lean toward her and whisper. "Shannon and Danny have moved in upstairs."

She wrinkles her nose. "I'm going to have to try and like the boy. He just reminds me of some of my least favorite students. The boys who knew they were the apple of every girl's eye and acted so sweet and innocent... Meanwhile, they were breaking hearts right and left." She folds her coat over her arm. "But I'm going to get over that, right? I mean, if he really is going to work here?"

I crush her hopeful look. "Starts in about ten minutes." Following her to the coatrack, I walk past her and behind the counter. "I think we're ready to open. I'll work with Danny this morning. I know you want to do some organizing of your decorator space."

"No worries, I'll keep an ear open and you can just give me a holler if you need me. Jackson is coming down around lunchtime to talk over what I want back there, and Gertie is meeting him here since she is the owner of the building."

"Oh, I didn't talk much to Jackson this morning. I left early to meet Susan, and he was getting a late start. It'll be good to see him. Maybe he can bring me a sandwich."

The door upstairs slams, and we look up. Danny comes into view. "Shannon will be here in a minute. She's not feeling so good. But here I am, ready to start, boss!" He laughs. "Or should I say 'bossettes'? I've never had a woman boss before."

"I'm not your boss," Bonnie declares before walking away, muttering, "Thank God."

I'm showing him the shelves and trying to explain our system of book categories, but he's a bit distracted. He keeps pulling out books and looking at them, then not putting them back in the space where he found them.

"No. Putting the books back where they belong is actually your job. You have to pay attention so you'll know where everything goes. These are nonfiction. We don't have many of them, well, outside biographies, so they go all together alphabetically." I hurry to add, "By the author's last name. Not the title."

"Doing it by title seems easier to me." He points to the book cover. "It's the first thing you see."

"But we want the books by one author together. So we do it by author's name. Last name."

He shrugs. "You're the boss." He grins. "And here comes my other boss. Hey, Shan."

"You feeling okay?" I ask while gratefully walking away from our new employee.

"I feel fine. I just didn't mean to get my hair wet in the shower, but…" She grins at her husband. "Things happen, I guess." There's that chuckle again.

He looks at me and shrugs. (He shrugs a lot, I'm noticing.) "Gotta keep my lady happy."

"He said you were feeling sick."

Shannon is wearing a blousy magenta tunic over black leggings. I notice when I say "sick" her hand jumps to her stomach. She drops her hand when I look at it. "No. I'm fine. Just fine. Let's get that open sign turned!" Danny is standing near the door, but he only looks at the sign. Obviously that is something for a bossette to do. Shannon obliges and walks to the door, unlocks it, and turns the sign over.

Danny claps his hands and startles us all. "Let the fun begin!" he shouts. "One of you make a pot of coffee, and I'll go get muffins from Ruby's for everyone. Guess we pay out of petty cash for muffins?"

"No," I snap. "That's not what we do."

Shannon frowns at me. "But for his first day? We bought them for Susie Mae's first day. Bonnie's too." She reaches under the counter and pulls out a brightly colored bag, something I got some free makeup in from a department store. It's been our petty cash bag since we opened.

"Yeah, you're right. I forgot."

He punches my arm as he strides by on his way to take the money from Shannon. "No hard feelings, boss. My mom has trouble remembering things too. Just part of growing old, she says!" He grins, winks, and, money in hand, waves on his way out the door.

You know, he's getting less and less good-looking by the minute.

Chapter 19

"Hey. Don't worry about bringing me anything," I tell Jackson with the phone cradled against my shoulder as I check out another customer. "Delaney called and wants to meet for lunch."

"Okay. I've got to go," he says and hangs up. I let my phone fall into my hand and lay it down. We've been steadily busy all morning, but we've noticed around lunchtime things slow down. Probably because there's nowhere to eat lunch here. I assumed Delaney and I would eat at her house, but she said she'd meet me here.

Danny is working out okay. He likes to talk and is interested in a lot of things, so that's a good thing, and everyone likes him. His big smile, sunny disposition, and enthusiasm for whatever you're enthused about have actually added a brightness in our place. Shannon is in hog heaven just watching him, so there's also that.

Needless to say, I can't wait to get out of here.

"Hey ho, Carolina!" Gertie blusters in the front door. She's bigger than life normally, but even more so now that she got a full-length, red leather coat for Christmas. She loves it. Wouldn't dream of leaving home without it. She sails in, bringing a blast of cold air, the aroma of good leather, and cheer. She's like the embodiment of the old-fashioned St. Nick in my mind: complete with the big, gray fur hat (you've seen those pictures, right?), except instead of a hat she's wearing her hair up in a messy bun. She says she's looking for an appropriate grandmother style. I thinks she needs to keep looking, but she's awfully happy.

Patty follows her, looking weak and gray. She comes straight to the counter. "Hey, Carolina."

"Poor thing. Are you still having morning sickness?"

"Yes, ma'am. Something awful. Momma said the fresh air would help, but I don't think so." She looks over her shoulder. "I'm gonna go sit down."

"Can I get you anything?"

"No, thanks. I've got a baggie of crackers in my purse and a Coke." She pulls away just as another customer comes to the counter.

"This sure is a fun place. Can't believe I never knew Chancey had a bookstore," the woman says, then leans closer to me. "Is that the woman who owns the moonshine place?"

"Yes, it is. Gertie Samson in all her glory," I say as Gertie's booming voice and laughter fill the store, even with its high ceilings.

"I thought so. There's an article about her place in the Roswell paper this week. Is the moonshine good?"

"Delicious. The Roswell paper, you say? Can I find that online, you think?"

She picks up her bag. "Oh, I'm sure. Thanks, and I'll see you this weekend. I'm bringing my husband back. Are there any good restaurants nearby?"

"Not yet. One's opening next door soon. Now if you're here early, then Ruby's café has great muffins, but that's really all she serves. But they are really good muffins."

A quizzical look passes over the woman's face, and then she smiles. "Okay, thanks. See you later."

You know, until I said it just now I didn't think about how

odd it is to only sell muffins. Maybe that's something Ruby should think about. Branching out a bit, serving some different things. That might get her out of her slump.

Looking for Shannon I walk back toward her worktable, but I find that Jackson has arrived. "I didn't know you were here already."

"Slipped in the back door. You were busy up front." He steps to me, and we kiss quickly. "We've pretty much sized up what we're going to do back here."

Bonnie is beaming. "It's going to be perfect. Shelves and cabinets, but all underneath the stairs. I don't think it'll infringe on the store at all. Where's Shannon? We'll show you both."

"I don't know. I was looking for her. Maybe she's helping Danny."

Gertie stretches to look up toward the bookshelves. "Helping him get his pants off if I had to guess." Then she yells, "Shannon Chilton Kinnock! Let go of that boy and get back here so we can all get back to our lives." Lowering her voice she says, "They are married, aren't they? I mean, I'm not sure he's actually divorced, but when has that stopped a Chilton?"

Shannon scurries around the back row of bookcases and makes a beeline for us. "What? What do you want?"

She looks guilty. Really guilty and, okay, really happy. "Oh, hey, Jackson." She looks at me and asks, "What time do you want Danny to take lunch?"

"How about now? There are no customers, and we're all here." Her face clouds at my words.

"Sakes, Carolina!" Gertie exclaims, waving arms and all. "She wants to know when she can take your employee upstairs and have her way with him." Gertie turns from me to the embarrassed florist. "Send him on up. He's a young man and needs lunch. Tell him you'll be upstairs before he's had time to wipe up the crumbs."

Jackson busts out a laugh, and though Shannon turns redder, she also turns to say, "Hon? You can go on up and eat. I'll be there in just a couple."

"Yeehaw!" Danny says as he dashes past us. "I'm starving!"

Bonnie frowns and says under her breath to me, "How old is he?"

Jackson doesn't wait for permission; he starts laying out what he and Colt will do, and in less than ten minutes he's gone back to his office at the house and Bonnie is manning the front counter. An empty store means I'm sitting and visiting with Patty and Gertie on the front couches.

Patty has perked up a bit and has some color in her face. "I miss being here with y'all. It's lonely at my house."

Gertie looks at me and then gives me a nod like I'm supposed to say something. Then she arches her eyebrows at me, and I *know* I'm supposed to say something. I just don't know what. Finally with a big sigh she does it for me, "Carolina would probably love for you to come over here and visit any time."

"Oh! Yes, of course. Any time. You enjoy books, and I'd love to see you more. We can meet at Ruby's too."

"I don't know. It's just so hard to get the energy to leave the house. And now that it's cold, what if there's snow or ice on the ground?" Patty is wrapped up in her thick coat, stuffed into the corner of the couch. I know she also got a new coat for Christmas, but here she is in her old, dull, brown one.

"Where's your new coat?"

Gertie makes a dismissive sound low in her throat and looks away. Patty sniffs. "What if I throw up on it? And I was just coming over here. Don't want to waste it." Then she rubs her nose with her sleeve, and I kind of see her point.

"Let me get you a Kleenex." I go behind the counter and bring her the box we keep there.

Gertie is sitting forward on the couch when I get back. She stands and takes the box from me to hand to her daughter. "Carolina, I need to show you something back here with Bonnie's new area." She pushes me ahead of her, and as we pass Bonnie, she says, "Bonnie, darlin', would you mind going over to sit with Sad Sack?"

Bonnie clicks her tongue. "No need to call anyone names. Much less the woman carrying your grandbaby. I'd love to visit with Patty." Bonnie is good at putting Gertie in her place, not that Gertie knows it, but it makes the rest of us feel better.

"Okay," Gertie says once we're alone. "You saw with your own two eyes what's going on with Patty. I've been doing some googling, and I'm thinking this has to do with being pregnant. There's that postpartum depression, but that's for after the baby comes. Lands-a-mercy! She's finally got all she's ever wanted, and she's acting like she's headed for the guillotine."

"Well, have you asked her?"

Gertie stares at me. "Asked her? She don't know anything about being pregnant."

"I mean about why she's feeling sad."

"Serious? If she knew why she was feeling sad, she'd just fix it and not be sad anymore, right? C'mon, think!"

I tug on Gertie's coat sleeve and pull her farther back in the big space. "Depression doesn't work like that. She needs to talk to someone."

The big woman slaps her forehead, setting her messy, gray bun to lobbing around her head like one of those balls on a rubber band tied to a paddle. "Duh! That's what this whole convo here is about. For her to come over here and talk to you and Bonnie and even that Shannon. She seems to be in a pretty good mood lately. Although if you'd told me sex with Danny Kinnock would beat sex with Peter Bedwell, I'd have had to call you a liar." She pats me on the back and starts walking back up front. "Okay. Good to know we're on the same page. I'll make sure she gets her lazy tail up and out of the house and over here. After that if you want to take her to Ruby's or whatever, that's up to you. I've got to go. I'll come give her a ride home before closing since it gets dark so early now." She lets off talking—instructing—me to start telling Patty what she's going to be doing.

It's nice and quiet back in the dark until I hear the door upstairs open. I hurry back toward the front just in time to see a tsunami of red leather leaving.

Patty looks up at me. "Momma says I have to stay here and help y'all today. Can you bring me a trash can closer in case I have to throw up?"

CHAPTER 20

"Are you ready? Our reservation is for one o'clock." Delaney finds me rearranging one of the shelves on the side of the shop farthest from the front door. Keeping the shelves full with our brisk sales is a problem I never even imagined having.

"Sure, but a reservation? Where are we going?" I push the box of books I was pulling from to the end of the aisle. "Those will wait on me there. Do I look okay for wherever we're going?"

"Of course!" She winks and swings around, saying "hi" and "bye" to Bonnie and Patty.

I brush dust off my black, tight-leg jeans and straighten my ice-blue sweater. It was a Christmas gift from my mom, and I'm glad I wore it today. It's long and not too thick. Perfect for working, but not what I would've worn if I'd known we were going somewhere that needed reservations for lunch. However, it does still look new. Delaney has on boots, ivory leggings, and a thick sweater in ivory, browns, and golds. Her hair is down, but held back with a headband, and she's wearing gloves that match her suede brown boots.

Shannon is nowhere in sight as I look around. Then Bonnie motions that Shannon is back by her florist table. At that moment Delaney says, "Ah, there you are." I thinks she's talking about me, but then I see she's headed straight back to the worktable. "Shannon. I just want to ease your mind. I will not be burdening you with our wedding flowers on your busiest weekend. My mother's best friend owns a floral shop and has always said she wanted to do my flowers. Plus she no longer actually works in her shop, so she'll be available all of Valentine's weekend. There are some standing orders I'll be needing in the future, but we'll talk about that, well, in the future!" She laughs and then pauses before lowering her voice. "I hope that's okay with you?"

Shannon swallows and nods. "Absolutely."

Delaney lets out a long breath and turns, catching my eye and shaking her head just a touch. Striding in my direction, she looks relieved, and I open the door so we can head out.

On the sidewalk, she stops and reaches out to grasp my upper arm. "Thank goodness that's over. Poor Shannon in the middle of all this. I just wanted to get it out in the open. Of course she doesn't want to do our flowers, and I'm grateful for the Valentine's excuse. Now, lunch!"

"Oh! I forgot my coat," I say, but she doesn't let go of my arm as I head back into the shop.

"You won't need it. We're already here." She points to the door next door. The door to Peter's bistro, or AC's, as it will soon be called. "We're having a tasting for AC's to cater the reception in the old train depot."

She pulls on the big, old door and holds it open for me to step through. I've not seen inside since the place was in the beginning stages of remodeling. It's very open, except looking around I see that strategically placed half walls make the tables feel private. There are strings of paper lanterns along the side walls, and more lanterns sit on top of the half walls. The floor has been painted in stripes of black and white, and it has very much the same bistro-type vibe Peter had in his store. There are even canopies over some of the tables and large potted plants forming their own walls. It's very nice, but not too nice; perfect for Chancey. As we walk farther in, Alex meets us.

"Hello! We have you at a table here beside the window and the fountain. Welcome to AC's." The wooden chairs are painted black but have striped cushions in them. Again, it feels very much like an outdoor place in the city. We are seated, handed a handwritten menu of what we'll be having today, and then he pulls over a wine bucket on a stand. "Can I offer you prosecco since this is a celebration you're planning?"

We look at each other and grin. "Sure!"

He pours, places the bottle back in the ice bucket, and then says to relax and that our first appetizer plate will be out shortly.

"This is so nice. I can't believe we're going to have this kind of restaurant in Chancey, right next to our shop." I take a sip. "Speaking of the shop, thank you for all the business you've sent our way. The pictures and write-up on the tourism site, and I just heard Gertie's is featured in the Roswell paper? I imagine that's you too?"

"Just helping out friends. Chancey is my home now." She lifts her glass. "To Chancey."

"To Chancey," I echo. "So, you're having the reception at the depot? The Parlor and Porch?"

"Yes. Vows at Peter's house for just family and a few close friends in the afternoon with an early dinner catered by another of my mother's friends also at the Bedwells'. Then the reception for more people that evening at the depot. Afterward we'll dash away for our honeymoon and be back before anyone even misses us."

We toast that, and then I ask what everyone wants to know. "I guess I'm wondering why the big hurry?"

"Here we are," Alex says as he places two small plates in front of us. "We'll start with some cold hors d'oeuvres, move on to hot ones, then end with sweet bites. You said you want a combination that evening, but I thought this would allow you to more easily judge between similar bites."

Delaney clasps her hands and smiles. "Perfect. Now, what do we have here?"

He describes in great detail each beautiful item, but I get lost in the encrusted and infused and embellished. There's a couple of large shrimp, a green slice of avocado on a square of toast, a citrus salad with toasted coconut and curry, or maybe the curry was on the shrimp? Something wrapped in phyllo dough and raw beef and salmon—except he didn't say raw, I'm just telling you what it looks like. I'm ready for him to go so we can start eating.

Alex gave us both pads of paper and pencils to write down our thoughts, but at the end mine looks like a harried teacher doing the last batch of grades before leaving on Christmas break—all hastily scribbled A's.

Delaney writes more, but then she lays down her pencil. "I agree with your assessment. They are all delicious. I want them all!" We laugh and sit back to wait for more while we drink. I raise my eyebrows at her, seeing if she remembers what I asked before Alex came to our table.

She does. "So. What's the hurry, you asked?" She looks around, but we're the only ones here. "Basically, I'm ready to be married. I'm done fighting my parents and grandparents and aunts and uncles."

"Fighting about what?"

"I need to be married. I'm the only heir on my father's side. His sisters didn't have children. One is mentally handicapped, and the other, believe it or not, gave everything up to become a nun. The family isn't even Catholic. She literally ran away to a nunnery to get away from the family. My parents had me and no more, and now for me to get on with my life, I need to get married. Back in college, the first time our parents tried to push it on us, an arranged marriage wasn't even thinkable to Peter or me. If only they'd left us alone we might've gotten together back then, but we were not going to let them get their way." Tears form in her eyes, and she looks out the window as she wipes them away.

Alex arrives with two more plates and detailed descriptions. I'm listening even less this time. I know I'll eat it all, and I know it'll all be good. Watching Delaney charm the young man with her praise and questions, I'm stunned she is in this situation. She has the world on a string. Beautiful, accomplished, nice. I don't get it.

As soon as the kitchen door swings shut, I say just that. "I don't get it. Forget them all. Why do you need to make them all happy?"

Her eyes are dry but weary. "That's sweet, but it's not reality. Oh, this crab cake is perfect. Put a dab of the sauce on it."

She's right of course, and once I start tasting, it's too hard to stop. We eat and compare, and again she says she wants it all.

I resist licking my fingers and picking up the tiny crumbs left on my plate. "I can't wait for this place to be open."

She nods. "I think they're going to do very well. I've arranged some publicity for them, which is very well deserved." She leans forward to pull the prosecco from the bucket and fill our glasses again.

"So, putting Chancey on the map, that's your reality now?"

Startled, she looks up, then smiles. "Something like that. I'm tired of living in the shadows of my family. Or in the shadows of my choices. I want it all, and it's available to me. Here."

Taking a sip, I pause. "At the risk of being told I'm sweet again, I have to say I still don't get it. What is so awful about your life?"

"Did I say it was awful?" She stops, then lifts her glass in salute to me. "Okay. I didn't say it, but I made it sound that way. It's more just what my life can be. It's like this: I'm tired of sitting at the kids' table. I want to be treated like a grown-up, and that means having my own house, my own family, being married."

"Those things don't make you a grown-up."

"They do in my world. First there's the money. I need to be married to get control according to my father. Until I'm married I'm just a kid with no direction, and he is holding the purse strings until I prove myself. Maybe if I'd gone into something responsible like banking or medicine, but I take pictures." She looks down at the table. "I didn't even finish college."

"But your photography does well. I mean, I've looked at your website and everything. You're very accomplished. They should be thrilled to have you for a daughter."

She sighs. "They are. They aren't monsters. I've given you the wrong impression. It's just, well, I'm ready. I'm ready to get this next part of my life started. To be married and settled. Oh, Alex! Everything was amazing!"

Again I watch them talk, and I'm struck by how little we know about what is going on in someone else's head. I thought Delaney had the world on a string. I thought she knew exactly what she was doing. I thought, well, a lot of things.

The front door opens, but we're in the corner. We can't see around the half wall beside us, but we don't have to wonder who entered for long. Alex takes a step back and holds an arm out. "We're over here. Glad you could join us, Mr. Bedwell."

"Peter. We're partners, Alex. Call me Peter. Hello, Carolina." He's striking in his dark gray dress coat, close-cut beard, and windblown hair. He leans down to kiss his fiancée's cheek. "Glad I caught you here. Was everything as delicious as I said it would be?"

I look across the table, and Delaney's face is flushed, her eyes bright, and her lips soft. Oh, here's the hurry. Something I hadn't thought about. She's flat-out, undeniably, knees-turned-to-jelly, insides-mushy in love with Peter Bedwell.

Chapter 21

"Seems like having money can keep you from growing up."

I'm sharing my opinions with my husband, who is ignoring me at the kitchen table while he works on his laptop. I'm chopping a cucumber for salad to go with a pan of lasagna my mother left when she and Dad were here to see Francie. She made a smaller one for Will and Anna's freezer; we planned on eating this one while they were here but never got around to it, so I stuck it in the freezer for a day like today.

Jackson doesn't look away from the screen but says, "Then I sure could use a little less growing up about now."

"Oh, didn't think you were listening. How is money going with the company? Colt & Company, I should say." The name still rankles me, but Jackson said it was fine with him, so I guess it should be fine with me. But still…

"Just an awful lot of outlay and not much coming in yet. Not sure we're handling taking deposits right. Just feels weird asking for money."

"Shouldn't that kind of thing be in the contract?"

He turns to face me. "Contract? Have you signed a contract since we moved to Chancey? Not the way they do business here. Or at least that's what everyone keeps telling me."

"Well, that seems like a red flag to me." I pull the lasagna out of the oven. "Can you yell at Savannah and Bryan? Tell them it's time to eat."

It's just the four of us for dinner, which feels strange, especially with this huge pan of cheese, noodles, and meat. I assumed we'd have our usual drop-ins and didn't ask until it was already in the oven. No Ricky, no Will and Anna, no Zoe. Susan and her family are up at Griffin's eating together—step one in her campaign to get her husband back—and even Colt had plans. I just hope his plans don't involve peeping in Phoenix's windows.

With the four of us seated and eating, Savannah whispers, "This is kind of creepy. It's so quiet."

I can't help but sigh. "Then talk. Quit answering my questions with just a yes or a no or a shrug." I nudge Jackson with my foot under the table. "That means you too."

Bryan looks around. His mouth is full, as it has been since he sat down. He's the only one with some semblance of an excuse for not participating in the conversation. He swallows, but before he can shovel in more I wave at him.

"You! Tell me how your new classes are this semester."

"Good. I mean. Not really, but it is what it is." And his mouth is full again.

Using my fork I point at his sister. "How are the college applications going? I know you don't want any help, but at least give us an idea of where you're applying."

She doesn't even look up or even answer my question. "My classes suck. I hate all my teachers. They took away my last-period study hall just because I'm not cheering now, and they cancelled my theater elective because Stephen is teaching up at Darien Academy."

"I heard he was just doing some tutoring on the weekend. Also, he's Mr. Cross to you. And do you need that elective to graduate?"

"I'm kind of tired of the whole theater thing anyway. Those

kids are so dramatic." I look to see if she's making a pun, but she's still playing with her salad. Then she jerks her head up, eyes wide and incredulous. "They gave me pottery. How lame is that? We're all going to protest in the principal's office tomorrow. They can't just do that to us!"

Jackson narrows his eyes at her. "You better not get in trouble. You're a senior; you need to think about college. It's an elective. What's it matter what it's in?"

"They can't just change things without telling us! Theater could've been my major!" She narrows her eyes right back at her dad. "Well, if I *go* to college at all. *If!*"

I reach out and grab Jackson's arm. "You two stop. We're not doing this at the dinner table." They go back to eating, and the silence falls again. Seems there's no happy middle with the two of them these days. I don't remember Will and Jackson sparring like this his senior year, but then again, Will is pretty easygoing.

"There's more salad," I offer, but no one even looks up at me. Okay, I'll try something else. "We have guests coming tomorrow."

More quiet. "Two retired couples heading to Florida from Illinois."

Maybe a question. "Guess where I ate lunch today?" No one appears interested, but I'm telling them anyway. "I ate at AC's. The food was wonderful."

"Good," Jackson responds. "Is there more salad?"

No. He's not joking. "I just said there's more salad. Here." I throw the bowl at him. Of course I didn't throw it. I handed it to him. Aggressively.

Savannah jolts alive. "Don't eat it all. I want some!"

"I'm not eating it all," he snaps. "Chill out."

She rolls her eyes, and Bryan giggles. I give the kids my warning look that says, "Shut up. Shut up now!"

"Whatever." She takes the bowl her dad passes to her by way

of her brother. "Was Angie at AC's? She's loving living down-town with Alex."

I think Jackson growls, but I rush to cover it. "No. She still has school. Your dad and Colt did a wonderful job on the place. It's almost like you're eating outside. And the food was delicious. We had plates of appetizers as a tasting for Peter and Delaney's wedding reception."

"I'm working that," Savannah says as she pours ranch dressing on her salad.

"That's enough dressing," her dad decrees. "You had a lake of it in there already." He points his fork at her. "And what do you mean you're working that? The wedding reception?"

"Why? You don't want me doing that either?" Shrill and mean already, her voice gets louder. "I mean, come on, it might look really good on my college applications. Shows I have life skills."

I stand up. "That's it. We're done here. No more family meals. Ever!" I might've shouted the word "ever," but does anyone blame me?

"Honey, sit down. I'm sorry," Jackson tries, but I really am done.

"No. I've worked all day, and I'm tired. Y'all don't want to sit together and have a nice meal, then fine by me." I point at Savannah. "If you roll your eyes you're getting a spanking! I honestly think I can still take you!"

Well, now it's a different kind of quiet, a wide-eyed, mouths-dropped-open kind of quiet, until Bryan bursts out laughing. Then I can't help it. I sit down and start laughing too. Jackson and Savannah join in, and we find it hard to stop because every time we almost do, Bryan mumbles, "Mom's going to spank you," or, "Watch out! She thinks she can still take you!"

Finally Jackson stands and comes up behind my chair. He takes my hand and lifts it up. As I stand he hugs me. "Thank you for dinner. We are sorry we acted so awful. Now, you go sit down, and we're cleaning up the kitchen. Right, kids?"

They readily agree and won't even let me take my plate to the sink. Bryan dashes into the living room, then back. "I put your book you've been reading in there on the couch. Go read it."

"Well, if you're sure. Sorry for yelling. Thanks." I leave the dining room, and hearing them chatting and laughing behind me feels so good. We needed that laugh to get on some solid ground again.

Families are not easy.

But I guess they're worth it.

CHAPTER 22

"Come on," Susan begs. "Let's go to Phoenix's juice bar. I want to check that place out." She swirls around in the middle of Blooming Books in the low light of the early morning. "I might take some dance classes."

"Looks like you had a good time last night. How's Griffin?"

She looks around before answering. "He was good. He misses me. I can tell." She lowers her voice even more. "And his mother is getting on his last nerve."

I chuckle. Rachel Lyles moved in almost as soon as Susan moved out. She's one of those mothers who always knew her four children would be better off with her than with their spouses. That kind of person not only makes for a bad parent; they are hard people all the way around. "Okay. I'll go with you for a smoothie at Phoenix's if you'll stop in Rachel's new pop-up shop with me."

Susan's face settles into a frown as she thinks, so I prod her. "Hurry. Anna is coming by to drop Francie off in about an hour." Now I lower my voice. "If Patty's going to be hanging out here, I might as well get some babysitting out of her. I get to see Francie, Anna gets time to herself, and Patty gets some supervised parenting experience."

Shannon has taken Patty and Bonnie upstairs to see the apartment while Danny is sweeping and mopping the back area. For an empty space it gets awfully dusty, and Danny doesn't mind doing the grunt work the rest of us avoid. The boy is growing on me.

By the time I get my coat on, the women are coming down the stairs and our first customers are looking around the store. I tell Bonnie I'll be back in a bit, and Susan and I are out in the cold, foggy morning.

"So, Campaign Griffin got started off well?"

Susan grins and peeks out from beneath her hood at me. She has on an all-weather coat in deep purple. It has a fake fur liner in silver gray and a big hood she has pulled up. Seems like everyone got new coats for Christmas, and my old, dark-green, wool one has seen better days. It feels even older and more out of fashion with the recent comparisons. "Griffin was the easy one. He fell right into laughing and strolling down memory lane. The kids seemed suspicious. You'll have to tell me what Susie Mae says about it all. Grant was almost hostile."

Her voice trails off, and we are quiet for a moment. Then she clears her throat. "And I guess I understand that. They don't exactly trust me."

"It'll take time. But you've got plenty of that, right?" We smile at each other and then look in the windows as we pass Ruby's. "Looks like the regular crowd. Today's Thursday, so that's the historical society ladies at the big table. I'm glad Missus has her back to the windows," Susan says, and I nod in agreement. Otherwise, Missus would find some reason to slow us down.

"Okay, pop-up shop first or smoothies?" I ask as we continue walking.

Susan stops, then plows on ahead. "Pop-up shop. Get it over with."

There's a lingering scent of pine since Rachel Lyles finally got rid of the Sexy Belles and all their exotic paraphernalia and let the Boy Scouts sell their Christmas trees in the space. With a fairly low ceiling, old linoleum on the floor, and beige paneling, it's not an attractive space to begin with, but now it might be even more unattractive.

Susan and I are stopped only a couple of feet inside the door. The jangle of the door alarm has Rachel coming from the back through the piles of cardboard boxes to greet us. Until she actually sees us.

"Oh. Susan. Carolina. What do you want?" Rachel Lyles is heavyset with dark hair and thick eyebrows. I can't help but think "hanging judge" every time I see her. She always looks like she's getting ready to sentence you to hang and not a bit sorry about it.

I smile anyway. "We wanted to see the new stuff." I take a step closer to the nearest box. "Opening is today, right?"

"I suppose. Although I don't think people here understand the concept of a pop-up store. Where's the cute mountain crafts, homemade jams, inspirational signs? Heck, I'd even take some of those rude, stupid hillbilly signs over this!" She waves her arms. "It's plumbing supplies! First all those sex toys and now this." She sounds like she could cry.

I look around to find Susan as shocked as I am. She pushes me forward, and I stumble toward Rachel, where she stands, arms folded and head hanging. Stumbling with my words, too, I get out, "Yeah. This is kind of, well, not good."

"I told Mr. Galvina we had to open today," she laments as she looks around. "He's been rather uncommunicative, and he refused to sign any contract, so I finally agreed against my better judgment. Then he shows up this morning at six a.m. and unloads this, this mess. What am I supposed to do with all this? I think he decided I was cheaper than taking it to the dump!"

I turn to look at Susan again, but she's got her back to us and is on the phone. Great help there. Not. "Rachel, I'm sure he'll come pick it all up if you ask him to."

"Oh, you're sure, are you? Well, I'm not sure. I'm not sure of anything in this awful place." She reaches into the closest box and pulls out a piece of pipe. Looking at it, she grimaces and drops it back in the box. "What am I going to do? He was so convincing that I'd sell it all, he got me to agree to him paying nothing up front and me only getting a percentage. My other shops aren't having this problem at all." She continues to poke around in the boxes and moan while I peek in a couple and find nothing good.

Susan finally strolls over to us. "That's because your other stores are in cities, not small towns like Chancey." She grits her teeth but manages to not sound too bitter. "It's not your fault. You didn't know."

The front door blows open, and in sails Andy Taylor, the owner—kind of—of Andy's Place, the big house on the square where he sells junk, both in person and online. It's a thriving business mostly due to Andy's knowledge of his trade and people as well as his personality. "Hey, Miss Susan. Carolina. Mrs. Lyles. Ya gotcha a bunch of stuff here, it looks like." Even as he greets us he's looking through the boxes. "Susan called and said you might be willing to give me a good price on it all."

Rachel's eyes pop out, and her mouth pops open. Then she shakes herself. "All of it? I don't know about that." She shoots a look of disapproval at Susan.

Susan exclaims, "Rachel, for the love of all that's good, give him a price. Learn something here."

I can tell the older woman is not used to being given ultimatums. She's drawn back and filling herself up with hot air and indignation. Then she deflates. "Okay. We'll talk, Mr. Taylor. Susan, can I have a word?" She motions toward the back of the store. The two walk in that direction, and I'm left radiating in Andy's energy.

"There is some good stuff here. You know I'll give her a good deal. And the junk, I'll get rid of that too." He looks around the room. "Maybe I ought to expand over here."

I laugh. "Bet you'd get a good price on the building. I think Rachel Lyles has about had her fill of Chancey."

The big, redheaded fellow rocks back on his heels as he folds his arm. "You know, some folks don't know they're happy in a place until they get somewhere else and find real unhappiness there. Only problem is, they just keep moving on."

Trying to unweave his words, I end up just nodding and agreeing with him. "You're probably right. I'm not sure she'll ever be happy."

He frowns at me. "I know. That's what I said."

Susan strides toward me, hooks my arm, and pulls me to the door. "Bye, y'all!" she calls out for both of us as she shoves me through the door and onto the sidewalk.

After a couple of steps she leans in close to me. "I have her blessing! She says Griffin and the kids need me."

I'm not sure I've ever seen Susan this happy. Pure joy radiates off her. I've seen her giddy with Silas, proud with her kids, having fun many times, but not this light from inside her. She pulls away and leans against the old, dark-red brick wall. "She said she had no idea Griffin could be so stubborn and bull-headed. Said she 'didn't raise him to be like that.'"

We both laugh out loud, and I shrug. "Yeah, wonder where he got that from?"

"My mother-in-law wants to go home where, and she did not say this exactly, she's queen of everything. She said something like 'home where things are under control.' She said she does not approve of my fling with Silas, but it's not often a woman gets a Hollywood star thrown in her face when she's going through a rough patch in her marriage."

"Wow, she really wants you back there!"

Susan takes a deep breath and looks down at the sidewalk. When she lifts her head her eyes are shiny. "Oh, Carolina, what if it doesn't work out? What if I've thrown it all away?"

I loop my arm through hers. "Let's not think that way. I believe you have a powerful ally in Rachel. She's always thought she makes her kids happier than their spouses. Just be grateful she's finally gotten the chance to see how wrong she was and that she's now on your side." I give her a tug to pull her away from the building. "C'mon, let's go see what Phoenix is up to and get a smoothie."

"Yes. I hope they're good. If they are, I'll take one to Rachel. I think she could use a pick-me-up."

Oh, Griffin doesn't know what he's in for. His wife and mother are friends.

Bless his heart.

CHAPTER 23

"Good, they're here," I say to myself as I pull into our driveway in the early afternoon. The white minivan with the Illinois tags is parked next to the sidewalk, so I park over to one side. Laney's black SUV is parked behind Jackson's truck, but she'll be leaving soon, so he'll be able to get out to go work with Colt. The kids are still at school, and Savannah knows to park out toward the bridge when we have guests. Doesn't mean I shouldn't text and remind her, though. I do that quickly, but I've already shut off the car. As I start shivering I get out and rush up to the door.

Pushing open the door, I exclaim, "It's cold out there!" but no one hears me. You know, because of the crying.

Cayden is screaming bloody murder, sitting on the lap of an older gentleman in the chair beside the window. Cayden's mother, and the person supposedly in charge of the B&B, is giving him a good run for his money, as she's sobbing on the couch between two women.

"Hello there!" says another man coming out of my kitchen, carrying two cups of steaming coffee. "You must be Carolina." Nodding in my direction, but veering away from me to the couch, he introduces himself. "Jim Tanner, and that's my wife, Deb. Thought we could all use some coffee."

The woman on Laney's right waves at me and gives me a

sweet smile as she pats Laney's back. She adds, "And they're the Boltons. Marian and Gary." The Boltons smile, and Mrs. Bolton gives me a little finger wave while her husband's smile is half grimace due to the squalling baby on his lap.

"Here's your coffee, hon. Yours, too, uh, Mrs. Conner? Right?" He looks back up at me. "Can I get you a cup?"

"Um, no. I'm good. What's going on? Laney, are you okay?"

"No," she moans. "Cayden won't stop crying."

I drop my purse in the floor and dump my coat on top of it and reach out for the baby. "Come here, sweetie." He comes to me but only because I'm closer to his mother. He is barely in my arms before he's reaching down for her.

Mrs. Tanner, Deb, gets up. "Maybe you should sit here?"

I take her place, and Cayden reaches out, clawing at his mother's arm. She grabs him and cuddles him, both of them still crying, but more quietly now.

The man who now has an empty lap shakes his head. "Poor thing just wanted his mom, but she was, well, you saw."

The woman on the other side of Laney—Marian, I believe—reaches her hand out to me. "Hello. You're Carolina?"

"Uh, yes, how long have y'all been here?" I ask as I shake her hand.

The gentleman handing out coffee answers. "Oh, about thirty minutes or so. Mrs. Conner showed us our rooms. We met your husband and were all chatting when he had to go downstairs for a conference call. Then the boy woke up from his nap and didn't like all the strangers, and he just started howling. Guess that set off his mother." He shrugs at me. "That's about when you came in."

Laney raises her eyes to look at me as she kisses the top of Cayden's head. He still has his head pressed into her and is clinging to her with both hands. He's no longer crying, just snuffling. Tears, however, still stream down my friend's face. "I can't be mayor. Look at me. I'm a mess. My baby's a mess."

Her chest starts heaving, and Cayden startles. Then he's sobbing again too.

I can hear Jackson coming up the stairs. Jim, who'd rested on the arm of the chair nearest the dining room, stands and waves a hand toward the kitchen, where we all hear the basement door open. "Your husband has been concerned, but I told him we could handle things until you got here."

Jackson rounds the corner of the kitchen, his eyes wide and a muted phone in his hand. At least I hope it's muted. "Oh, you're here. Is she okay? What's wrong?"

With a quick smile I assure him, "She'll be fine. Are you still on your call? Go back to it."

"If you're sure?" All of us, except for Laney, who is crying more quietly now, tell him to go back to work. The man who'd been holding Cayden also stands. "Jim, let's take a walk out to the bridge."

"Good idea," Jim says, and they are gone in a flash. Deb sits in the chair that was just vacated. Laney reaches for her fancy leather diaper bag, and I hand it to her. She's snuffling now, but she digs in its depths and brings out a baggie of Cheerios. Cayden shifts around on her so his hands are free, and he reaches into the bag as soon as she opens it. He sighs and eats, and after one more shudder he gives me a tiny smile. All's right in his world again.

Laney shifts around and reaches out a hand. "Can you hand me my coffee, Mrs. Bolton?"

"Marian, honey. Just call me Marian."

"Thank you." Laney gives us a sad smile before she takes a sip. Then Cayden turns his face into her and rubs his nose on her, giving her a glazed coating any Krispy Kreme doughnut would be proud to sport. She tries to laugh. "Well, so much for this blouse."

After a sip, she hands her cup back to Marian to sit it on the end table. "I'm so sorry about all this. Some way to start out your stay, isn't it?" With the sheen of tears, her purply-blue eyes are even prettier, and she apologizes with them as well as her words. "It's been a rough day, and when Cayden started crying like that I just couldn't take it. Carolina, you know what?"

She waits, so I do my part. "What?"

Her eyes get even wider. "I don't want to be mayor! I just wanted to win—you know, like when I was doing pageants. Everybody voting for me sounded great, but I got to thinking what all Jed had to do. No, thank you, ma'am!" She looks down, kisses Cayden's forehead, and then gives him a smile when he looks up. "I figured it out this morning, and now I don't know how to get out of it without Missus winning."

Marian and Deb both swing their heads toward me. I'm sure this is way more entertainment than they planned on getting at Crossings B&B. I shrug. "Not sure there is any way around Missus winning if you don't run. But that's not all bad. Missus will drive us crazy, but she'll do a good job. Plus, she did just lose her husband."

Marian gasps a bit, then sucks in a breath. Deb tsks and shakes her head.

I watch Laney take in their reactions, her eyes narrowing and brain wheels spinning. "That's true… I mean, poor thing probably *needs* to be mayor a lot more than I do, right?"

With a big sigh—hope it wasn't too big, don't want to over-play my hand—I slowly nod. "Bless her heart, she has had a rough year."

A sheen of victory replaces the sheen of tears, and my friend and partner even straightens her shoulders. "Why, everyone would probably be so very thankful to me. So appreciative of my sacrifice." She looks to our guests. "I mean, what else would a good Christian do?"

Okay, now we've gone too far. Gotta reel her back in. "But, Laney, poor Missus would never accept anything like charity.

You know how prideful she is. If she thought you felt sorry for her—well, that would be worse than ever."

Marian nods briskly. "You must leave this woman her dignity. Sounds like she's lost enough already."

I give Marian a side glance of gratitude, and she wrinkles her nose quickly at me with a tiny eye twinkle.

We watch Laney struggle to figure out a way to quit and still win. And be humble—but not too humble.

The front door opens, letting Jim and the other man, Gary, push inside with a blast of cold air. "It's getting colder out there. Good thing there's no snow in the forecast."

Marian stands. "Yes. We've seen enough snow already this winter. We like to stay in Illinois until after Christmas, but this year we got so much snow I was ready to come south weeks ago."

Deb is playing peek-a-boo with Cayden. Between boos she says, "We're going over to Poole's BBQ for dinner. The place with all the little pig signs on the hill. We usually stay in Blue Ridge on our trip, but the guys wanted to try Crossings out for the train stuff." She sits up and looks back at the guys, who are still standing near the door. "I can be ready to go in ten minutes. Is that all right with the rest of you?"

As they all agree, she joins them in heading back to the rooms. I focus on my friend. "So, you're good? You look like you feel better."

"Honestly, Carolina, what was I thinking? Sure it was fun to play mayor in the movie, and it'd be such a hoot to out and out beat Missus, but then I'd have to be mayor!" She shudders. "Go to all those meetings, and you know better than most that I don't have an issue with stretching the truth, but political lies just don't sound all that fun." She moves to get up, and Cayden whines. "Shh, baby. Mama's just getting up. You wanna go home and see Daddy?"

Cayden likes that idea and lets me take him after I stand.

140

Bouncing him I say, "Seeing as you're in a good mood, I'm going to go ahead and tell you that I went to Angie's restaurant yesterday. It was really good."

Her look at me is sharp. "I heard. With Delaney, tasting for her reception. So the food was good?"

"Delicious. Of course Angie was at school, but I think it's going to go over well. Not too fancy, but different from home cooking. Inside is really comfortable. You can see Angie's decorating influence."

Her whole face softens. "Really?" She walks over to the entryway to get her coat. I follow with Cayden and the diaper bag. Laney shakes her head as if things keep coming up to think about. "I think not wanting to deal with Angie moving in with that boy was another reason I was running for mayor. It was easier to fight with Missus than think about all that." She pulls on her coat, and then, while I hold him, she puts Cayden's coat on his wiggling arms and thick, knitted socks on his feet. "Angie always has marched to her own drummer."

"I remember when we moved here and I met her at the Piggly Wiggly. I knew there was no way she was your daughter! Her hair and the goth makeup." I laugh. "She kind of scared me!"

Laney laughs loudly. "She scared me too. Still does!" She stuffs her purse into the diaper bag and puts it on her shoulder. "Give me that boy." Cayden goes happily to her, and she squeezes him tight. "Guess I'll just focus on raising this one and let Angie be Angie."

I open the door, and she steps onto the porch. "Law, it is cold!" She turns at the edge of the steps. "Tell you what: Lunch the first day AC's is open. You, me, and Susan."

"It's a date! Drive safe. I'm going back inside!"

From the entryway window, I watch her strap Cayden into his car seat. Then Laney gets in and backs around to pull across the tracks.

I don't know whether to hit my knees in gratitude or open a bottle of champagne. Laney is out of the mayor's race, and she'll never have to know how badly she was going to lose.

I've not met one person who was going to vote for her. Including me.

Chapter 24

"You're not going out in this, are you?" Laney stands at the front door, blocking the Tanners and the Boltons from leaving the B&B on Thursday morning. "It's still in the teens out there! Come on. Got muffins in this cooler to keep them warm." She pushes through the two couples, already in their coats, and heads for the dining room.

The four turn around, but they don't follow her. Jim Tanner speaks up. "We're going out for breakfast and then driving around. Maybe up to Amicalola Falls State Park for a little walk later."

"A walk?" Laney stops and turns around, staring at them like they just said they were going to jog up the Appalachian Trail a few miles naked. (The Appalachian Trail does start at Amicalola Falls. Naked hiking is not encouraged.) She squawks, "It's not getting above twenty-five today. Did you know that?"

I step over to her. "Yes, they know that." I don't say how I repeated the same numbers to them multiple times earlier.

"Like we told Carolina," Marian Bolton tattles on me, "we're used to it being cold. We like it when it's more temperate here, but we came prepared!" She laughs and gestures to her husband and friends, who are all decked out in gloves, hats, boots, and serious coats—parkas, I think they call them up north.

Laney's bottom lip sticks out. "But I wanted to make up for

how awful I was yesterday. Did you know they delayed school this morning? Didn't want any school buses to break down on some country road and have kids freeze to death."

"Yes, we heard. Carolina was also telling us that," Marian says, rolling her eyes as she does. "Never heard of that, but I guess it's different down here."

Deb smiles at Laney's growing frown. "You guys just aren't used to such cold weather." Her smile and words do not help. As Laney's mouth opens, Deb laughs loudly. "Well, I'm starving!" She turns and begins pushing her companions toward the door. They are out and the door behind them is closed in record time. Laney's mouth still hangs open, but with the door closing she shuts her mouth, looks at me, and shrugs. "Want a muffin?"

"Sure. Shannon's at the shop, and she says downtown is like a ghost town, so I'm in no hurry to leave." Laney heads for the kitchen table, and I follow, then walk past her to the counter, where a freshly made pot of coffee waits. "I'll text Jackson in the basement that there's muffins up here."

Bringing our coffee to the table, I detour by the thermostat and move it up a couple more degrees. "I can't get warm this morning. Can you believe it's going to be cold like this through the weekend? It was a nice thought, you bringing muffins up here, but really, why are you out in this cold?"

Laney is still wearing her thick, black coat and white scarf, but she has taken off her gloves. I sit down saucers, and she pulls out a basket of muffins from the cooler. "Before you ask, no. I didn't steal this basket from Ruby. She said I could borrow it. Like Shannon said, there's no one downtown. Libby and Ruby were sitting at a table working on something. They were real secretive about it."

"Libby did say she had something in mind to get Ruby's mind off Jewel moving to Florida. So come on. What are you doing out? Where's Cayden?"

"I really did want to apologize to the Tanners and Boltons. I feel awful about yesterday." She shakes her head. "They didn't seem too bothered, did they?"

"Nope. They're pretty evenhanded. I think that's how Midwesterners are."

She breaks open a muffin and puts one half on her saucer. "These are lemon blueberry. The savory ones are some kind of herb." She picks one up and smells it. "Yeah. It smells like herbs, but I have no idea what."

She holds it out for me to sniff, and I do but then shake my head. "Smells good, but I don't know." I hold out my hand. "Here, I want it. I'm going to heat it up a bit. Want me to heat yours?"

"Sure," she says, her voice muffled with muffin. "Half of that one. Then we'll heat up another one in a minute."

I set the timer, close the microwave door, and lean back on the counter. "So, where's Cayden?"

She wrinkles her nose at me. "Home. With Shaw. He's only opening the showroom this morning with it being so cold, and his assistant manager can do that." She wiggles in her seat, and I see she's wearing her jeans, the stretchy ones that just look tight but are actually comfortable. Guess the non-stretch, natural-fiber pants went the way of her mayoral hopes. "I've got to say, Carolina, I'm a bit confused at the lack of, well, consternation at my announcement about not being mayor. Shaw and Jenna seemed right giddy, and thinking back you didn't try to talk me out of it at all. Mother practically said Missus was going to win anyway! What kind of a mother says something like that?"

Luckily the timer dings, and I turn away to get our muffin. "Everyone just wants you to do what you feel is best." I grab the butter as I pass the refrigerator.

"You were going to vote for me, weren't you?"

With only two things in my hands, a saucer and the butter,

it's hard to make it look like I have to concentrate, but I do anyway. Wrinkled brow and walking gingerly, I get to the table.

And lie. "Of course. But I did think it was going to be an awful lot on you. And honestly it would be a waste of some of your greatest talents."

"Like what?"

"Your muffin is hot, better get your butter on it. Let me see if Jackson wants me to heat him one." I scoot around the table and hurry to the basement door. As soon as I open it, though, we can hear him on the speakerphone, so I softly close the door. "You don't belong behind a desk in a stuffy office. Look what a great job you did in the movie and with this place. Maybe we should plan some more events up here as soon as it warms up a bit."

She stares at me for a moment, and I match her gaze. Everything I've said has been the truth, except for that one little thing about voting. With a sigh, she looks down, picks up her knife, and butters her half of the herb muffin. "I guess. I went to the city office to take my name off the ballot, and you should've seen some of the looks I got. Right up until I said I was withdrawing." She bangs down her knife. "I worked day in and day out with those people when I was the treasurer. How dare they act like I wouldn't be a good mayor?"

I'm eating my muffin. I'm drinking my coffee. I'm not saying a word. Especially not any word about a certain treasurer having to resign because she was playing with the books. Granted, she was adding money, but still…

"I added money to this town. I didn't steal any!" She folds her arms over her bosom and huffs.

I'm eating my muffin. I'm drinking my coffee.

Laney grumbles, "I took a quick look at the mayor's office, and it would be nice to have that big desk, but you know it's really a tiny little office." The city offices are next to the depot at the edge of the park and across the street from the library.

It's a one-story, concrete-block building that houses the police department, city offices, and the mayor's office. The only windows are on the front walls, and then there's one long, boring hall with offices on each side. It's completely utilitarian, and no one goes in unless they have to. Lots of chalk-yellow walls, fluorescent lights, and unhappy people.

The basement door opens. "Did I hear there are warm muffins up here?" Jackson steps into the kitchen. "We've got to get another heater for down there. It's freezing. Hey, Laney, sorry to hear you're dropping out of the mayoral race, but it's probably for the best."

She whirls around in her seat. "Why? Why is it for the best?"

His eyes pop wide, and his mouth opens, then shuts. Then opens. "Just because it's better to know what you want now than to find out later, right?"

Her shoulders drop, and she turns back to face the table. "I suppose. But just so you know, I'd be a very good mayor. Even with a baby."

With a duet of "Of course you woulds," Jackson and I meet over a saucer of muffins near the microwave. I leave him to watch his breakfast treat circle in the microwave, one of each kind, and I wander back over to the table. "So, what else is on your agenda today? Sounds like you've gotten your big item done, withdrawing from the race."

"Except it's too late to get my name off the ballot." She rolls her eyes. "Oh well, it'll be fun to see my name on there, even if I don't get any votes. But that wasn't really my big thing to do, and well, since you're both here, I guess I should tell you."

I don't like how serious she sounds. I can tell Jackson picked up on that too. He brings his saucer to the table, but sits quietly at the head of the table between us without first refilling his coffee cup.

Laney reaches over and puts her hand on his, and he flinches. My heart jumps along with my voice. "What is it?"

She sighs. "You know I said I called Mother to tell her about me not being mayor, and well, she had some news."

Jackson tilts his head to the side. "What kind of news? News for us?"

Her frown deepens, and she pauses. "I think so. I mean, I can only assume so." She looks past me out the back doors. "Yeah. Gotta be. Anyway, just want you to know. Then you can do with it what you will."

"What? Tell us," I plead.

She takes in a deep breath, then lets it out. "Ricky bought a ring. Borrowed some money from Mother."

Jackson pulls his hand away from hers and sits back. "So? He wanted a ring. He probably shouldn't be borrowing money for jewelry, but what's that got to do with us?"

"The ring isn't for him," I whisper.

"Who? Oh. Oh, hell no!" Jackson leaps up. "For Savannah? That's not happening. Where is he? The real estate office?"

Laney looks from him to me. "I don't know. But settle down a bit. We don't know what he means to do with it." She looks down, then back up at my husband, who is leaning forward, both hands gripping the back of the chair he'd been in. Her voice takes on that Southern belle vibe she does so well. "So, I'm guessing he hasn't talked to you, Jackson? You know, asked for her hand in marriage?"

"Laney!" I hiss.

"I'm just asking. I figured y'all would want a heads-up." She clears her throat, then stands. "I better be getting back home." Reaching out to Jackson, laying her hand on his arm, she says, "Don't kill him. Learn from us. Angie's barely speaking to me and Shaw. Don't make Ricky look like the good one, and don't make her choose."

She backs away when Jackson just narrows his eyes at her. Then she reminds us, "Savannah is a smart girl."

She waves goodbye, saying she'll get the cooler later, and

hurries into the living room. I notice she never took off her coat. Never unwrapped her scarf. She came all the way up here just to tell us this. To give us a heads-up.

Well. The muffins were a nice touch.

CHAPTER 25

"What are y'all doing out in this cold?" I'd seen Will pull in the driveway, but was more surprised to see him open the back door of their car and emerge with a bundle of pink at the same time the other back door opened and Anna struggled out with bags, blankets, and a hood pulled so far over her head that I don't know how she saw to get up the sidewalk. I jerked open the door as they approached and asked my question as I helped them get in the front door.

Once inside, with their pink cheeks and full arms, Will speaks up. "The cabin is too cold. We can't keep it warm enough with just the fire. The heaters keep tripping the breaker and so..." He shrugs, but I reach to take a bag hanging over his shoulder. He sits Francie's carrier on the floor and unbuckles her. I lean over to pull her out. She weighs next to nothing, but I can only see her eyes occasionally with the blankets, from inside her tied hood and under her stocking hat.

I carry her into the living room, and I sit in the middle of the couch. "Of course you'll stay here. There's a semi-fresh pot of coffee in the kitchen. Laney just left, and she brought some muffins, there on the table." I let them help themselves in the kitchen, as they seem to be doing just fine, and I unwrap my girl. Francie's eyes are wide as she looks around, and then she wriggles as she discovers she's no longer bound up. Her stocking hat is pink with black-and-white penguins on the edging, and it's so cute that I don't take it off right away. Loudly I tell them, "Your daddy has a conference call, so he's downstairs working."

Anna sticks her head in the living room. "You want me to warm up your coffee?"

Francie's forehead wrinkles, and her head twists a bit in the direction of her mother's voice. "Oh, she heard her mama. Yes, please, if you don't mind." With some close-up baby talk I regain my granddaughter's attention, and the wrinkled forehead smooths out.

"Will's still fixing his muffin," Anna says as she comes in and sits beside me on the couch.

I can't help but giggle as the forehead wrinkles immediately return, deeper this time. Francie knows her mama is near. I move her in my arms so she can see Anna, and the wrinkles deepen and spread. How dare Mama be so far away! Just sitting there eating a muffin! Her sweet cry makes me laugh, and as Anna prepares to put her muffin and coffee down, I stand up. "Oh, she's fine. You relax. We'll walk around, and she'll forget you're in the room—for at least a minute!"

Will sits on the other end of the couch. "Sorry, but I just couldn't leave them to go work on Peter's office knowing how cold the cabin would be. Plus, my classes start tomorrow, so Anna would be there dealing with the fireplace and Francie and everything all day."

"We're happy to have you here. Since the B&B rooms are full, you'll all three be in your old room together. But then I guess y'all are kind of used to that."

Anna pushes back on the recliner in the couch and stretches out. "Yes. We'll be fine. Warming the cabin by fire seemed romantic at first, but it's exhausting keeping it going. I don't know how people did it in the old days. At least I didn't have to also build a fire in the oven." Her voice gets slurry as she closes her eyes. Oh, those days with a newborn when you fall asleep at the drop of a hat. I look over to grin with Will at his dozing wife, but he's picking birdseed with his half-full cup of coffee still in his hand. I hurry over to take the cup out of his hand, and he lets me take it with only a try at opening his eyes. "Here, put this behind your head," I whisper, handing him a small pillow while keeping Francie balanced on my shoulder. He secures the pillow behind his head, then stretches his legs out. I leave the two of them and go to the kitchen to call Shannon and tell her I'll be even later than I thought.

Will warmed my van for me, so my ride to town is pretty toasty. After about a twenty-minute nap Anna and Will were refreshed and Francie was starving. After we finished the muffins and Francie finished nursing, Anna and Will went upstairs to set up their room. Jackson was in charge of our sleeping baby while I got dressed. Anna said she'd make grilled cheese sandwiches for her and Jackson, so everything was handled when Will headed off to work on Peter's office and I headed to Blooming Books.

Downtown is still super quiet. There's lots of parking, so I pull in across from the shop and dash across the street. My weather app says it's still only twenty-three degrees. At the front door I'm stopped by the "Closed" sign. I think Shannon must've forgotten to turn it over, but as I try to open the door, it doesn't budge. It's locked. I knock and look inside. I really don't want to have to dig out my keys. It's too cold. Then I see Shannon walking slowly toward me. She unlocks the door and then turns away.

"Why are we closed? I just talked to you before I left the house."

I reach to turn over the sign, but Shannon says, "Can you please relock the door?" She's slowly walking to the sitting area and doesn't look back at me.

"Okay. I guess it's just as well." I follow her and watch her ease herself onto the couch. "Are you okay?"

"No. Can you sit down?"

I sit in one of the chairs across from her while pulling off my gloves and unbuttoning my coat. "Shannon, what's going on?"

She presses her lips together and then looks back toward the stairs to her and Danny's apartment.

"Is Danny here?" I ask while looking in that same direction.

"No. He can't be here." She takes a deep breath and stares at me. "We're not married."

That stops me. I sputter, "But, but I thought you were."

She throws her hands up. "So did I. Well, almost. So did Danny. Remember when Mrs. Bunch and Alison came here? They said the divorce could be final in a month?"

"Yes. They seemed pretty certain."

"Well, they were because they'd done their part. Danny just never actually signed the papers!" She's dry-eyed, but her eyes look pretty crazy. "I had this all figured out. Me and Danny have to be married. Have to be! That's the only way to pro-tect—" She comes to an abrupt stop and stares right through me.

"Protect the baby?"

She's very quiet. "This baby can't be Peter's. It has to be Danny's. Legal and, well, in every way."

I scoot up to be closer to her. I look at her from across the coffee table. "Honey, you can't change some things no matter how much you want to."

"I know. But I just don't need people asking questions. I need to keep this all under control."

I think, but do not say, that it's a little too late for that. "Where is Danny?"

"At the courthouse trying to fix things. We snuck away and got married, so that part is legal, except we didn't exactly get the license first. And, well, of course it's not legal if he wasn't divorced. Do you think we'll get in trouble?"

"No. Well, I don't know, but… Not if it was an innocent mistake, right? And I don't think anyone will believe Danny was trying to fool people." Again, I think but do not say, *Like you are actually trying to do.* "Does Danny know you're pregnant?"

She freezes, then shakes her head. "No. Danny's not that perceptive. Plus, he can't know the truth." She freezes again, but this time with a look of horror. "And you can't tell anyone. Matter of fact forget this." She jumps up. "Forget all this. I'm opening the store. You didn't hear any of this!"

"Yes, I did. I'm not going to tell anyone, but you need a friend." I follow her to the front door. "This is crazy. Everyone in town can do simple math, and counting the months of a pregnancy is a small town's favorite kind of math."

She falls back against the door. "I know! Believe me, I know. It was all going so smoothly. Then Danny's not-yet-ex-wife, Alison, calls him this morning. Apparently her lawyer had contacted her to tell her Danny hadn't signed the paperwork. Danny just isn't very good at paperwork stuff."

"Shannon?" I keep my voice low, nonthreatening, like I'm talking to a scared animal. "Maybe you want to slow down and really think about what you're doing? Maybe Danny isn't right for you."

And this is why you never corner a scared animal. Her arms fly up, and she yells, "Of course he's right for me! Just because you hate him doesn't mean anything! He's sweet and he loves me and we're going to be fine." She blasts past me. "I'm done talking about this with you!"

She stomps up the stairs and slams the apartment door.

I look out on the blue, cold day and turn the sign over to

"Open." To think I used to actually spend hours each day watching soap operas. Who knew all you have to do is move to a small town and you can live in one!

Chapter 26

All afternoon the bright sun and blindingly blue sky told a different story from the temperature reading on my phone. It went all the way up to twenty-five for less than an hour, and for the last hour it's been falling. It's now four o'clock and nineteen degrees. Shadows stretch across the street and park, and although I've climbed the stairs to Shannon's apartment twice, I've not made it past her door even with all my knocking. She has music playing and I smelled something cooking earlier, but that's it.

No one else is coming to work because there is nothing to do here. Up at the house Anna has put the roast I had out in the Crock-Pot, and now she and the baby are taking a nap while the house is quiet. Will and Jackson are both at work remodeling Peter's office. Bryan is at basketball practice, and Savannah is at work over at Andy's Place, so everyone is taken care of.

My big question now is, do I follow the instructions in the text I just received from Gertie? Leaning on the counter, I look around. No one has entered the front door since I arrived a little before noon. The shop is in perfect order, and I'm bored.

Gertie must be bored too. She's having a party.

"Close up your shops and come have an apple pie hot toddy on the house. It's warm but mostly ginger tea, so no worries about driving home. See you soon."

She'd sent it to the chamber's texting list. I'm pretty sure this isn't what Retta had in mind when she made it for emergencies. No one has responded, so I don't either. I just turn off the cash register and begin putting out the candles around the shop and locking up. A hot toddy sounds wonderful, and I bet the Moonshine Cave is toasty warm.

One last look up and over my shoulder toward Shannon's apartment, and then I plunge out into the frigid temps, lock the door, and hurry down the sidewalk. My old coat feels like it's doing a good job until I'm past Ruby's dark windows, and then I realize it's not. Shivering, I start to run and almost plow face-first into Phoenix's door as it suddenly opens.

"Oh! Carolina! Are you okay?" Phoenix asks as she grabs my arm and then shuts the glass door.

"Yeah, I didn't actually hit it with anything other than my hand. You going to Gertie's?"

Her back is to me as she locks the door. "Yes. I assume that's where you're rushing to?"

"Yes." I wait for her as she's pulling on her gloves and ask, "Have you had any customers today?"

"Not a one. And these huge windows are great for advertising what's going on inside, but they sure do let in the cold. Let's go!" We dash on to the corner, cross the street, and then turn up the sidewalk to the porch stairs. The house is freshly painted in garish orange and neon green with touches of bright purple and accents of ice-cold white. Where the old wooden doors once stood, there is a door like you'd find on a big-box store in any strip mall in America. Glass and metal. Inside it's like nothing else in Chancey. Wide open with shiny floors, small kiosks with laptops, and shiny, plastic orange, purple, and green chairs. Off to the right are doors to Gertie's living area in the house. Off to the left is a hallway to the basement stairs leading to the Moonshine Cave.

We pause and take a breath. Phoenix sighs. "It feels so good in here." Her phone chimes, and she immediately grabs it out of the back pocket of her white jeans. She's also wearing a white sweater with a burgundy coat over everything. It's more like a ski jacket than her usual dress coat. She's also wearing low-heeled boots, which are awfully casual for her these days. She smiles and turns away to talk on her phone.

"What are you doing here?" I'm queried from above.

Savannah is on the landing, staring down at me.

"Gertie invited me."

I know I've had all afternoon to figure something out, but I still have no idea how to handle the idea of Ricky buying a ring for my daughter. Dealing with a cornered animal or a pregnant Shannon is nothing compared to a smart-as-a-whip teenager who's lived with me her whole life and often knows what I'm thinking before I do.

"Daddy called me but then hung up. Almost sounded like he was on the phone but wasn't saying anything?" She's talking as she's walking down the long staircase. All the modern decorating of the first floor ends at the bottom step. From there up it's a typical old house with lots of rooms that are all full of junk. Savannah has been working here since the fall, mostly with the online sales. Her eyes never leave mine as she asks, "What do you think he wanted?"

I did not think coming here through. Really didn't want to talk to her this soon. "I don't know. Did you call him back?"

She shakes her head as she steps onto the floor. "What's going on?"

Told you. She knows what I'm thinking before I do. I chuckle. "Nothing. I mean. I don't think anything is going on. What do *you* think is going on?"

But instead of answering me she looks up as the door chime sounds, and smiles. "Hey there."

Ricky's deep voice—he's actually sounding like a man these days—says, "Hey there," back to her. "Hey, Mrs. Jessup."

Before I can respond Phoenix speaks up from the beginning of the hallway. "You coming?"

"Sure. Just a minute." I turn back to where Ricky has Savannah tucked under his arm. "I'm going downstairs to Gertie's. Where—"

They start toward me. Ricky winks. "Yeah, so are we. Of course Savannah will have to have a hot toddy without the moonshine, but—"

Savannah elbows him. "And so will you." Her big eyes remind him he's not twenty-one yet and her mother is standing there.

"Oh, that's right. After you ladies." He gallantly waves his arm toward the hall, which Phoenix has already started down. I follow her, and Savannah follows me. The hall is narrow, but not as narrow as the stairs going down to the Moonshine Cave. At the bottom the door opens into a dark space with a roaring fireplace on one side, a long bar on the other, and low tables in between. Everything is gray, like a cave, but it's also plush. It's cozy and comfortable. Gertie has a huge selection of flavored moonshines, and I can smell the warm cider, which she has on a burner on the bar. Ricky says, "Ladies," again and waves us to the bar area.

Gertie looks right past Phoenix. "Well, here's Ricky Troutman with two Chancey ladies on his arm. Hot toddies all around?"

"No!" I shout.

Gertie bursts out laughing. "I'm just jerking your chain, Carolina. You look way too uptight to be in a moonshine cave. Loosen up! I have this wonderful cider here for those not imbibing and those too young to imbibe—well, at least in a public place."

"Good one, Gertie," Ricky says with another wink. "Two ciders." He looks at me. "A hot toddy for you, Carolina?"

"Sure." Gertie's right. Just watching Ricky and Savannah has gotten my neck in a mess of knots. I stretch, trying to loosen them, and smile as Ricky hands me my drink.

He puts his now free hand around my daughter and then lifts his mug up. "Everyone, I have an announcement to make."

I've got a mouth full of hot toddy, so I can't yell as he looks at Savannah and says, "Congratulate me. I sold my first house today!"

Now my neck is a tighter mess of knots and my throat is scalded, but he didn't say what I was afraid he was going to say. Savannah is staring at me. "Are you okay?"

"I'm fine. We just have to talk. Soon." I take a smaller sip and try a smile. "That's great, Ricky."

"Now I'm still in training, so I don't get the full commission, but it's the first of many." He squeezes my daughter again. "Just the first, right?" He stares into her eyes, and she stares right back at him.

Oh, we have to talk. We have to talk really soon.

But right now I need to sit down. My knees aren't feeling so steady.

Phoenix has taken a seat at a nearby table, and when she sees me look around, she pushes out a chair. "You can sit here. I'm alone—apparently."

There's not anyone else I know that well in the small crowd. Plus, I've enjoyed Phoenix when I can forget that she broke Colt's heart. I know Colt and Jackson won't be here. They are in the middle of something at Peter's office that they didn't want to stop.

She nods at the cider-drinking couple I left at the bar, chatting with Gertie. "Those two look quite smitten with each other. So, he's working real estate full time now?"

I shrug off my coat behind me in my chair. "Yes. Another one that feels college is just holding them back. Ready to start the adventure of living!" I roll my eyes and she laughs.

"Oh, how to tell them it's a really, really long adventure. Take your time and figure things out a bit."

"Exactly!" I tip my drink at her, and we clink glasses.

She looks tired as she stares into her cold drink. Moonshine on the rocks, it looks like. She sighs. "I didn't have the opportunity to go to school, but I sure didn't have to grow up as fast I decided to. I knew more than everyone around me and now... Well, now I'm just trying to pull things together as best I can."

"And that no longer includes Colt?"

Her head snaps up and her eyes narrow. "He and I..." Her voice trails off, and then she shrugs and takes a drink. "I should've left him alone, but when he wanted to charge in on his white stallion and save me from that mess in Kentucky, well... waiting has never been my strong suit, and he was just too cute and too good to let pass." She meets my eyes. "But I'm letting him pass now." She pauses, then speaks firmly. "For his own good."

I actually gasp. I wasn't thinking that.

She smiles at me. "He needs kids and a girl to sit in the stands on Friday nights cheering the team on." She turns up her drink and finishes it. "You should see the way he watches you and Jackson and your family. He's incredibly jealous of you all."

My back is to the door, but it's déjà vu watching her eyes light up as she looks over my shoulder, just like Savannah's did when Ricky came in upstairs. But then the light dies, and with a look behind me I see why. Peter has entered the cave, and he's holding the door open for the person who is coming down the stairs behind him.

Gertie shouts, "Peter! Delaney! Glad you could make it."

Delaney loops her arm through Peter's and pulls him toward the bar. She has on a full-length leather coat, high-heeled boots, and a soft-looking, emerald-green scarf that even in the dim lights from the bar I can see make her green eyes sparkle.

Her hair is full like she just had a blowout, and all in all she looks like she stepped out of a magazine. I've never seen this Delaney. She beams at Gertie, then at Peter as she talks… perhaps a bit louder than necessary? "My wonderful fiancé worried it was too cold for me to be out, but I told him we needed a cocktail, and where better than at Gertie's? Thank you for the special invite."

Gertie leans her ample bosom on the bar. "I know you're not on the chamber list, but with all the good you've already done for business here in Chancey, you should be! Isn't that right, Peter?"

He pauses, and Gertie studies him. "You are aware your wife-to-be is single-handedly responsible for the shopping boom here?" As she's talking to him, she lifts off the bar and stands straight so she's on eye level with him.

"Why, I guess I must've missed the news," he says and then mumbles something I can't hear.

Delaney laughs at whatever he said, and then, without loosening her grip on him, she slides onto the closest barstool. "I never get to visit with Gertie. Let's sit here for our first hot toddy, don't you think?"

Phoenix makes a disgusted sound, and I turn around to face her. She's draining whatever bit of liquid might be left in her drink. I say quietly, "You know they're getting married, right? Like soon."

"That's her problem. Won't be a problem for anyone else," she says as she stands up. "Thanks for the drink, Gertie," she cheerfully exclaims. "It's been a long day, and I'm going home to get comfortable and cozy!" At the door she waves at me and says loudly, "Bye, Carolina. It was great to get to catch up. We'll get together again soon!"

I wave, but turn quickly back and pick up my drink. Grabbing my coat, I move to the bar to take the stool next to Delaney. "Hey, y'all." Delaney and Gertie both give me a bit of evil eye, which is why I came over. I have to make it clear I'm not choosing sides in whatever is going on. "This hot toddy is fantastic. I don't think we have a bottle of the apple pie moonshine. Can I buy one tonight? And you say it's ginger tea? Can I get that at the grocery store?"

Gertie rolls her eyes. "Quit babbling, Carolina. The answer is yes to all your questions. Now Delaney and Peter are telling me all about the wedding plans."

Peter looks as confused as I do. I'm confused because I'm trying to remember what exactly the questions I asked Gertie were. Peter is confused, I bet, because he has no clue about the wedding plans.

Our confusion doesn't slow Delaney's roll one bit. "My mother's friend, the florist, is a genius with heirloom roses and making bouquets and arrangements not look stiff and planned. Peter and I don't want things to be too Valentine-y, you know?" She laughs again and leans against an unsmiling Peter. "We're doing dusty pink, cream, and a grayish-green for our colors. Isn't that right, darling?"

Gertie sighs and reaches out to pat Peter's arm, which is still entwined in Delaney's. "It'll be the social event of North Georgia, I'm sure."

Delaney lowers her eyes and smiles demurely. "Oh, I don't know about that. All that matters is that in only a few weeks I will be Mrs. Peter Bedwell for the rest of my life." When she looks up she doesn't look at the man whose name she's taking, but she turns to me. "Carolina, we'd decided we weren't going to have attendants, but I just realized I'd love to have you be a part of all this. Will you be my matron of honor?"

Her green eyes really are striking next to that scarf, and them being shiny wet doesn't hurt. But mostly it's the desperation in them that makes me nod.

"Well, of course. I'm honored," I stammer.

Then she lets go of Peter's arm and wraps her arms around my neck.

Over the bride's shoulder, Gertie toasts me with her bottle of water. Peter is back to looking confused. And me?

Well, look who just chose a side.

Chapter 27

"I need this," Jackson says from his seat on the bottom of our bed as he pulls on a pair of thick socks. "You're sure everything is good here?"

Still snuggled under the heavy bedclothes, including an extra quilt, I stretch and venture an arm out. "Turn up the thermostat on your way down the hall. And yes, we're good here. Go have your fun watching trains with Tim." Jackson worked with Tim years ago, and his friend is spending the weekend here at Crossings. They'd bonded some at work, but mostly from watching trains outside of work when the kids were small. Tim got in from Kentucky last night after I got home from the Moonshine Cave. Tim's daughter and wife are doing a mother-daughter church retreat, so he is visiting with us in the third B&B room. Frigid temps will not hinder this long-planned railfan weekend.

"I'm getting up soon. With school cancelled again, Friday feels like Saturday. Grant and Bryan were up late last night. I heard them come upstairs after midnight, so they'll sleep late. Savannah is working but not until later." Jackson and I didn't get a chance to talk last night, given Tim's arrival. I weigh messing with his good mood against bringing up Ricky and his ring, but then Jackson bounces up off the bed and strides around to lean down and give me a kiss.

A fast kiss. He has trains to catch. "Thermostat!" I remind him before he closes the bedroom door. He closes the door too loudly in his exuberance, but I don't hear anything from Francie or her parents next door, so maybe they've slept through his leaving.

There's thin light coming in around the edges of the curtains. The temperature is close to the single digits this morning, and we've left several faucets dripping so the pipes won't freeze. This cold wave should be over Sunday night, but until then virtually everything's been cancelled, including church. Something about not being able to heat the big old building. Thankfully we're not also getting snow or ice.

Another casualty of the cold is that our Midwest guests are heading on to Florida this morning although they've paid through Sunday. I reluctantly offered a partial refund, but they refused. They said they'd come south for warmer weather and would miss their time in the area, but that the cold snap wasn't our fault.

I roll over onto my back and push the covers down a bit. The heat is working hard, and I'm so glad we have the new system even if it meant going without air conditioning for a while last summer. Will and Anna can move down to the B&B, and Francie will have her own room for the next couple of nights. It's nice having them here, but they are falling back into old habits, with Will acting like a teenager and Anna working like a servant who is grateful to be allowed to stay. Although it was nice to have her take care of dinner last night. For the next couple of nights I'll get up with Francie so they can both catch up on some much-needed sleep.

My phone chimes with a text, and I go ahead and sit up before checking it.

"Bridesmaid???" Laney's text says, and I see she has included Susan on it. Susan responds with a single question mark. I ignore them both and get up, go to the bathroom, and then enter my closet, deciding what to wear. My phone is silent while I get dressed in thick, navy corduroy pants, a beige turtleneck, and a brown-and-blue sweater. They think I'm still sleeping since I've not answered. Seeing as it's only seven, they know better than to text this early. However, it is usually a school- and workday, so I'll cut them some slack—in a minute.

Downstairs is quiet, and I look around. Fresh muffins would be nice. I bought some pastries from the grocery store, but nothing beats fresh muffins from Ruby's. I lift my phone and smile. Let's see just how curious they are. "Coffee at Ruby's? Ten minutes?"

I don't have my shoes on before both have responded with thumbs-up. They are just too easy. I pull on my coat, hat, and gloves. My smile is big, and I can't help it.

I'm pretty lucky to have them for friends.

No snow or ice, but a thick frost makes the world sparkle as I drive down the hill into town. The roofs are solid white, the grass, too, and even each limb on the trees. The leaves of the big old camellia bushes just before I hit town look as if they've been coated with white sparkle paint. The bushes had been blooming before this cold front, but I bet this will make all the bright pink blossoms turn brown and drop. These evergreen camellias are big, and Missus says they're really old. Planted in a grouping right before the downtown area begins, they are babied by the garden club. Somebody planted them, probably the first garden club, to mark the entrance to Chancey. These are all one variety, with pink flowers that don't last very long. I love the name "camellia," and the flowers are so perfect they look artificial, but this far north they require a lot of work, so we aren't going to have any at Crossings.

There are plenty of parking spots, so I take one right across from Ruby's. The sun is barely up over the mountains, but there is nothing else in its way. Bare limbs and clear skies don't impede its warmth, but I still don't feel it when I jump out of my car and hurry across the street.

"Hey," I say, catching Libby's eye as I enter the half-full café. There are more people here than I imagined given the early hour, cancellations, and did I mention it's really cold? There's the usual table of older men near the front, but there's enough of them to fill two tables. All but one booth is full, and with a quick nod toward it, Libby tells me if I want it, I better grab it. She beats me to it and is filling a cup for me when I get there.

"What's with all the people?"

She shakes her head and sighs. "Power's out over behind us, up the hill. Just a couple streets. Guess a branch took out some wires, and it's gonna take the power company a couple more hours to fix. Police called Ruby, so she opened up early to give folks a place to come be warm."

I shiver and don't take off my coat right away. "Can't imagine not having heat in all this. Tell Ruby she's a good one."

Libby pauses, and a grin steals up her face. "You can tell her yourself. She'll be out in a bit to tell you her news, I bet."

"She's not moving to Florida, is she?" I dare to whisper.

Her grin shifts to a smirk. "I'm smiling, aren't I?" Then she moves on to the next table.

Susan scurries in the front door, waves at me, and then turns to look outside. As her sister comes into view she pushes open the door, and then they both come bustling to the table.

Susan slides in beside me and motions to Laney. "You can have that side to yourself, Nanook of the North. I thought you got rid of that coat years ago."

Laney is wearing one of those huge, balloon-type coats that were popular, oh, about twenty years ago. Laney's goes down past her knees, and it truly does look like she has a team of sled dogs waiting outside for her. And it's white. Bright, well, kind of a dingy bright white. The hood is up, but she pulls it back to reveal a green stocking cap, which, when it's pulled off, reveals a big old head of hair, due to both static electricity and general wildness. Her hair is thick, and with the short cut it easily can become its own entity.

"Shut up," she directs her sister's way. "I'm not meant to be cold, and since I'm no longer going to be mayor, I can look however I want."

I raise a bit of an eyebrow, and I think Susan did the same because Laney rolls her eyes at us both. "Okay. Well, I don't care today. And tomorrow. Cold ends Sunday, right? So I don't care Sunday either. Matter of fact I wasn't leaving my house, but, well, Cayden and Shaw both being babies and Jenna waiting to hear from University of Georgia, those people I live with are driving me crazy. So here I am in all my winter glory." She tips her chin up. "Take me or leave me."

I jump in before her sister can get in another smart comment. "We take you! You look fine. All that matters is being warm. Did Jenna apply to any other places?"

Laney nods. "Yes, but she's got her heart set on following her cousin Leslie to UGA."

"Not to be around Leslie, though," Susan adds. "Those two are not a thing alike. Leslie also applied and got accepted to Georgia Tech, but she's really happy at UGA. I'm sure Jenna will get in." She turns to me. "Anything more on Savannah's plans?"

I avoid looking at Laney. We are not talking about that ring. "Just that she says she's not writing any long essays, and she's got everything under control. She's seeming really wishy-washy on the whole theater thing."

Laney is waving to get Libby's attention, but she fills us in on her observations. "Savannah doesn't fit in with the theater kids from what I've seen when I've been at the school." She bends toward me. "Sure the jocks and cheerleaders are cliquey, but so are the theater kids. Her swooping in and taking lead roles was not considered kosher."

Susan ponders that, then nods. "I can see that. So, what's with all these people here this early?"

Libby arrives at the table as I tell them about the power outage. She looks excited. "Muffins are to die for this morning. Ruby got an early start baking, and she's feeling good. We have peach crumble; sausage corn—not corn bread, but corn; maple nut; and maple oat. She's also just now putting in some German chocolate ones. Ruby's going to join y'all when she gets them in the oven."

Susan frowns. "Join us? Like, come out here with the peons?"

I jab my elbow into her side. "Hush. She has some news. No, she's not moving to Florida."

Libby lowers her head and looks over her glasses at Laney. "And I told her Laney had joined you and she said that was fine, so try and behave, okay? Give me that coat so she has somewhere to sit."

Laney has shrugged the coat off but is cuddled in it. "There's room for her. Besides, I'm still cold."

Libby just stands there with her hand out.

Laney ignores her but places her order. "I want a peach crumble. Susan, you probably want the sausage one, right? Can I have a bite of it? Carolina, let me guess, one of the maple ones? How about maple nut? I'd like a taste of that one too. We're going to want a coffee refill next time you're by." She sips her coffee, looking straight ahead.

With a sigh, Libby moves on. Susan clicks her tongue. "I kinda miss you running for mayor. At least then you were nice sometimes."

"And let me tell you, it was exhausting! Since I figure you

don't know anything more about Ruby's news, what's this about you being Delaney's bridesmaid?"

I lean forward and whisper, "Who told you?"

"Ricky. He said he was at Gertie's and everyone was talking about it?"

"Oh, Gertie's yesterday?" Susan asks. "The chamber thing? Griffin got that text. If I'd known you were going we might've come down."

Laney's head, and mind, jerk sideways at her sister's comment, but she drags her thoughts back to me. "We'll talk about that in a minute. What chamber thing?"

I explain Gertie's impromptu cocktail party. "It was kind of a neat idea, and I sat with Phoenix for a bit until Peter and Delaney came in." I drop my voice back to a whisper. "I'm pretty sure Peter had told Phoenix he wasn't coming. She talked to someone on the phone right as we got there. When Peter showed up with Delaney, Phoenix got ticked off. She was dressed like she had been working in her shop all day. Fine of course for Chancey, but really casual. Delaney, however, looked like she had stepped out of a complete makeover. Her hair was blown out, full makeup, the whole nine yards."

"Good for her!" Laney exclaims. "Gotta do battle for your man sometimes. Do not look on my current state for evidence of this. Shaw's as tired as me, so I know he's not making comparisons. But, sister dear, you might want to take notes."

Susan concentrates and then nods. "I think you might be right. I need to find out where Delaney went to get all gussied up. Oh, look at our muffins."

"Are they bigger than usual?"

Libby answers, "Yes, ma'am. Ruby changed up some things, and she's getting a bigger crown on her muffins. Plus she's putting a shine on them at the end. See how pretty they look? She's really outdoing herself this morning."

"Thank you, Libby. You make all my baking look good. Can

I join you ladies?" Ruby being nice to Libby at the same time that she asks permission for anything makes us all pause. She not only asked, she's standing at the end of the table waiting for our response.

"Sure." I gulp.

Laney scoots against the wall, pulling her coat toward her but steeling herself for a comment.

Ruby seats herself, then pats the coat. "Oh, this is perfect. So cozy and warm over here. Where did you get this coat? I need one like it."

"Um, I don't remember."

Ruby plants her elbows on the table. "Go ahead and eat while I tell you my plan."

We all cut our muffins in half so they're easier to eat and share. Susan tilts her saucer toward us. "Look. There really is corn in here. I know Libby said it wasn't cornbread, but I still wasn't sure what to expect. It's like an almost sweet bread but with the spicy sausage."

Laney shows us the peaches in hers, and I lift my plate for them to smell the maple. "These look like they could be in a magazine."

Ruby beams. "That's what that doll Delaney said. Not all she said. She said pies. I should sell pies. And so I'm going to." She lightly slaps the table. "That's my big news."

"Your pies are amazing. So, like, whole pies? All the time?" I ask quickly so I can take a bite.

"Sure. Sure. Whole pies but also pieces. In the afternoons right here. Every day—well, of course not Sunday. But every other afternoon from one to four."

Laney doesn't wait to empty her mouth. She just holds up a hand in front of it and talks anyway. "But you close at noon. Always have."

"Things change. It's time I change with them. Why should this place sit empty all afternoon? Wouldn't y'all love to occasionally come in here of an afternoon, get a piece of pie and a cup of coffee?"

We all nod. Susan stops her nod and tips her head. "Ruby, won't that wear you out?"

"I won't be here. I'll make the pies, of course, but I'm hiring a manager to run the afternoons. Someone to just serve the pie, make the coffee, and then clean up and close up." She slaps both palms emphatically on the table and scoots to the end of the bench. "So I'm hiring. If y'all know someone, send them my way! Now I better get back to my kitchen. Spread the word. We'll be opening Monday afternoon."

"Monday!" Like Laney, my mouth wasn't empty either but… "You can't mean this coming Monday?"

A grouchy countenance takes over the unfamiliar cheery face we'd been looking at; then Ruby takes a deep breath and the grouch is gone. "Of course I mean this Monday. I'm being positive and happy. Someone will come along, and it will all work out. Spread the word: Ruby's Pies will be open on Monday!" She smiles at each of us, then sails off toward the back.

"Can I taste y'all's muffins? I got all caught up in what she was saying and ate all mine, but we can order another one for y'all to split." Laney reaches over and pinches off part of my maple nut muffin.

Susan shoves her plate into the middle of the table. "Sure. Have the rest of it. Who in the world is Ruby going to find this weekend?"

"No one," I say with a laugh. "She's decided to be positive and happy, and has plowed right on into delusional."

Laney pulls Susan's saucer to her side of the table. "Speaking of delusional, why is no one talking about Shannon being pregnant with Peter's baby?"

Chapter 28

Our stunned silence causes Laney to look up, a piece of Susan's muffin on its way to her mouth. "What? I mean, everyone knows that's what's happening." Shifting her eyes between me and her sister, she finishes with, "Right?"

Susan's eyes are squinted as I look side-eyed at her. Then she pulls back to turn toward me. "Is that true, Carolina? It is, isn't it? Oh my word, it is!"

Laney rolls her eyes. "I figured everyone knew. I mean, she's pretty short, and her weight is usually all in her hips. Plus, you know how hiding something is the best way to get folks to pay attention to it? A good liar knows that. Shannon's definitely not a good liar." She takes a bite and talks through it. "Just put bad stuff right out there for folks to see, and most will look right past it. Those that do take a second look will figure you want them to ask, so they ignore it or don't believe it."

Susan and I, not being good liars, try to think through this theory but with a glance at each other, give up and just take the liar's word for it.

I hold my hand up. "To be honest, she's not actually told me that."

Laney groans and rolls her eyes even more dramatically. Susan frowns and asks, "So what does she say about, well, you know?"

"Nothing. She won't talk about it." Shannon and Danny not being married comes to my mind, but I'm not mentioning that. I claim my final bite of muffin. With a glance at Laney I see that she knows I'm not saying something. She barely shakes her head to let me know she's not going to say anything. Not yet. But we both know she'll be around asking before long.

Whispering, Susan asks, "Do you think Peter knows?"

I open my mouth to say no, but Laney beats me to it.

"No way. Peter believes he knows more than everyone else. Wouldn't dawn on him that Shannon Chilton, much less Danny Kinnock, could pull a fast one on him." Then her eyes narrow. "Wait... I'll bet Danny doesn't know either, does he?"

"I don't know," I blurt, then stop myself. "No. He doesn't have a clue. About much. But he doesn't mind sweeping, so..." I shrug. Lifting my hand up I wave at Libby, and then when she looks at me, her eyebrows raised in question but still halfway across the café, I yell that I need a dozen muffins to go.

"But what about this bridesmaid thing?" Susan asks. "How can you stand up there at Delaney's side knowing all this?"

Laney shakes her head at her sister as she pulls her green stocking cap down over her mess of hair. "Are we really related? Besides, aren't you a tad late playing the morality card to anyone? We know you were with Griffin last night, and there's still an indent on your finger from Silas's engagement ring."

Susan glares at her sister. "You're being hateful. And ugly." Then she looks down at her naked hand. "Besides, the indent is from my wedding rings. The engagement ring was a tad big."

I grab her arm before she slides out of the booth. "Are you and Griffin back together?"

She points across the table. "Ask her. She seems to know everything this morning." Then she pulls away from me and out of the booth. "I've got some work emails I need to get out. Thanks for letting Grant spend the night last night." She winks at me. "I might send him up there again tonight." Then she hurries away, pulling her coat off the coatrack beside the door and putting it on while chatting with the men at the front tables.

"My sister is something else." Laney struggles into her big coat and joins me in standing. "And if she doesn't watch out she might just end up being happy."

I bump fists with her, and we both chuckle. "I think that's her plan," I say. "And we all know how Susan Lyles likes a plan!"

"I need a weekend," I say, still prone in our bed on Monday morning.

"We just had a weekend," Jackson groans. He rolls over to stop his alarm clock from buzzing again, as it was getting ready to do for the third time.

Tim and Jackson had been on the go all Saturday and Sunday, then stayed up late last night talking and looking again at all the pictures and videos they'd taken of the trains. Due to the cold and lack of shoppers, Shannon was able to take care of the shop mostly by herself, thank goodness. Francie didn't like sleeping next door in her nursery all by herself apparently because she didn't sleep worth anything the last three nights. Her parents, on the other hand, have enjoyed full nights of sleep down in the cozy Chessie room.

"Did you look at the weather?" I ask Jackson, who is now sitting on the edge of the bed looking at his phone.

"Forty. Hallelujah. Going to be into the fifties today and even near sixty by the end of the week. Did Francie sleep last night?"

With a grunt I tell him what you'd think he'd know since he slept right beside me. But we established Saturday morning that he thought it was great how Francie slept right through the night and didn't make a peep! Yep, that's what he said in front of

God and everybody—including his exhausted wife who heard every single peep and got about three hours of sleep total.

"You should've woke me." He dives back under the covers and wraps me in a cuddle. "I told you I'd gladly get up with her. I just don't hear her." He kisses on my ear and squeezes me until I giggle. Then he pulls away, tucking me in. "You stay in bed. I'll take the monitor downstairs and get her when she wakes up."

"Maybe for a bit," I mumble. He gets up and then comes to my side of the bed to unplug the monitor before he heads into the bathroom.

But the day is already started in my head. The break from routine last week's cold weather gave us will have everyone starting slow this morning, but I don't care. The kids are most definitely going to school. Wonder if Savannah set her alarm? Bryan and Grant spent Thursday and Friday nights here but then were up in Laurel Cove from Saturday afternoon until Susan brought Bryan home last night, and of course only then did Bryan start his delayed homework. He was still working on it when I was up with the baby at midnight. He was asleep the other times I was up; at least I think he was. Either way, he's going to be a bear to deal with.

Will and Anna are moving back to the cabin this morning with a brand-new kerosene heater Colt got them, which he said will make the cabin toasty warm. I probably should make them breakfast before they leave. Plus Will has taken the finances of the construction business under his wing, so it'd be nice to show my appreciation.

While Jackson and Tim were going through train pictures in the basement, Will and Colt spent most of last evening around the kitchen table with Will's laptop. I'd kind of forgotten Will's major before he decided to go to law school had been business, and he's always been pretty good with numbers. Once Tim retired for the night, the three Jessup men also divvied up the duties better to fit each of their schedules. I could tell they were all feeling pretty good about the future of Colt & Company by bedtime.

Savannah's shower begins to run, so I know she's up. She worked most of the weekend at Andy's Place doing online sales. Ricky went with his mother to a real estate seminar, which was good because I've been too tired to deal with all of that. Besides, they aren't getting engaged. Laney doesn't know what she's talking about.

Jackson creeps out of the bathroom into the dark room. "You can turn on a light," I tell him. "I'm getting up."

"You sure? Stay in bed."

I sit up. "No. I'm wide awake now, and everyone else will be up soon. Think I'll make some French toast."

"Oh, that would be awesome." He sits on the bed beside me and pulls me into a hug. "Thanks for this weekend. It's been crazy, but things will be back to normal in just a couple of hours."

I laugh. "That's exactly what I'm counting on!"

On his way out our door, he sticks his head back in. "Francie's already up apparently. Her door's open, and the crib is empty."

"Okay," I say, then add, "Wait. Leave the monitor up here then." The kids don't need a monitor at the cabin, so they said to leave it here for us to use. I love being able to check in and see that sweet baby bundle all cozy and fine, but it sure makes getting any sleep at all difficult. "Every time she turned over or coughed, I was grabbing for it. I don't see how I missed her waking up?"

Coffee is heavy in the air along with the smell of bacon by the time I get dressed and head downstairs. Will greets me as I walk in. "There she is. Dad said you were making French toast, so I put a pan of bacon in."

"You? Or Anna?"

"Me. I've learned a thing or two over the years." He wraps

me in a hug. "I feel like a new man. Three nights of sleep were miraculous. Thanks, Mom."

"Where is Francie? I'm assuming she didn't come downstairs herself."

"Anna's cuddling with her in bed. When I got up she asked me to go get Francie and bring her down to her. I was super quiet so you wouldn't hear me on the monitor. She didn't even wake up."

Funny, but his renewed energy is better than sleeping in for my own energy levels. I pat his back and open the fridge for the eggs and milk. I see the bread is already out on the counter.

He gets down a mixing bowl. "Dad's downstairs. Savannah and Bryan up?"

"Yes, and they know there will actually be breakfast. Not that we have to all sit down together since they'll be in a mad rush. Is Tim up? He wanted to get an early start home."

"Yep. He's already loaded up his car and is downstairs with Dad. Probably downloading more pictures to the computer. I'm going to go check on Anna, and then I'll come take the bacon out. Table is set too."

Well, this is almost too easy. For almost half a minute I'm alone in the kitchen, then they come from below and above to fill the space with chatter and bodies.

The French toast gets eaten almost as fast as I can flip it as each wave comes through. Savannah and Bryan are done and out the door before I take the second round off the griddle. I'm thinking they might've just taken theirs to go, but I didn't see them out the door, so who knows. Will and Anna are eating while Jackson holds his granddaughter and Tim makes another pot of coffee. The three old folks sit down to eat while Anna and Will go finish packing up. They leave Francie with us, sitting on the table in her carrier. She's fascinated by the birds on the new, squirrel-proof feeder I got for Christmas, which hangs right outside the dining room window.

"Next time, Colleen is coming with me. She'd love this place. Plus, I think you and her would enjoy getting to know each other better," Tim says as he picks up his plate and heads into the kitchen. "Thanks again for everything, but I better get on the road. There's snow coming in at home, and I want to beat it."

His truck is barely over the tracks before Will and Anna are turning around to pull their car out too. Jackson dashes downstairs to get on a conference call, and there I am, alone with syrup-scented air, a full tummy, and quiet.

Yes, there's also a kitchen to be cleaned, beds to be stripped, and a bookstore to be opened, but... have you ever seen a couch so inviting?

Grammy needs a nap.

Chapter 29

Bonnie grabs me before I get fully in the front door of Blooming Books. "Finally! I thought you were coming in when you finished breakfast." She's pulling me past the bookshelves, where our customers are, back to her desk and decorating area. "This'll only take a minute. Danny's up there."

"But we don't let Danny run the register. Do we?"

She waves her hand that's not gripping my elbow above her head. "He'll smile and charm them for another minute or two until we can get back up there. I need your help now." She turns me to sit down in her desk chair and then pulls a stool over and sits right in front of me, our knees just inches apart. "Peter wants to hire me for another job," she whispers through gritted teeth.

Before my smile gets a good start, she shakes her head at me. "Wait. Don't smile. I don't know if I should take it." She scoots toward me and motions for me to lower my head closer to hers. "It's to decorate Phoenix's bedroom."

My head jerks back. "No!"

Her head bobs up and down, then sideways, and she sighs. "It's her Christmas gift, and depending on how it turns out he'll decide whether to hire me for his whole house. Well, Missus's house."

"Delaney and Missus might have something to say about

that." I sit back and think for a moment. "Does Phoenix even want someone decorating her bedroom? I mean, I've seen it, and it's going to be beautiful with big windows and all but..." I lean forward again. "What are you going to do?"

"I don't know. I mean, this is completely strange, isn't it?"

"Completely. It's like he doesn't even care that people think he's, you know."

"Having an affair? Exactly." She stands up and looks to the front. "Okay. I just had to get it out there, but now I need to go up front. Danny's charm does have an expiration." She turns back to me, hands on her slim hips. "Think about it. I need to give him an answer by two."

"Two today? That's, like, in a couple of hours."

She walks away, saying over her shoulder, "Yep. I'm meeting him at Ruby's for pie." She turns back toward me. "Did you know Ruby's is open for pies in the afternoons now?" Then with a little jog she hurries to the front. "I'm coming. I'm coming!"

Peter is hiring a decorator for Phoenix's bedroom?

I'm beginning to think he doesn't actually want to get married.

"Missus is buying everyone pie," Patty announces from near the front windows. She showed up right after I got to the bookstore, with an old-fashioned feather duster her mother ordered on Amazon, so she's wandered around dusting for the last couple hours—that is, when she can remember where she last laid the duster down. "No, seriously," she yelps. "We need to get down there." Holding her phone, she walks up to me and the lady I'm helping.

The woman's interest in Victorian cozy mysteries fades at

the thought of free pie. "Pie? Is this Missus buying for anyone, or just people she knows?"

Patty pushes her phone at us. "Mama says everyone. Missus is buying everyone pie. We should go." She focuses on me. "Can I go?"

"Patty, you don't actually work here. You can do whatever you want."

My used-to-be customer hands me back the book I just handed her. "Is it close to here? We didn't have any lunch."

"Oh, yes, ma'am." Patty points to her left. "Just right down there. Y'all can follow me. Want me to bring you a piece back, Carolina? Bonnie's already down there, ain't she? Lucky thing." Patty heads to the coatrack, moving faster than I've seen her move in a month of Sundays. "Hope they don't run out."

Shannon looks around, then says, "Danny, come on. We don't want to miss this. Carolina can handle things here. I mean, I had to all weekend, right?"

"We didn't have any customers this weekend, remember? But I'll be fine. Go on." And I will be fine since most our customers are heading to Ruby's. Except for an older man looking at books and a bride-to-be going through Shannon's flower books. Of course, she's been here for a solid hour already and doesn't actually have a wedding date.

I lean on the counter and look out the front windows. It's like I'm the only person in town not honed in on the free pie. There go Angie and Alex; of course they're not open yet, so they can just lock the door and leave. My phone dings, and I see Missus is now using the chamber of commerce contact list. So this is merely her congratulations to Ruby on a new business venture and has absolutely nothing whatsoever to do with the mayoral race. Right. Surely she knows Laney dropped out of the race, so she can quit trying so hard.

The bell over the door dings, and I look up, ready to smile, but it's Peter with Bonnie in tow.

He opens his arms. "Much quieter here. Who knew my mother was going to cause a madhouse at the opening of Ruby's Pies? Well, my fiancée knew. She's apparently become Mother's campaign manager."

"Oh, Delaney didn't tell you something that important?" I can't help but smirk. "Imagine that. Keeping secrets."

He grins and walks over to lean his hip on the counter. "Oh, Carolina. You're so righteous these days. So, did you advise Bonnie to not work with me?"

Bonnie and I both object.

"And yet..." He looks from me to Bonnie.

She pulls on her stern teacher look. "Peter, you know how this looks. I told you it's just not a good idea. For you or for me."

He straightens up and turns to face her. "And I told you I'm no longer worrying about how things look. I tore the bedroom in that house apart before I leased it to Phoenix. I told her I'd take care of getting it put back together. That includes things like flooring and wall covering, wouldn't you agree?"

Bonnie moves around him to be able to see me. "That does kind of make sense, doesn't it?"

"Of course it does," I agree but tack on an eye roll. "Anything we want can be made to sound reasonable."

Peter nods at me. "Exactly. Like, are you concerned that your husband spent so many, many hours in Phoenix's bedroom? No. And you shouldn't be. It's just a job, right?"

"This doesn't really concern me." I move out from behind the counter. "Bonnie, do whatever you want." With eyes narrowed at Peter I add, "Because Lord knows everyone else does."

He grins again and leans back on the counter. "I do now." He puts out his hand to Bonnie. "So we have a deal?"

When she hesitates he tips his head at her. "You're a very good businesswoman, Mrs. Cuneo. You want to know about doing the Bedwell mansion before you commit, don't you?"

"Oh!" Bonnie jumps. "I wasn't holding out or anything like that. I'm just…"

Peter gives her a small bow. "Just wanting to know where you stand. Okay, I like what you've done with my new office, so let's go ahead and make it a grand deal. You have all my business."

Bonnie sucks in a deep breath. "Oh. Okay." Her eyes dart to me, but I quickly turn away and walk over to the gentleman examining our Civil War books. Behind me Peter laughs, and it hurts because I used to love to hear him laugh.

"Can I help you find anything, sir?"

He creaks up from where he was bent over looking at the bottom shelves. "Not really. Think I'll take these to that table there and look at them. You have quite a good collection of Civil War books."

"Thanks. We had a local man here give us a lot of his collection. Let me carry those for you." At the small table I pull out the solid wooden chair for the gentleman. With the books still in my arms, I can't help it. I open the front cover of the top one. There's F.M.'s name on the upper corner of the first page in his straightforward signature, half script, half print. Francis Marion Bedwell.

Peter and Bonnie are headed back to her desk, but he stops when he sees the books. "Those were Dad's."

I turn and hold the book in my hands out to him. "Yes. He cleaned out his collection last summer. Do you want to take a look at them, too?"

He backs away from it, his face paler than before. "No. I'd just… I'd just forgotten."

"F.M. was a special man." I step toward him. "He's not someone we should forget."

Peter shakes himself. "And we won't! Bonnie, make sure your decorating plans include Dad's library. Making it a place to remember and honor him."

Keeping my voice low I lean closer to him. "He'd be happier with you honoring his memory in the way you live."

He stares at me. "Probably. But we know that's impossible, right? My genes come more from my mother's side, don't you think?" Then, with squared shoulders, his grin is back, and he turns, putting out his arm in a dramatic flourish for Bonnie to precede him back to her desk space.

I lay the book down on the table and smile at the man seated there. "Here you go. These belonged to a very special man."

"I can tell." He opens the book on top. "Thank you for letting me look at them. I'm afraid I can't afford to buy any of them, but I hope it's still okay if I look at them? Besides, perhaps the young man will change his mind and want his father's books back one day."

"I don't think so. Matter of fact, the man who owned them would love to know they were being treasured." I take in a slow breath. "We'd be honored if you'd take one with you. If you want?"

"Oh no, I couldn't just take one."

"Please. Whichever one you'd like. It would make me very happy. Let me get you a bag."

I dash to the counter, wiping my eyes. F.M.'s legacy should live on somehow.

It's sure not living on in his son.

Chapter 30

"Hope there's some pie left," I mutter to myself. However, walking in the opposite direction of all these happy, pie-filled people, I'm afraid I'm too late. Peter finally left just before Shannon, Danny, and Patty came rolling back in. Our customers from earlier also returned, along with a few more. Bonnie joined Shannon in rushing me out the door to not miss out. No one knows for sure how long Ruby is going to be open in the afternoons, though everyone seems to have a different idea.

The door to Ruby's opens when I push it, so that's a good sign. "I made it! Any pie left?" I say, but my voice trails off under the torrent of words coming from back near the counter. And it's a torrent from three different founts—Laney, Missus, and Ruby. At least I'm the only other person in the café.

"Who gave you permission to give away my pies, anyway?"

"Give it away? I paid for every single bite of that crummy pie. Even the burnt one!"

"None of my pies were burnt!"

Laney decides she's feeling left out. "Well, that sweet potato one was a little dark…"

Ruby sticks her tongue out at Laney. "Thanks to you two fighting over being queen of this lousy town, I don't have pies for the rest of the week. I'll be here all night baking." She whirls away from them and leans on the counter, braced on her scrawny but steel-like arms.

With a giant eye roll Laney exclaims, "I don't want to be mayor!"

Missus bravely, or foolishly, steps right up to her. "You don't fool me one bit, Miss I-Don't-Want-to-Be-Mayor. Coming in here all schlumped up with your hair a mess and wearing that, that, what is that coat? Salesman giving them away to dealerships that sell those tires? You should've told Shaw to keep it to use for insulation on that old house he got from his parents." She sticks a finger in Laney's face. "No, ma'am. I've got your number. You're going for the pity vote."

"I withdrew from the race!" Laney shoots through gritted teeth. "But you are right about this coat. I'm burning up." She fights to get out of it and then drops it in the floor. "And no one pities me. I may not be on top of my game right now, but at least I would never have stooped to giving out free food to get votes." She smooths down her hair and then her hands rest on her flushed cheeks. She mumbles. "I don't think I have on any makeup."

I'd slowly, slowly, walked back to them. Laney turns to me. "Carolina, do I not have on any makeup?"

"No, honey, doesn't look like it, but you know you still look good."

She pulls her hands together to cover her face, and she shakes her head while she talks from behind her hands. "I came down here determined to start taking a dance class at Phoenix's—you know, those deals she's doing for the new year?—and then, well, everyone was coming here for free pie." Her hands fly away from her face, and she glares at Missus. "It's your fault I ruined my diet already!"

Missus opens her mouth to object but then sees that Laney is crying, and she takes a step back. Then we hear sobbing from

Ruby. I step through the mayoral debate panel and go to put my arm around her.

"Ruby, what's wrong? Everyone loved your pies. Your new idea is a great success."

She shrugs off my arm and sits on one of the stools. "Look at this mess. Every saucer and fork I own is dirty. Every coffee cup. I'm out of pie supplies and had to put milk in the creamers for the last round of customers because I ran out of half-and-half." She lays her head on her folded arms. "I'm so tired."

"I'm assuming you didn't find anyone to work this afternoon?"

"No, and I never knew how hard Libby works. I'd give her a raise, but I've sunk all my money into pie stuff." She whirls on the stool to face Missus.

"This is that daughter-in-law of yours' fault. You and her, with all your cockamamie ideas about this town. She ought to spend a little more time making that boy of yours happy and a little less time worrying about Chancey."

Laney sniffles one more time, but there's a new light in her eye. This is one conversation she wants to hear, makeup or no makeup. However, Missus's jaw is set firm and her lips are crushed closed.

I try to wave Laney off, but that light in her eyes is growing brighter—and meaner. "Yeah, Missus. How are the wedding plans coming? I hear Carolina is the matron of honor? Think Phoenix will serve as Peter's best—oh, I don't know. Best, um, I bet they'll come up with something she's best at."

Missus ignores her and focuses on me. "You're in the wedding? Why did I not know this? Carolina, you insist on keeping secrets."

"Me? How about the two people you live with? How about all their secrets?"

Ruby and Laney draw in breaths, eyes glued on Missus. A survival skill from years of small town living comes into play as she notices the attention from the two women she's fought with her entire life, and she pulls back. Then she straightens her shoulders and looks around. She pushes up the sleeves of her powder-blue turtleneck as she plows past Laney, avoiding actually touching her, and walks around the counter. "Where are your extra aprons, Ruby? This is partially my fault, and the least I can do is help clean up a bit."

Laney doesn't say a word, just stomps to the front door and leaves. Ruby gets off her stool as she points to a rack near the back door. "Some extra aprons back there on the rack. You staying, too, Carolina?"

I look at the clock on the wall. "Ten minutes. That's all I can do, but please tell me there's at least one piece of pie left."

Missus stares at me as she ties on her apron. "Don't be so thick. Didn't you hear a word we said? There. Is. No. More. Pie. Now pick Laney's coat up out of the floor and throw it out back. Maybe some feral cats need a new home."

"Your coat is my van. Can't believe you left without it," I tell Laney. I'm driving home after closing the store. After helping clean up at Ruby's.

Her sigh comes through the phone. "Like I can ever wear that coat again. Give it to Goodwill or the church donation box. I've got to get my groove back. Pains me to say it, but Missus was right. Not about me wanting the pity vote, of course. I can't believe I ever thought I wanted to be mayor, and with the way Missus jumped in to help Ruby, she obviously deserves to win." I hear a choke in her voice, and it's husky as she adds, "How petty can I be?"

I laugh. "Give yourself a break. I stayed to help for a few

minutes, but as I was leaving I passed Charles Spoon from the *Vedette* on his way to Ruby's. Missus had called him."

"What did she do that for?" Then she sucks in a big breath. "Oh my heavens! That glory hound! She called him to get pictures of her helping Ruby for the paper, didn't she?"

"Yep, that's exactly what she did. I couldn't believe it."

There's silence.

"Laney, did I lose you?"

"No, I'm here. I do hate the idea of her winning, but you know? Missus is as sly as Jed is dense. Maybe she's just what this town needs."

See? Even Laney wouldn't have voted for Laney.

CHAPTER 31

"We're making brownies!" Savannah announces when I walk in the kitchen to the loud chatter and laughter of a bunch of high school girls.

"Jenna got into UGA!" her friend Allie announces just as loudly, then calms down a bit to add, "Hey, Mrs. Jessup."

"Hey." I speak to my daughter over the heads of the girls. "Your dad still working downstairs?"

"Yep. He told me we could order pizza when you got home, so I called when we saw your car pull in."

"Everybody staying for pizza?" I lift my eyebrows, pull my lips into a smile, and force my voice up to a more cheerful octave to show how much a part of the fun I am.

Savannah frowns as she looks around. "Yeah, I ordered a ton." She flips back around to her mixing bowl. "We're going to take the brownies to Jenna after we eat. She's celebrating with her parents first."

The girls turn back to their task, and I debate talking to my husband or getting changed. I leave the kitchen and head upstairs. Wait... I stick my head back in the bright, crowded room. "Who's going to get the pizza?" We don't have delivery except on the weekends.

"Dad. Unless his call goes long. Then he said to ask you." For a quick moment I wait to see if one of the girls, all of whom drive and whose cars are filling up my driveway, will offer, but of course they don't. Okay. Well, if I have to go back out, which is better than cooking dinner, I might as well get something out of it. Like information.

I walk back inside the kitchen and pull out a chair at the table. "Sure. I'll go get it." Sitting down, I fold my arms and lean onto the table. "So Jenna's going to UGA. What are the rest of you girls doing after graduation?"

"I knew it. Savannah is the only one who doesn't have any idea what she's doing."

The brownies are out with the girls for delivery. Bryan and Zoe had pizza with us, and now he's walking her home, so it's just Jackson and me on the couch, waiting for our pizza to digest so we can enjoy the brownies sitting on the coffee table in front of us. The girls bought cans of decorator icing to write on Jenna's treats, so ours are also decorated, with a heart on each one.

Jackson mutes the television. "I had no idea Allie was going into the army, did you?"

"Nope. Savannah hasn't said a thing. Usually I'd get info from Laney or Susan, but they're both so preoccupied lately."

When we sit quietly for a bit, he unmutes the TV, but I don't think either of us are watching it. It's a rerun of a sitcom we've seen many times, so it's easy to tune in or out.

When a commercial begins he hits the mute button again and asks, "Did you ever talk to her about Ricky and that ring thing?"

I can't help but bristle. "No. Did you?"

"Hey, I just asked, and no, I didn't either. I'm nervous to mention it and make it real. You know, force her hand."

"I do know. To think I was worried about her majoring in theater; now I'd be happy for her to major in underwater basket-weaving if it would keep her from getting engaged."

He nods, then sighs. "You know she talked to Silas about acting?"

"She did?"

"Yeah, I kind of overheard them one day, and then I asked him about it. She thought it was fun, but apparently she found it frustrating, too much waiting around for her. Silas said he explained to her it's like with any career: you need to like the stuff surrounding it or it gets old real quick. Also, apparently the other actors drive her crazy." He grins at me. "Good to know it's not just us."

"Amen. But that makes a lot of sense. Watching her shoot scenes at the store, I felt she was agitated. I guess just being a good actress isn't enough to want to make a career of it. Something like that takes a lot of passion."

"Exactly what Silas said. He just doesn't see the passion for it in her." Jackson lifts his hands in a shrug. "As long as she doesn't decide marriage is her only option."

I shudder, and we watch the ads one after another in silence. Then he laughs. "The girls sure were cute tonight. Laughing and acting silly." He pauses. "I missed things like this when I traveled. Impromptu pizza parties, no big thing just…" He shrugs and then unmutes the TV for the show.

He's right. It was fun. And it was nice of the girls to want to celebrate Jenna. They'll all be dispersing into the world in a matter of months. They'll make new friends, then have adventures their current close friends will only experience through Facebook and Instagram posts. I spent too much of tonight comparing and contrasting instead of simply enjoying. Shame on me.

I scoot forward. "Want some milk or decaf coffee with your brownie?"

Jackson nods. "Good thinking. A glass of milk would be awesome." Then he once again hits mute, lays the remote down, and reaches up to put his arms around me. He pulls me back toward him. "I also missed this when I was on the road all the time. Just sitting on the couch, watching another episode of *The Office* with you."

We're still snuggling when Bryan opens the front door. "Mom, Zoe's mom wants you to call her."

I scoot forward and stand up. "What for? Why doesn't she just call me?"

He comes around to flop into the chair by the front window. "I don't know. Something about Ruby's? Says she doesn't want to disturb you, but I told her you weren't doing anything."

"No. I'm never doing anything." I don't bother with an eye roll. They're wasted on teenage boys. Older boys too. Men in general. "She want me to call her tonight?"

He looks at me with wide eyes and an exaggerated shrug. He's sprawled across the chair, but he suddenly springs forward. "Hey! Can I have one of those brownies?"

His father sticks out his arm. "No way! Those are ours. You had more than a few as I recall."

"And they let you have all the burnt edges," I add.

"But I'm still hungry. Those girls were like piranhas on that pizza." He gets up and follows me into the kitchen, where he asks his dad loudly, "Oh yeah, Dad! Did you leave your phone downstairs again?"

"Probably. Only way I can get some peace working with those folks on the West Coast. It's the middle of the afternoon to them. Why?"

Bryan has both the fridge and freezer doors open. I reach past him to get the milk as he yells back, "Ricky's trying to get hold of you. Says he has something to ask you."

Good thing the cap was nice and tight on the milk when it fell right out of my hand.

Chapter 32

"Hey, Kimmy," I say when she picks up the phone. "Sorry I didn't call you last night."

"Oh, that's okay. Bedtime around here gets kind of crazy, and by the time they're all in bed I'm beat. Are you already at the bookstore?"

"No. Not yet."

"Why don't you come have a cup of coffee on your way in? That way we can talk."

"Well, we can talk now." I really have no desire to sit in the Kendricks' house with all those kids running around. It's always a madhouse.

"But I'd really like to show you something. Come on by on your way in. You usually pass here around nine thirty? Come over at nine. See you then."

She was already arguing with one of her children before she could hang up. Zoe is her stepdaughter and just a jewel. Bryan is crazy about her, as most of us are. And now that her parents are in counseling and have worked out some of their issues, she doesn't have to act out like she did last summer with the vandalism that drove Chancey crazy. The other three kids are Kimmy and Kyle's, and are all in kindergarten or younger.

The Kendricks bought Susan and Griffin Lyles' old house, and I still miss having Susan that close. I also can't help but feel that selling that house was the beginning of all their marriage problems. Susan says they had issues from the get go, but still, they seemed happy.

I didn't call Kimmy back last night because hearing that Ricky wanted to ask Jackson something stole all my attention. Jackson finally got a hold of him, and they are having coffee at Ruby's this morning at nine. At least going to Kimmy's house of fun will help keep my mind off what they're talking about.

And who knows? Maybe Ricky just has something he wants remodeled.

"What's going on?" Kimmy asks because I'm still staring at my phone. I've only been here ten minutes, and Jackson just texted me that he'll meet me at the store to talk. I'm staring at my phone because he's not answered my desperate line of question marks.

"Um, just kind of a weird text from Jackson." I stand. "Listen, thanks for the coffee and cookies, but I've got to go."

The petite mom with thin, light-brown hair and almost colorless gray eyes frowns at me. "But you just got here. We didn't get to talk."

I quickly sit back down. "Okay, just another minute. What did you want?"

"This pie thing at Ruby's. What's up with that? Is she really looking to hire someone?"

Blinking I try to corral my thoughts of Ricky and Savannah. "Yes. To serve pie and coffee for a couple hours in the afternoons. Why? Are you interested?"

"I might be. I can't do it every day, but the days the church has Mother's Day Out in the afternoon I might be interested."

"Great!" With a big smile I stand again. That was easy. "Well, I better go."

She frowns again. "But I need you to talk to Ruby for me. She's not my biggest fan." She dips her head to indicate I should sit back down. I sit back down.

"But you have to ask her for the job. I can't hire you for her."

"Oh, I know I eventually have to talk to her, but can't you tell her how much me and the kids have changed? Ruby practically banned me from coming in there."

I was there the last time the Kendricks' kids were let loose in Ruby's. They weren't "practically" banned. They were full-on banned, and I was a big proponent of the action. I look into the living room where three-year-old Katherine and the baby, Kevin, are watching television. "They are being really good. But you said the kids would be at Mother's Day Out, so they wouldn't be a problem."

"Yeah, but she might think if I can't control my own kids, how can I run her restaurant? I just need you to put a good word in for me. Okay?"

"Okay!" I stand and this time start walking to the door. "I really have to go. But wait…" I turn around. "What did you want to show me?"

She smiles and spreads her arms like Vanna White on *Wheel of Fortune* displaying a new car. "This. My clean house and well-behaved kids. Me and Kyle are doing good, aren't we?"

I look around and see that the house is clean and comfortable. There are pictures on the walls and other comforts that say it's a cared-for place. Kevin crawls to his mother, and she picks him up. There's none of the anger or disinterest she often displayed before. She's right. The house feels… it feels like a home. "You are doing well. I'm real happy for you. I will definitely talk to Ruby. Then you'll need to call her, okay?"

"Sure thing. Thanks, Carolina. I just set a lot of store in you and your opinion."

I start the van, get the heater going, and then pause. Kimmy has really gotten her life in order, and I'm impressed she had the guts to seek out affirmation. How easy it is to think people should change and even to talk about it, but I guess it's import- ant then to acknowledge it if it actually happens. I feel good as I back out of their driveway and head downhill to town and to Jackson.

Well, kinda good. Jackson never did answer my question marks.

Jackson is measuring the shelves for Bonnie's work space when I come in the back door. Since Bonnie and Shannon are up front, I go straight toward my husband, asking, "What did he want?"

He turns to me, puts his hands on his hips, and hangs his head. My heart sinks, but as I hurry to his side he looks up and grins. "He wants to know if we're interested in selling our house."

That stops me in my tracks. "What?"

"Exactly what I said. He said he has a buyer looking for property like ours, and so he wanted to officially ask. Also to say if we ever do want to sell, he'd like to handle the sale."

After a deep breath I lean closer and whisper. "The ring? Did he say anything about it or Savannah?"

He shakes his head. "Nope. I asked about the two of them, and he said everything was good but that he's concentrating on his career."

I sink into Bonnie's chair while Jackson leans against the desk. "But he wanted to meet with you for that?"

"Said he's trying to be professional. And he was. Gotta say I was impressed. It was only when I brought up Savannah that he seemed like the Ricky that hangs out at the house." He leans over to pick up his travel mug and take a sip. "Maybe that was the idea. Wanted me to see him in a different setting."

"Huh. You know, the same thing happened to me this morning. Kimmy Kendricks wanted me to come by. Had something to show me and ask me, and I ended up impressed too."

"With Kimmy Kendricks? Must not have been any kids around." He laughs and steps back to finish measuring.

"But there *were* kids there. That's what she wanted to show me." I rise from the chair and give him a kiss on his cheek. "And while I have my coat on, I'm going to go talk to Ruby for her. She wants to work some of the pie shifts and wants me to put in a good word for her."

He laughs. "Look at us. People wanting us to have good opinions of them. It's like we've grown up or something. Now let me get back to this. I'll be gone by the time you get back from Ruby's, so see you tonight."

I don't stop to talk as Shannon and Bonnie are both with customers. It's a partly cloudy day, but it's well above freezing, so I'm not complaining. Old leaves rustle in the square in a bit of a breeze. I feel more a part of this town today than ever before. I belong here, and my family belongs here. I'm going to talk to Ruby real quick, then get back to my bookstore.

I step inside Ruby's and walk to the back, nodding and saying hello to other customers, though there's no one I know well. At the back counter I speak to Ruby quickly. She gives me exactly thirty seconds as she's watching meringue brown on a batch of pies. She nods and says she looks forward to hearing from Kimmy, and then she's back to the oven.

Okay. That was way easier than I imagined.

Back out on the sidewalk I look in both directions at the empty sidewalk. Just as I get to our door, it opens and Missus comes flying out. She grabs my elbow and then stops, looking up and down the sidewalk as I just did.

"We need somewhere to talk," she says.

"Let's go back in the store."

"No. Private." She lets go of me to take two long strides to the door of AC's. She jerks it open, looks inside, then motions for me to go in. Alex meets us before we get very far inside.

"Sorry. We're not open. Oh, Mrs. Bedwell. Mrs. Jessup. Can I help you?"

Missus points to the row of tables by the front window. "We need to talk in private. Believe me, young man, you'll make enough off of me in the future to pay for my use of one of those tables for a little while. Are there any workers in this area?"

"No, ma'am. We're in the kitchen, but uh…" He looks at the tables, then at me, but I only shrug at him. He shrugs back, saying, "Sure, I guess it's fine."

"Come, Carolina. We'll sit at the last table there."

"Can I get you ladies a glass of water?"

"No. Nothing," Missus says, marching away from us. "I will need you to lock that door. I will not be interrupted. You can use the back door if you or your staff need to leave."

He gives me a smile and steps to the door to twist the lock. "I'll leave you ladies alone. Just let me know when you leave."

Missus sits on the far side of the table, and I take the seat across from her. I shrug off my coat, although I immediately regret it as it's chilly. So it's halfway back up my arms when Missus taps the table in front of me with a gray-gloved finger. "Quit playing with your coat, Carolina, and look at me."

I stop, arms bound to my sides, and glare at her. She's dressed in all gray, a suede-looking jacket and slacks of dark gray with a light-gray, high-necked blouse. Her hair has lost all its blonde highlights from the fall, so it's gray also, but the most striking gray is that of her face. If she has makeup on (and she *always* has makeup on), it's not masking the pallor. Her lips are thin and stretched tight, colorless. I drop my glare and my shoulders, but before I can ask her what's wrong, she shushes me with a sharp hiss through those tight lips.

She clenches her gloved fists on the table between us and squeezes out, "Peter. My son, Peter, is having a baby."

CHAPTER 33

"What?" is all I manage. Boy, I wish I had some water. I swallow a couple of times while she stares at me. "What makes you say that?"

Tears come to her eyes. "That girl is pregnant, isn't she? You know she usually carries her weight in her hips and bottom. How can he do this to me? Planning a wedding and a master suite when he should be putting in a nursery."

She's still clenching and unclenching her hands, so I reach out and put my fingers over hers to keep them from closing again. "Missus, you have to relax. You're going to give yourself a stroke." I look over my shoulder. "Maybe we can get some of that water Alex mentioned."

"No!" she says, pulling her hands away and putting them in her lap. "I'm completely embarrassed. My own son doesn't want me to know he's going to be a father." She stares at the table, slowly shaking her head.

I hesitantly try. "You know Shannon's with Danny now. Maybe it's his."

"No. I've done the math. Besides"—she shifts her eyes to look up at me—"he can't have any more children."

"How would you know that?"

She looks back down and clears her throat. "Well, I was in a Bible study group with Marjorie Kinnock, Danny's mother, a couple years ago. She and I were slated to do refreshments one week, but she had to bow out because Danny was at her house recovering from, well, his surgery. She was quite thrilled, as Danny never has really financially supported his family without help from his parents, and the Kinnocks thought three kids were more than enough." Clearing her throat again she says, "Some water might be nice."

Shifting to get up, I say, "I'll find Alex."

"No! I don't want him up here. I don't want anyone knowing that I don't know about my own grandchild."

"Missus, we don't even know there is a-a… child."

She gives me that arched eyebrow look. "What is Shannon saying? I can't believe Peter is agreeing to share his child with Danny Kinnock. We have to get a handle on this, and first thing to do is call off this wedding. I will not be made a laughing-stock. My son with a bride on one arm and his, his baby mama on the other!" She lightly pounds the table. The clenched fists are back.

I look outside and wait to be excused. Maybe we can get through this without her realizing I've not actually said anything. But then the silence drags on, so I say, "Listen, I have to go to work." I try a laugh and a graceful exit as I slowly stand. "I've not gotten anything done at all today." I pull my coat the rest of the way on and lean back over the table. "Missus, you shouldn't say anything about all this. You don't really know if Shannon is actually pregnant."

"I have eyes, Carolina, and I can count. Plus…" She scoots back her chair. "I just know. That's my grandchild." She stands and pulls the belt on her coat tight. "As usual no one knows what to do. Everyone is dithering, so I must take charge." She strides past me, head held high as she spouts, "Also as usual, you've been no help at all."

"Peter doesn't know."

She stops, her hand on the lock. I wait for her to turn around and face me. Instead she twists the lock, pushes the door, and is outside by the time I'm ready to say something.

Well, I wasn't actually ready, but I was going to say something.

Shannon was out delivering flowers when I got back to the store. Then it was lunchtime, and she and Danny went upstairs and she stayed to take a nap. (Like pregnant women do.) Bryan has a JV basketball game right after school, so I can't stay here much longer.

"Bonnie, are you and Danny good here? I need to go upstairs and talk to Shannon."

"Sure. It's usually slow this time of day until close. You're leaving soon anyway, right?"

"Right. Bryan's ballgame."

I start to tell Danny I'm going upstairs, but he's busy reading one of F.M.'s history books. The boy sure likes to read, I'll say that for him. As I head up the stairs I kick myself. I have to stop calling him a boy. He's a father of three. He's been married and divorced and is now living with my business partner. It's just that he looks, and acts, like a boy. Oh well. I knock on the door and open it when she says, "Come in."

"Hey, Shannon. It's me." It's the first time I've seen the apartment since she moved in, and it looks really cute. When Patty lived up here by herself it was a mess; then when she married Andy he did a lot of fixing up and decorating. It looks pretty much the same as it did then except there's more purple. Shannon loves purple.

There's a little pass-through kitchen, then a couch and chair, and in the corner the bed. There's a sheer purple curtain around the bed, and she comes out from behind it. "Everything okay downstairs? I'm ready to come down. I can't believe I slept so long."

"Well, it's because you're pregnant." I've decided to quit asking and just assume. Plow on through.

She frowns and walks over to the couch. "I guess so," she says as she sits down.

"Oh! Okay. So you are."

"Yes. I am. I took a test, and I'm going to the doctor soon." She takes time to slide on her shoes, then looks up at me and smiles real big. "Danny and I are very happy!"

"Shannon. It's not Danny's."

"Of course it is," she says with a laugh. "I know I lied about us actually being married, but we will be soon. Just having a quiet ceremony. No need to have the whole town talking."

"The whole town is already talking. Everyone knows you're pregnant, and well, what's Danny have to say?"

"He's happy. Hoping for a boy."

"Does he ever have his other children? What's he like as a father?"

"His ex-wife is very controlling. She has full custody." She stands. "That's not his fault."

"Of course it's his fault. Shannon, look at me."

She stops as she heads to the bathroom but avoids looking my direction. "Don't worry, Carolina. He's, ah, matured. We're going to be fine. I'll see you downstairs." She enters the tiny bathroom and closes the door.

Okay, this might even work better if I don't have to see her face. I step up to the closed door and lean in close. "Shannon. I just heard from a very reputable source that Danny had a vasectomy a couple years ago." I wait, but there's nothing. "Shannon? Did you hear me?"

All I get is a flush. So if I can hear that, she heard me. Okay. Well, that did work better.

I may start having all my hard conversations through a closed door.

Chapter 34

"Our guests for the weekend have cancelled." Laney is clearly perturbed as she flounces from the B&B office into the kitchen and drops into one of the chairs. "What are you doing?"

"Putting together chicken soup in the Crock-Pot for dinner tonight," I tell her from where I'm working at the counter.

Everything's been quiet in town for the last couple of days. Everyone seems to be staying inside and staying in their lanes. I've had no response from Missus on finding out Peter doesn't know he's about to become a father. No response from Shannon on finding out Danny has all the kids he's going to have. The store's been busy. All of downtown has been busy, and the big ski weekend for the church kids begins tomorrow with them crowding onto a bus to West Virginia. I wash my hands and turn toward Laney as I grab a towel. "Why'd they cancel? It was three couples, right?"

"Yeah. The couple that made the reservations is sick with the flu, and I get the feeling the other couples don't like each other that much. They're paying the cancellation fee since they were supposed to get here tomorrow." She takes the banana I offer. "Good. I'm trying to eat more fruit. So with that and the kids leaving, you and Jackson now have the whole house to yourselves this weekend."

I sit across from her and peel my banana. "Hey, that's right."

"You can sleep in one of the B&B rooms. Be like you're off for the weekend."

"Except I'd know it was me that would have to wash the sheets and redo the bed. I know Jenna's going on the ski trip. Anything new from Angie?"

"No." She sighs and finishes chewing. "We're at least talking now, so we offered to pay for her to go on the ski trip, but she's so beyond those children." With a roll of her eyes and a flourish in her voice, she lets me know those are her daughter's sentiments, not hers. "She has a restaurant to open. She can't be playing around!"

"Some kids grow up faster than others. Have they set an opening date?"

"Actually they have set a, what's it called, ah, little opening? Or a small, no, a soft opening Tuesday night after the election. They're doing a set menu. Shaw says we're going, but…"

"But what? Is the problem that it's election night or that it's Angie's new life?"

She flings up her hand. "Oh, I don't give a fiddle for the election. Missus can have this town. And I've decided if Angie's happy, I'm happy." She leans forward and plants her chin in her palms. "Look at me. I cannot get rid of this weight from having Cayden. I was never a stick like Susan, and I liked my curves. But this is different. I feel so bloated. I can't wear any of my nice clothes. All those stupid outfits I bought to run for mayor aren't me. Blah colors and natural fiber pants that won't stretch. But my old clothes aren't me either anymore apparently." She widens her hands and lets her head fall to the table, then pulls it right back up.

"And my hair. Yes, it was my stupid idea to cut it, but the texture since I was pregnant is just gross, and it won't do anything. Plus, who has time to *make* it do anything?"

"Maybe you and Shaw need a weekend away? Time to recharge. Or maybe just a spa appointment with Beau. You used to get your hair and nails done all the time. Didn't you go to that luxury place when we first moved here? Remember? I couldn't get hold of you about the permits. The old place on the other side of the interstate?"

"Oh, Barnsley Gardens. That was years ago. But maybe that is what I need."

She grabs her phone, and before I've eaten my last bite of banana, she's talking to someone at the resort. But quickly the conversation takes a sad turn, and she hangs up.

"They're full this weekend."

"But you don't have to go this weekend." She looks at me with all the confusion of a puppy being told the walk is over.

"Why would I wait? I don't need a weekend away sometime in the future. I need it now." She stands, gathering her phone and banana and bottle of water. "I'm going to figure this out in the office with the computer. Are you headed to the bookstore?"

"Yes. Jackson is downstairs—oh, actually I hear him coming up the stairs now."

"Hi there," he says as he pushes open the door, but he remains only halfway through the doorway. "Tim's on the phone, and he wants to know if I can meet him and some other railfan buddies up in Chattanooga this weekend. They're running a special engine on the Tennessee Valley Railroad. Kids are going to be gone, right? But I know we have guests coming."

Laney speaks up. "Not anymore."

"But that doesn't matter," I say with a smile. "Go on up there. I'll enjoy a weekend alone."

"You sure?" he asks, but his face has already lit up. "I already checked with Colt, and he can handle the workload with the remodeling, so I guess I'll tell Tim I'm good to go." He blows me a kiss, closes the door, and pounds back down the stairs.

Laney slowly turns to me, her mouth open and eyes sparkling. "Girls' weekend here. I'll call Beau and set us up for the works. We'll have Phoenix come do yoga in the morning. You know, like they do on those girl trips on the Real Housewives shows."

"You do yoga?"

"Not yet. We can even hire Phoenix to come cook healthy food for us, and then as soon as she leaves we'll break out chocolate and wine." She giggles. "This is great. What a fantastic idea, Carolina!" She hurries toward the B&B office, but then stops and turns. "Of course we'll invite Susan. Who else?"

My eyebrows are drawn down, my lips are pressed together tight, the word "no" reverberates in my head, and I know I do not want to do this. Yet I've lived here long enough, and known Laney long enough, that I know I *am* doing this. I can argue and fuss and stumble through it as I usually do or…

"Beau, and what do you think about Delaney?" I spurt. "I'm not working at the store either this weekend. I'll hire extra help, but I'm taking the weekend off!"

My enthusiasm catches Laney off guard, but then she grins. "Okay! I'm liking this. Definitely Beau, and Delaney works for me. You call her, and I'll call Beau, see what she can set up for spa treatments." She yells, "Yahoo!" and heads toward the B&B hall.

On the table in front of me is my to-do list for the day, and even though I know I just made it twice as long, I don't care.

I'm having a girls' weekend. My first.

Let's just hope it's not my last.

"This is the last time I'll ever do this! No one understands 'no.' No one understands 'We only have room for a few' means 'You're not invited!'" I'm growling at Jackson, but he's packing and can't get out of here fast enough.

His comments swing back and forth between, "Really?" and "Wish I could help," though I can see he doesn't actually want to help; he just wants to get out of here.

"Even when I say there's nowhere left to sleep, they just giggle and say they'll bring a sleeping bag. Shannon has claimed our couch. I mean, actually claimed it. On Facebook. So of course that brought a whole new wave of attendees. Then I say there's no food, and everyone offers to bring food. At this point there will be more people here than on that bus going on the ski retreat!"

As he zips his suitcase he varies his grunted responses to ask, "What's Laney say?"

"You know Laney. She's never met a party she didn't like. She says it'll be fine and that, well, that I need to chill."

"Then try that. Just chill. These are not kids; they can take care of themselves. You have your bed and bathroom right here, so let the rest of them fight it out. Sounds like the women of Chancey need something like this." He sits on the bed beside me and pulls me into his arms. "It's one weekend. I'm going to bring you an iced cooler full of Diet Cokes for up here, and you can gather a bag of snacks. If things get crazy just lock yourself in up here and read."

I burrow into his shoulder. "I like having an escape plan. And it's really not my job to feed everyone, is it? They've all been warned."

"Exactly. Now I'm getting your cooler, and then I'm going to hit the road. I'll drop off the kids for the ski trip, so once we leave, you are on your own, and I'm pretty sure you'll have fun."

"Probably."

We hug once more, then get up. The hug and the pep talk help. A lot.

Plus, I'm putting a bottle of wine in that cooler.

Chapter 35

"Feels kind of like the end of one of those murder mysteries, where you bring all the suspects together for the big reveal," Laney says from our perch on the stairs, looking out over my buzzing living room.

I give her a warning look. "There will be no reveal, big or otherwise. You hear me?"

"I hear you, but have you told them?" The wave of her arm covers Missus, who is standing near the front door, watching the room much as we are; Delaney, who is laughing with Beau and Gertie at the dining room table, which is crammed with dishes, bags, and boxes of food; and Shannon, who has decided to embrace her pregnancy and is pelting Patty with first trimester questions and Anna with birthing queries.

We can't see into the kitchen, but I know Phoenix is in there making pan fajitas, whatever they are, for a healthy meal. Which is a good thing since I'm pretty sure there isn't a healthy option on the entire dining room table.

"Well, now that we've gotten upstairs squared away, let's go get something to drink," Laney suggests. "We have to go past Missus, but the drink will be worth it."

Getting upstairs squared away basically meant setting Susan up in Bryan's room. Susan had originally claimed the Chessie room, but when Delaney showed up with Missus and her luggage, Missus called dibs on it instead, informing Susan that she was young and could find somewhere else to sleep. Delaney was apologetic, but after Missus saw that all the other women in Chancey were coming, she refused to be left out. However, she hasn't done much more than wander around the edges of the party and watch Shannon. Shannon doesn't seem to have a clue she's got a stalker.

"Missus, what are you doing way over here?" Laney threads her arm through Missus's as we leave the stairs. "Come into the kitchen and let's see if Phoenix is about done. I'm starving." I follow them and can't help but shudder as Missus gives Shannon the evil eye as we pass behind the couch. The kitchen is full of people too. What I'm noticing, however, is that this group is made up of the real Chancey women—no one from Laurel Cove and no one from the new neighborhood of younger couples, where Athena Markum and her group live. They probably already have a women's group. And it being Friday night, I'm sure the Laurel Cove ladies are at the clubhouse up there for the weekly seafood buffet. Maybe Jackson's right, and the women in Chancey need something like this occasionally.

"Phoenix, that smells delicious," I say as I move closer to the oven.

"It's really pretty easy. Especially for a crowd." Her red hair is pulled back into a ponytail, and she's wearing a lime-green apron from her smoothie bar. She motions me toward her. "I've laid out the wraps here. These are the low-carb ones, which I'd normally only suggest, but since you said there were going to be so many here, I also had to buy some regular ones. Piggly Wiggly doesn't appear to keep a good stock of low-carb anything. There's also tortilla chips if we run out of wraps. Over there I put the black beans, Greek yogurt, salsa, and other toppings."

I make a mental note to sneak our container of sour cream onto the table before someone squawks about the yogurt. But

I also make a commitment to try the yogurt, my nod to being healthy this weekend, to counteract the box of chocolate-covered cherries leftover from Christmas that Susan brought and opened earlier.

Phoenix looks around and then comes closer to me. "Listen, if you'll let me take some pics and use this event for advertising on social media and such, then you don't have to pay me. Just cover the expenses."

"Advertising? What are you advertising?"

"Personal chef duties. It's all the rage now, and this could really get me started. Cooking for dinners and parties, but also helping people get their own meals in shape." Her eyes widen. "I don't mean I'd only do healthy food, but you know that would be my specialty."

"Of course. And since this has already been all over Facebook, you might as well use it and save Laney some money. Also, if you want to stay you know you're welcome."

She grins and slowly shakes her head. "Thanks, but no. I have other plans." Her sharp, green eyes flit around the room like she's taking a head count. Her grin grows, and then she winks at me before turning to check the oven. "You can let the ladies know dinner is served."

"Facials and nails. Tomorrow at three, okay?" Beau asks as she pulls on her coat. "I hate to leave, but Angel's not been sleeping well, and when ya got four kids, overnight help is hard to come by. I have a full day at the salon tomorrow, but I'll be here and ready to party at three." She pauses and sinks her hands into her coat pockets. "Y'all don't look like this party is going to last much longer anyway."

She's right. She's the last of the guests not staying for the night. Even some who planned on staying decided their own beds looked better than claiming a spot on the floor. Patty's been gone for a while. Same for Anna. I really thought Shannon would leave when they did. Everyone still here is older than she is, and it's impossible that she's not aware of Missus's obsession with her. However, she's staked out one end of the couch with blankets, pillows, and is already wearing her long, purple nightshirt with fuzzy, purple socks. Her belly is really pronounced in the snug gown, and Missus can't stop staring.

Laney is in the Orange Blossom Special room getting changed. Susan is tucked in one of the chairs beside the fireplace, feet up under her, blanket draped over her, and her phone front and center as she focuses on it. Delaney is nodding off in the rocking chair in the corner. I'm on the other end of Shannon's couch. Gertie and a few more cleared off an end of the dining room table and are playing cards. I think it's poker and they're playing for money because they are being awfully serious.

Before Beau can open the front door, it swings open. "Hey! Am I too late?" Betty Taylor says as she pushes inside. "Oh, hey, Beau. Did you just get here too?"

"Nope, I'm actually leaving. Got too many kids at home, you know."

Betty laughs. Loudly. "Don't I know all about that! I promised Jed I'd stay home until the youngest got in bed. Kimmy's walking up the road here. She didn't want a ride because she said she was still trying to calm down from the knock-down, drag-out two of hers were having. Hey, everybody!" Betty is a chunky woman with a new personality we're all trying to get used to. When her husband was mayor she kind of stayed in the background and was always busy with their five kids. Then two things happened: Jed quit being mayor and Betty made manager level in Sexy Belles.

She lifts her hands, which each hold several bags. "I brought my old sample bags. Lots of good deals in here!" She laughs loudly again and smacks her bright red lips as she swerves into the middle of the living room and sets down her bags on the floor. "Now someone grab me a glass of wine while I get these laid out for y'all to see."

Laney swirls into the room, but is stopped when she's not the center of attention. It's understandable that she assumed she would be the center of attention, as she's wearing a red satin robe, which is not closed, over a short, red satin nightgown that is straining across her bosom. Matter of fact, that's not the only place it's straining. She tugs on the front of her robe, and once she gets it closed somewhat she jams her fists on her red-satin-covered hips. "What in the Sam Hill is all this?" She shakes her head and frowns. "Perfect, just perfect."

Missus, coming from the Chessie room, creeps up behind Laney, then steps forward. She has on a pair of blue flannel pajamas that look like she just took them out of the package. They have white buttons and white trim. She's carrying a book in her hand, ready for a night of light reading. "I agree with Laney. A lingerie party is absolutely the last thing this gathering needs. Betty, try and control yourself."

Laney scowls at Missus's back. "First of all this is not a 'gathering.' It's a slumber party. Second, a lingerie party is exactly what we need. My concern is that samples mean the small, left-over sizes. There won't be anything at all in there for me."

Betty smirks, and she looks nothing at all like the mild, plain, quiet woman I met when I moved here. "Au contraire, my busty friend. You just take a look in that pink bag there."

Missus rolls her eyes. "Laney, don't you think you've already shown us enough of yourself in that getup you're wearing? Pull your robe closed—if you can."

And that does it. Laney jerks off her robe and throws it in Missus's direction as she passes her. "Give me that pink bag, and Carolina, put on some better music. Norah Jones is good for a sleepy, rainy day, but I'm ready to party!"

I open my phone to open my music app, but then Shannon grabs it out of my hand. "I'll find something good. I can't drink, but I'll have to if I'm punished with anymore of this old lady music."

Delaney laughs as she stands and stretches. Then she dances her way over to the bags. "Maybe I'll find something for my wedding night."

Missus shakes her head again, or did she ever stop? "In this pile of trash? I don't believe any of this is what my son would expect for his wedding night."

Gertie guffaws from the poker table. "Yeah, Missus, tell us what a Harvard-educated man likes his woman to wear to bed!" She gets up and lumbers over to the rocking chair, where she leans over it, glass full of moonshine in hand. "I think this lingerie business is for the birds. Just ends up wadded up on the floor. A real man don't need nothing like that to get his motor running. But now wait a minute…" She's perked up, her glass halfway to her mouth. "Laney, turn back around this way."

Laney sashays in front of us all. She's put a black lace dress over her red nighty. It has a full-length, flowing skirt with long sleeves that are tight to the wrists but then drape down, ending in fringe. The V-neck is low, but there's a shelf built in to hold up her breasts. She sways, holding out the full skirt, then twirls, letting her sleeves dangle and shimmy. "It's all stretchy, except where it's holding up my boobs!"

Gertie takes a big slug of her drink, then straightens up. "Betty girl, you got that in red? Or maybe pink?"

"Oh, good Lord," Missus exclaims.

Gertie pushes past her to where Betty is holding out a bag. "That's a start, Missus. But I'm hoping Bill will have a bit more than that to say when I show up in this!"

CHAPTER 36

"You want to ride to town with me?" I whisper to Missus, who is sitting by herself, fully dressed, in the kitchen in the dim, early morning light. "Ruby called and said she's offering a big basket of muffins if I come pick them up."

Missus frowns at me, then shrugs. "I suppose I might as well go with you. Get a breath of fresh air. No one else is even awake."

"You want a cup of coffee for the road?"

She shakes her head at me. "I made a full pot, and you can see how much I've already drunk. I didn't sleep well last night."

We tiptoe through the living room, where, along with Shannon on the couch, there are a couple of others in sleeping bags on the floor. I see Kimmy Kendricks's hair sticking out of one near the cold fireplace. I have to smile; she was actually funny last night. She has a real dry sense of humor. She and Laney played off each other and had us all in stitches. I softly close the front door behind us, and the fresh air is bracing. It's cloudy but not too awfully cold, though there's a light frost on the ground.

I wait a minute for the van to warm up, and then we pull out of the driveway. "Sorry you didn't sleep well. It's always strange being in a different bed."

"It wasn't the bed so much as it was worrying about Peter. I'm convinced Shannon is carrying his child. I must tell him."

She's turned toward me, even leaning forward to try and get me to glance in her direction.

I open up my hands against the steering wheel like I'm excusing what I'm about to say. "I'm not saying anything about whether the baby is his, but do you think he'll care either way?"

That makes her lean back. And scowl. "Of course he will care. Of course. That is *not* Danny Kinnock's child." She pauses as I continue down the hill. Quietly she says, "I even did some more checking."

"More checking? On what?"

"I called Marjorie Kinnock."

"Oh, Missus, Danny's mother? What did she say? Have Shannon and Danny even told her?"

"The Kinnocks are out of town on some cruise. I talked to their other son, who said they won't be back until later this week."

"But you said you did some checking."

"When I could not get hold of Marjorie, I called Wilma. Wilma Bunch, Alison's mother? Danny's ex-wife Alison?"

"Yes. I know who Alison is. And Wilma. I met her around the holidays, and she's been in shopping. But why would you call her?"

"Just because Marjorie is off on some pleasure cruise doesn't mean I should have to wait on desperately needed information. Wilma and I have not always been on good terms, but now that I'm going to be mayor she was most accommodating. Really quite chatty."

I press the brake pedal hard, perhaps a little too hard, at the stop sign at the bottom hill. A bit too suddenly also. We jerk to a stop, and I take a deep breath. "What did you find out? Just say it."

"Danny Kinnock has not had his, you know, his surgery, or his, uh, procedure, undone. He can*not* have more children."

She sniffs. "It was a rather uncomfortable conversation, but it had to be done."

I don't know if it's the lack of sleep, or the surreal state of leaving a house full of sleeping women, but a snort leaps out of my mouth, followed by a laugh. "So just what in the world did you ask her? 'Hey, is your ex-son-in-law shooting blanks?' 'Did your ex-son-in-law get his vasectomy reversed?' No, wait, 'His *procedure* reversed?'" Now I'm laughing out loud and having to work to catch my breath. Thank goodness there is no traffic this early, as I'm having trouble seeing the road in front of me as I pass the camellias with their new crop of pink buds welcoming us to downtown.

Then, miracles of miracles, I hear laughter from my passenger. Missus is laughing, which turns into coughing as she tries to talk. "It was rather comical. It took forever for her to figure out what I was asking." She laughs and bends forward. "At one point she thought I was calling to tell her he was in the hospital now and his member had been cut off!"

We are both laughing so hard that I drive right past the front of Ruby's, but there are three empty spots on the side of the square on my left, so I just slip in across all three of them for a minute. "I need a tissue to blow my nose," I say as I turn to dig around for the box of tissues I carry in the car.

"You can't park here, Carolina," Missus warns. Laughing is over; she's back to bossing me around. "You're taking up three spots."

"I know. I'll move in a minute. Want a tissue?" I ask as I offer her the box.

She doesn't answer, so after I wipe my nose and eyes, I look at her and shake the box. She's staring straight ahead, so I look out the windshield. My van is pointed at her house, and then I see what she's looking at. Her salmon-colored front door is open, and standing in it is Phoenix. We can see her red hair, but not much of it because a man's hand is holding the back of her head. Then as the hand drops, she pulls away and turns to walk across the wide porch. She's wearing the jeans and black turtleneck she had on last night, and in her hand is her lime-green apron. She hurries down the sidewalk toward her house and is soon out of our sight.

Well, Phoenix *did* say she had plans last night.

CHAPTER 37

"I'm not spending the night," Ruby declares. "Libby, you can do whatever you want, but I don't think you should either."

"Of course I'm not spending the night. I'm only going up there because you want me to bring my ham sliders and I need some girl time. Here ya go, Carolina. It's right heavy."

She slides the big basket across the counter, and I pull it toward me and ask, "Are y'all going to spend the night?" They both stare at me, and I realize they've already answered that question. I shake my head. "Sorry. I'm just distracted. Missus is in the car, so I better go."

Ruby steps to the counter across from me. "What's got you so distracted?"

"Nothing. Wow. This is heavy."

"I warned you. Here, let me get the door." Libby runs around to get ahead of me, and she pulls open the door. I hurry out yelling behind me that I'll see her later. I'd parked the van in one of the three spots I'd been straddling. I struggle to open my door and then punch the back door button on my key fob, which is hanging in the ignition. Missus is scowling out the windshield, but there's nothing to see out there; I checked before I even got out because she was looking out of it then too. She hasn't moved since we watched Phoenix scurry away toward her own house. I get the big basket secured in the back and climb into my seat.

"Ready to go back up to the house?" I try a smile, but I don't have much hope it'll get a response, as nothing else has in the last ten minutes. It's like she's frozen, made of stone.

Before I back out of the parking spot, I wait for a car to pass, then pull out behind it. Morning sun is creeping over the mountains and causing the frost to sparkle. "Ruby and Libby are coming up around dinnertime. Neither one of them are staying the night."

Nothing.

"Think the camellias buds will open after the cold? They looked pretty done."

Nothing. We cross over the bigger road going out to the schools and the Piggly Wiggly, still behind the same car.

Missus gasps. "That's her car. That is her car."

"Who? Oh, Phoenix. You're right. Oh, the yoga. I kind of forgot about that."

"How can you associate with that woman? She was at my house. With my son!"

"So she was probably invited, right?" Of course Phoenix is going to be given the scarlet letter to wear, not darling Peter. "And she's not the one engaged."

"But she knows he is. She knows that he's... Oh, never mind." She huffs out a disgusted sigh. "I shouldn't be surprised. She's just his type."

I slam on my brakes. "Just his type! Peter has a type?"

She raises an eyebrow but doesn't look at me. "Not Peter. My father."

That pretty much kills the conversation as I slowly drive through the neighborhood on the hill rising out of town, leading to our home at the top. Sunshine and clouds greet us at the big curve, and I give us time to enjoy the view before turning into our drive.

"Carolina, I know what you are doing, and it's ridiculous," Missus spits at me.

With a huff and a big eye roll, I answer her. "I'm just trying to give her time to get inside. Or do you want to have a little chat on the front porch?" I punch the gas, but at exactly the wrong moment, and we almost bottom out on the railroad crossing.

"That was completely uncalled for. I would not be surprised to discover you've just damaged your van. If I had only known what a disaster going for this little jaunt with you would be."

"Get out. Get out and don't talk to me again today."

"Gladly!" She opens her door before the van completely stops and then steps out stumbling along as the car is still moving.

"Missus!" I yell and reach out toward her swinging door, but she regains her balance and looks at me like a cat just doused with water. I stick my tongue out at her, but she doesn't see, of course. She marches in front of the van, then down the sidewalk. Phoenix and Missus both move quickly, so I take my time. Hopefully I won't have to engage with either of them if I dillydally long enough.

"Are you out there baking those muffins?" Laney yells from the front porch as I come around the van with the heavy basket. "How am I supposed to do that yoga stuff on an empty stomach? My coffee is gonna be cold by the time you get in here."

"How about, 'Do you need some help?' Or, 'That looks heavy. Can I carry it for you?'" I'm out of breath from trudging up the walk, but I'll never be so out of breath I can't yell back at Laney.

"I'm holding the door. You sure are grouchy for someone on a retreat. Did you get good muffins?"

"They're free, so yes, I got good ones." I push past her holding the huge basket out in front of me. After I get a quick look inside the living room, I whisper over my shoulder at her. "Where's Phoenix? Where's Missus?"

"Phoenix is in the kitchen making smoothies, or at least getting stuff ready to make smoothies. That's why I thought I'd better come check on the muffins. I thought Missus was with you. Least that's what you said in your note." She looks back outside. "I haven't seen her."

I sit the basket on the bench beside the stairs. "She stormed in here. I was afraid she was coming in to confront Phoenix."

Laney laughs and reaches for the basket. "Oh, that's why you were hiding out there. I'll take these in the kitchen. Oof, it is heavy!" She slogs toward the kitchen while I take off my jacket and look around at the mess. Kimmy is still asleep, most likely, because I see she has earbuds in. Shannon is no longer on the couch, but I hear her voice in the dining room. The other sleeping bag is empty, and I hear voices down the B&B hall. Laney announces there are muffins and a fresh pot of coffee in the kitchen.

Phoenix adds, "Yoga begins in fifteen minutes downstairs."

"Oh, downstairs. That's a good idea, Laney," I say, walking into the kitchen. "I wondered where you were going to do it."

"I'm not doing it. I changed my mind." She's seated at the kitchen table, muffin and coffee ready for action.

Susan waltzes in behind me, reaches over her sister, and takes her muffin. "You can have a sip of coffee, but you are doing yoga with me this morning. Then you can have your muffin. Or a smoothie. You made a deal."

The fact there is a deal is evidenced by the way Laney doesn't move a muscle to reclaim her muffin. She doesn't yell, curse, threaten. She just yawns and stretches. I notice she's wearing stretchy leggings and a long T-shirt. Maybe she is going to do yoga. My money is still on not.

"Maybe I'll try it, too," I say. "There should be plenty of room downstairs."

Phoenix claps her hands as she announces, "I'll be setting things up downstairs. Everyone interested in finding out more about yoga, please make your way in that direction in the next few minutes. I assure you everyone is welcome." Her smile seems a bit searching as she looks around, and I wonder if she's looking for Missus or Delaney, neither of whom are near. I've done my own searching.

She opens the basement door and leaves it that way for us to follow. I say, "I need to go upstairs and change into something more stretchy than these jeans. I'll be right down there." Leaving the kitchen I turn and ask behind me, "So, Laney, what's the deal you struck with Susan?"

She grins as she stands. "She helps me get into my hot-pink suit by Valentine's, and I'll help her get Griffin back."

I pause. "But those are both things you want."

With a tiny shrug she winks. "Only kind of deals I make."

Trudging up the staircase I think about it. "I've got to figure out how to be more like Laney," I mutter. Then I laugh. "But I probably shouldn't mention that to Jackson!"

Chapter 38

"Of course we can't do a full-blown beauty routine here at Crossings." Beau tips her head in my direction. "It's a lovely, inviting place, Carolina, but it's not my salon, so we'll be going over some trouble spots you individually would like help with first. We can each do a facial with my handy-dandy little kits here, and then I brought a whole case of nail polishes. Try something new for the new year—purple, green, glitter! You can paint your own nails or take turns with a friend. I know it's not a real, true spa day, but it's fun with lots of people, right?"

Laney widens her eyes at me. Beau isn't exaggerating. There are a lot of people here this afternoon. We've picked up some of the ladies from Laurel Cove and the younger women from the new subdivision out of town, Summerfield. Retta went and picked up a load of folding chairs from the funeral home and brought the funeral director's wife and the secretary too.

Delaney is seated on my other side. She's leaning forward, elbows on her knees and chin in her hands. I found out her glamour session last weekend came from Beau. Delaney says Beau is a treasure. That of all the makeovers and beauty sessions she's ever had, none were so honest. Beau is very opinionated, and apparently that's not common in the more luxurious establishments down in Atlanta and the suburbs.

And here all this time I thought all this small town honesty was a drawback.

It's been a rather quiet day after such a weird morning. One of the weirdest parts of it was Delaney arriving downstairs late for yoga and taking a spot right in the front row. Watching her ask Phoenix for pointers and then watching Phoenix give her pointers was almost too much for me. Luckily, despite the front row scene, I found the class calming and the pace slow enough I never felt like I was lost. That happened to me with jazzercise. I'd get to daydreaming and watching the other people, then lose track.

I did have to move away from Laney because she wanted to just make snide comments from the back row, and while I've heard laughing is good exercise, Susan's dirty looks weren't worth the extra workout.

Throughout the rest of the day people came and went. We grazed on the abundance of food and drink. Athena and her friends arrived right after lunch with two containers of already made margaritas. They set up a little bar in the kitchen complete with salt and limes. The first salty toast was to the second anniversary of Athena's divorce. She apparently moved up here from Atlanta just her and the kids, which I don't remember knowing. She seems happy, but Chancey is really not a good place to look for a new husband; not many single guys around.

Gertie hadn't spent the night, but she and Patty came back around that same time with a bag of games. Before long there were little groups all over the house playing games. I found myself at a table with a couple of ladies I didn't know well playing Apples to Apples. Between the game's questions and the margaritas, we felt like old friends in just a matter of time.

Missus has stayed in her room most of the day. Occasionally I'd spot her skulking around the edges of the laughter. I keep trying to put myself in her shoes after what she saw this morning, but my imagination's just not that good. Your son is sleeping with one woman while another woman carries his child, which he doesn't realize, and he's marrying a third woman in a few weeks.

Nope—can't do it.

So I just focused on the game in front of me. Or the puzzle. Gertie's bag included a huge, thousand-piece puzzle of the Eiffel Tower. We set that up in a corner of the living room, and guests have worked on it all day. It's really been a special kind of day, cozy and friendly, and I'm feeling very warmly toward grown-up slumber parties.

"Me! Me!" Laney yells while punching her hand high in the air. "Pick me!" I jump and realize in my reminiscing about the day I'd dozed off. There's Beau at the front and ladies seated all around me. Oh yeah, spa time.

"Okay, Laney, come on up, and we'll get a drape on you and wet your hair down," Beau says as she motions to her aunt Pearl who's along to help. All the Bennett women work at the family beauty shop, Beulah Land.

I lean toward Delaney. "I missed something. What's Laney volunteering for?"

"A hot oil treatment for her hair. I got one last weekend, and they make your hair feel so soft and luxurious." She straightens in her seat, crosses her legs, and looks at me. "So, what were you daydreaming about?"

I actually feel my face flush, and my throat goes dry as my thoughts about Missus's morning jolt return. "Oh, I don't know. Just this. All these ladies having a nice time."

"I know. I'm not as familiar with Chancey as you are, but did you expect this many to show up?"

"Are you kidding? Do you think I would've done it if I'd had any idea? I was picturing just you, me, Laney, Susan, and Beau. We planned on going to Beau's for our beauty treatments. No, this is all a huge surprise." I lean closer to her. "Missus coming shocked me."

"Me too, honestly. I thought she might like some time alone, well, just her and Peter, but she didn't want any of that." She looks down at her empty wine glass. "Want to take a walk outside for a minute?"

I hold up my empty margarita glass. "Yes. A breath of fresh air might be just what the doctor ordered."

We sit our glasses, which have been marked with our names so we'll not need clean ones, in the empty kitchen. Well, empty of people. Every flat surface in here is covered with food or dishes. The dining room table had to be emptied for the beauty session, so everything was crammed onto the kitchen counters.

"I hear Phoenix is making white chili for dinner tonight," Delaney says as she opens the back doors.

"Yep. It's actually in two Crock-Pots in the Orange Blossom Special room. Laney's staying in there, so we cleaned off the dresser because there's obviously no room in the kitchen until the beauty session is finished." I laugh and walk over to lean on the deck railing. "Who'd've imagined?"

"Not me. Not in a million years. Chancey is just full of surprises."

In the quiet we enjoy the sunshine on the deck, and I stretch my neck muscles.

Delaney stares toward the weeping willow and the river. "I checked into F.M.'s will, and everything Laney said was true. Missus doesn't own anything." She shakes her head. "I don't mean she's poor by any stretch of the imagination. But the house and the family investments are all in Peter's name."

"Did Peter tell you—"

She jumps in. "Oh, heavens no. My father. He knew everything because, well, that's just who he is. And let's just say I know how to work him." She gives me a lopsided smile. "He can't resist bragging about the deal he made for me and my future. Well, he couldn't resist after I made him some special brownies. *Very* special brownies."

"Delaney! You didn't!"

She shrugs and grins. "He holds his liquor too well, and I thought it couldn't hurt to try. Gotta fight fire with fire; this is my life we're talking about."

"I wouldn't have any idea how—"

"Oh, me either, but I do have a couple of friends who were more than delighted to pull a fast one on my father. He's one of those people who always thinks he's in control. Besides, he never had any idea. He ate, he drank, he bragged, and then probably had the best night of sleep in his life. And I had my answers." Her last sentence fades off.

"So, are you happy with your answers? Do you think you'll be happy with Peter?"

"Happy with Peter?" She rocks back and forth on the heels of her boots for a minute. "I've not been happy without him. I believe he's the one for me. Will we have what you and Jackson have?" She softly laughs. "Probably not." Then she laughs louder. "No, no probably about it. We will not have what you have. But it's what I want. *He's* what I want." Then she leans forward on the railing, her weight on her folded arms. "With all his foibles. All his mistakes." She tips her head and face toward me. "*All* of his mistakes."

"What if you don't know all of them?"

"Then I deserve what I get. I'm like my father in that. I believe in knowing the details." She shivers and steps away from the railing. "Think I'll take a walk around to the front of the house. Follow the sun." She pats me on the back as she walks by. "Don't worry about me, Carolina. I'm going to be very happy here. I know what I'm doing."

She jogs down the four steps from the deck and walks below me. I watch her walk to the corner of the house and then around it.

"Where's Delaney going?" Susan asks as she takes her place beside me at the railing.

"Just taking a walk. She gets more interesting the more I get to know her. "

"I sure hope she's interesting and not dumb."

"Dumb? About what?" I turn to lean on my elbow and face my friend.

"About Shannon and about Phoenix and just about life in general with Peter and Missus."

I stare at her, and she winces. "Yes, I know about him and Phoenix. I mean, I don't actually know, but he's at her house too much for anything else to be happening. They're not discreet about it either."

I sigh. "That's part of the interesting I was talking about. I think she knows. I think Delaney knows everything that's going on."

"Naw. You think so? And she still wants to marry him?"

"She says she loves him and she's not been happy without him, so..." I shrug, and we both turn to look back down toward the river. As the last sliver of sun leaves my shoulders, I straighten and wrap my arms around myself. "I'm going back inside and going to say a prayer of thanks for my simple, simple life."

"Speaking of which..." Susan flips around and leans back on the railing. "Mother told me Ricky borrowed money from her to buy a ring."

Closing my eyes, I sigh. "I know. Laney told us. I'm trying to ignore it. It can't be for Savannah, can it?"

"I don't know. Jenna doesn't know what to think, and that's not a good thing. Jenna usually has a pretty good read on what her friends are doing. She's given me full rundowns on everyone's plans after graduation, but as for Savannah..." Susan lifts her shoulders, then drops them with a grimace.

"I don't think Savannah knows either. That's why the least little thing her daddy or I say, especially her daddy, sets her off.

233

Jackson pushes every one of her buttons these days. Of course she can't see that he's just nervous for her."

She comes alongside me as I near the back doors. I butt her shoulder with mine. "Thanks for nothing. I'd managed to put that drama way in the back of my mind, but now it's reclaimed front and center."

"Sorry. Just wanted to give you a heads-up. Now, let's go try some wild fingernail polish. I'm thinking purple with glitter."

I laugh and push her ahead of me inside the door. "Purple with glitter? I thought you were trying to win back Griffin, not send him running for the hills!"

Chapter 39

"She said yes," Kimmy tells me in a whisper as she quickly takes the seat beside me on the couch, which opened up when Susan went into the kitchen to get more popcorn. We're watching *Steel Magnolias*, and the living room is dark. Kimmy is pressed up beside me, her voice practically in my ear. "Miss Ruby. She hired me."

"Oh!" I exclaim too loudly, though I quickly shush. We about had a knock-down, drag-out fight when we first started watching the movie. Who could've imagined Laney and Gertie are screen talkers? Yeah, everybody who's ever met them could see that coming. Missus blew a gasket at them, though I believe she was taking out some of her other frustrations. Susan threw pillows at them and knocked over Retta's soda, which drenched Patty, who was seated on the floor trying to get comfortable. Gertie then got mad at Susan about Patty needing to get changed. Retta got sad because, as she loudly informed us, her soda had contained the last of the Jack Daniels she'd brought. And not shared. Which set off Betty because she *loves* Jack Daniels and didn't know we had any. In truth, neither Retta nor Betty needed any more of anything alcoholic. Luckily, once they both calmed down and the lights were turned down, they proceeded to sleep their buzzes off. They are still asleep, and the only problem with that is I'm afraid they're going to wake up raring to go when the rest of us are ready for bed.

Giving Kimmy a big smile I nod enthusiastically at her. She gets back up into my ear.

"I'm going to be in charge of Mondays and Wednesdays and maybe Fridays if she decides to do Fridays too. I can still write some for the newspaper, but this will pay a lot better and be more steady. Mr. Spoon ain't used to having someone working with him at the paper, and he forgets to call me. I'm going to like working at Ruby's. It'll be like having my own little restaurant. You know?"

My ear is hot and moist from her talking right into it, and it's grossing me out, so I pull away, smile, and nod at her again. I abruptly get up, mouthing at her that I need to go to the bathroom.

I decide to use the bathroom down the B&B hall to see what folks are doing down that way. Gertie has a card table set up in the Southern Comfort room, where Delaney is sleeping. Except right now she's abandoned that room for the Orange Blossom Special, where she's stretched out on the bed with her laptop. I knock on the almost closed door that I was peeking through. "Hey, can I come in?"

She quickly shuts her laptop and twists around on the bed. "Sure. Movie over?"

"No. I just needed to get up and move around. Whatcha doing?"

"Nothing. Wedding stuff." She shifts to sit cross-legged on the bed. She has on comfy lounging pants with a big, hooded sweatshirt. I walk over to sit in the window seat. It's dark outside, but there's an almost full moon out the window. "Pretty night out there." I twist to face her. "Elon? Who do you know who went to Elon?"

She jumps. "Why are you asking about Elon?"

I point to her hoodie. "Your shirt."

She looks down, then grabs the front of the hoodie and wads it up. Suddenly she laughs and releases it. "Oh, no. A friend's kid goes there." She looks down at the logo, smoothing it with her hands. "I forgot I had it on."

"One of Savannah's friends got accepted there, but I guess it's pretty expensive, so I think she's waiting to hear about scholarships."

"From Chancey? A friend from Chancey?"

"Oh, no. From Marietta. She's a really sharp girl, and although her parents aren't hurting for money, I guess it's really pricey. Private, too, right?"

Delaney shakes her head as she moves her laptop behind her. "Oh, I think so. I don't really know. You going back out to watch the movie?" She scoots to the edge of the bed, letting her feet dangle off. "I might go watch it."

"Are you okay?" She seems nervous, and while I would be surprised if anyone in her current situation didn't feel nervous, it's the first time I've ever seen her this jumpy.

"Me? I'm fine. Just tired." She folds her arms across her chest. "Missus has me on edge, you know?"

"Oh, I know. She's been on edge, and that makes everyone miserable. She's one of those people who doesn't believe in suffering in silence. All will suffer with her."

We laugh, but it's short-lived. Delaney leans back on her elbows. "I just wish the wedding would hurry up and get here. I want things to be settled down. I'm ready to get on with my new life."

"Your new life living with Missus? All the time? I know you don't stay over there as much as you act like you do."

She goes still. "Why do you think that?"

"Because I've seen you leave when I've dropped you off at night. Jackson is working just up the street, and he's asked about where you go. You're out and about early in the morning when I've had to take Bryan to school." I glance at the door to make sure I shut it. "If you're in such a hurry to start this new life, why don't you go ahead and move in with Peter and his mother?"

She sits up. "It'll be different when we're married. Besides, I have things I need to wrap up back home. You know I did have a life before I came to Chancey."

"Speaking of which, I do kind of want to talk to you about me being in your wedding. Are you sure? Don't you have some older friend, well, I mean friends you've known longer, that you want to be there?"

"But I asked you."

"I know." I shift around to rest my elbows on my knees and be closer to her. "But maybe that was just an impulse move. You know things have been pretty tense with you and Peter. I just want you to know it wouldn't hurt my feelings if you change your mind."

She frowns and nods. "I know, but my old friends belong to my old life. Not that I'm ignoring them. They're actually throwing me a shower, but I don't want all the bridesmaid weekends and such. I just want to make a new start." She sighs with her whole body and looks wrung out. "Believe me, I'd really like for you to be in my wedding. This place, Chancey, is my new world. I see how you've made it your new world. Your son has even moved here and is raising your granddaughter here." She looks down at her hands in her lap, and her spirit seems to lift.

She stands up and walks to the door. "I'm tired of talking. I'm going to watch the movie." Her eyes hit on her laptop. She looks at me as she walks over to the bed and picks it up. She turns around, but then just as fast turns back to face me. "It's kind of a mess, the whole thing, but it'll be better soon. Remember what I said this afternoon? I know what I'm doing." With a smile she tucks a hank of hair behind her ear with the hand not holding the laptop against her stomach, and then leaves the room.

I don't have a chance to get up before the door is pushed back open and Missus comes in, closing it behind her. "Were you telling her about what you saw this morning?"

"You mean what *we* saw this morning? Of course not." I soften my voice. Missus probably needs a friend. Whether she deserves one is up for debate, but oh well. "How are you doing? That had to be upsetting for you to see, uh, that."

She prances to the edge of the bed and sits. She has on the blue pajamas from last night, but with a soft, thick, white robe over them. "My son is only participating in the time-honored tradition of sowing his wild oats. Nothing for me to be concerned about. He'll be a married man soon, and all will be well. However, there is no need whatsoever for Delaney to hear of anything sordid. Don't you agree?"

"So you think the wedding is a good idea? You weren't so sure the other day when you were concerned about Shannon's pregnancy."

"I've thought through this entire situation, and for reasons that are none of your business, the wedding must go on. You see, Carolina, in families like the Bedwells and the LaMottes, there are concerns outside the mundane, daily issues most people worry about."

"Oh, do tell. I'd love a glimpse outside my mundane existence." She either is so deep in her delusion she missed my sarcasm or she believes she is truly giving one of the little people a genuine thrill.

"I can allow Shannon and Danny to enjoy this pregnancy because my lawyer has assured me we have ample evidence on which to demand a paternity test once the baby is born. With the upcoming wedding, honeymoon, and the happy couple getting settled in their new life, there's no need to find out until after the child is actually here. Don't you agree?"

My mouth has dropped open and is hanging in that state.

That and my silence seem to have completely confused Missus. "Of course you agree. What could there be to disagree with?"

My mouth closes, the wrinkles across my forehead smooth out, and I take a deep breath. "Whatever. You're going to do whatever you want anyway, so why waste my breath."

She tugs on the belt to her robe. "Exactly. So, what is on your agenda for the rest of the evening? I fear I was out of sorts most of the day and missed some of your planned, uh, things."

I stand up. "I think bed is next on my agenda." Walking to the door I add, "Have a good night. See you in the morning." Abruptly I spin around. "There will be no run to pick up muffins or anything else in the morning," I announce with my hands held up in front of me like I'm testifying.

She smirks and shakes her head as she stands. "Oh, Carolina. You are such a drama queen."

Chapter 40

"We just need the snow to hold off until later tonight. It cannot, absolutely cannot, ruin our grand opening!" Laney makes her announcement as she blows in the front door of Blooming Books on Tuesday morning.

"*Our* grand opening?" I ask. "Besides, it's a soft opening. The grand opening is next weekend."

"Whatever you want to call it. It simply cannot snow until later. Do you understand me?"

Bonnie laughs. "Oh, we all understand you, but why do you think we, any of us including you, have any sway over when it will snow?"

"Don't get on my nerves. I'm worried enough with everything I have to do for the opening." She stresses the word "opening" while giving me a stern look. "And yes, I'm completely on board. Shaw is too. We are determined AC's will be the best restaurant in North Georgia." She waves a hand and then shrugs off her beautiful black leather coat. "Make that all of Georgia. Atlanta included."

Shannon guffaws from back at her worktable. "Everybody say an extra special prayer for Angie and Alex tonight. Laney is now on their side!"

We all laugh. Surprisingly, Laney laughs too. "You know it. It finally dawned on me I might enjoy being the parent of a grown-up. I can make lots of suggestions, give all kinds of advice, but I bear none of the responsibility. Besides, now that I'm going to be a downtown merchant, I am all in on wanting a good restaurant here. Right, Carolina?"

Bonnie and Shannon look from Laney to me. I nod at them. "Yep. We're getting a new neighbor right here on Main Street."

"Laney's Retreat!" she announces as she hangs her coat up. Then she turns, her face screwed up in thought. "Or maybe Laney's Spa, except it's not a spa, is it? Come on, ladies, I'm here for your creative help."

Shannon heads for the coffee table where an electric teapot has been added. "I believe I'm going to need another cup of tea. This 'no coffee' part of being pregnant is making it hard for me to decipher what it is exactly you are saying."

"That's not it" Bonnie says. "I've had plenty of caffeine and I don't have a clue."

Laney grabs the big, insulated cup she'd set on the counter. "Over here, ladies. Gather round and I'll fill you in."

"Wait, isn't that the suit you wore for filming last fall? Playing the mayor?" It's a rich, deep-purple suit with a peplum jacket and skirt.

She does her model walk, twirling, head held high, disinterest dripping off her every move. She looks down at us, her closed eyes giving us a good look at her fake eyelashes and heavy eye makeup. Then her deep-pink, pouting lips burst open with laughter as her eyes do. "Yes! Here I was trying to fit back in my old clothes, completely forgetting what that movie wardrobe lady helped me with. I'm the new Southern belle; my old clothes are for a different woman. A different time. And then I got all caught up in thinking I could be the 'real' mayor and lost my mind. All those boring clothes! I'm heading to Atlanta for a couple days tomorrow, for the shopping trip to end all shopping trips. I'd invite you, Carolina, but you would only slow me down. Now, ladies, sit. Sit. We have things to get in motion before the opening tonight and me leaving town early in the morning."

We all sit, with me and my coworkers on the couches and Laney in one of the wing chairs. Danny is talking to a customer in the book racks, and I notice Shannon and him making eyes at each other. My stomach rolls when I think of Missus letting them have this time to enjoy and what damage she's planning to inflict when the baby comes.

"Carolina? Are you paying attention? I need you." Laney condescendingly smiles at me when I nod and mumble that I'm sorry.

"Okay. After this weekend I've decided the ladies of Chancey need relaxation like that every day. Well, except Sunday, Monday, and Tuesday when I'll be closed. I've also learned about this soft opening thing from my daughter the restaurateur, and so at first we also will be closed on Wednesday and open only half a day on Thursday."

Shannon giggles. "So you'll only be open two and half days a week? That sounds like a place where I could work."

Laney dismisses her with a frown and a wave of her hand. "No. I'm not selling flowers. Like I was saying, it's for women to come and relax. Chat, have some kind of food, although I've not figured that out. Maybe tea." She slaps her hands together. "Like tea parties!"

Bonnie raises her hand. "There's a lady, a company that comes and does tea parties. We had her up at Laurel Cove for a ladies' day. You could hire her or someone like her."

"Excellent idea, Bonnie. Someone write that down. Carolina, you're not busy."

I get up and grab a notebook from under the front counter. "Yes, you could have the ladies pay for their tea party and even make reservations."

Shannon speaks up. "My favorite part of the weekend was watching the movies together. Even if I didn't watch it all, it was fun to be together watching chick flicks. Are you thinking of showing movies?"

"I am now! Well done, Shannon. Yes, it's a place to come and visit and hang out. I'm going to have games and cards. We can have a schedule of what games will be going on if you want to drop in. And it'll be a real pop-up shop, not like that plumbing disaster Rachel has going on down there now."

Bonnie holds her hand up again. (She was a teacher, you know.) "Is that where you're going to be? Rachel's place?"

"Yes, ma'am. I spent hours on the phone yesterday with her daughters, who run successful pop-up shops, which focus on things women actually want. Rachel just didn't know how to explain the concept to folks here in Chancey, but I'll take care of that. I'm an excellent communicator. Shut up, Carolina."

"I didn't say anything."

She raises an eyebrow at me. "But you wanted to. The walls will be filled with purses, or makeup, or perfume—"

"Candles and lotions!" a lady says as she steps out of the bookshelves and heads to the counter to buy the books in her hand. "I have friends who would love to sell their things in your place, uh, or shop. This sounds wonderful. Where is it? And what's its name?"

Laney beams at the woman. "Thank you. It's not open yet but will be just down the street here. Before you get to the corner."

As Danny rings up her sale, the customer picks up the pen on the counter and turns over one of our business cards. "What's its name?"

Laney's smile slides some. "That's right. We have to come up with a name." She says to the lady, "You'll have to check back in with the bookstore here. That's what I'm actually here to do today." She turns back to us. "Carolina, you've had all night to think. What did you come up with?"

"I like the word 'retreat.' Retreat on Main? Chancey Retreat? I agree that you can't call it a spa. Ladies' Day Out?"

Shannon shakes her head. "No, that sounds too much like a babysitting place. Plus, it's for staying in, not going out. How about Home Away from Home?"

Laney axes that one. "No. Home is where the dirty dishes and diapers are. I like Retreat on Main. Day Retreat?"

Bonnie holds up her hand but doesn't wait to say quietly, "What about some kind of club?"

The rest of us turn to her but don't say anything; then we begin nodding and jump in all at once: "Yes!" "Perfect!" "It's a club!"

Bonnie smiles, then speaks without holding up her hand at all. "It is a club. I don't know if there'll be membership, but still…"

Laney thinks for a moment, her long lashes fluttering. "No. No, I don't think we'll do memberships that you pay for, but it is still a club. Oh, this is the bit I was missing, Bonnie. It's a club! Ladies' Club. Not women's club; that makes me think of blue-haired church ladies."

I stand up and dart into the bookshelves. "Wait. We have a book here about a club. I've not read it yet. Here it is. …*And Ladies of the Club.*"

Shannon whistles. "That's a huge book."

"It's supposed to be really good. An older lady wrote it, I believe. You know, maybe I have read this. Yes, I did. It is really good. It's about a group of ladies that start a book club."

Bonnie agrees. "It is a good book. I read it years ago. You know you could drop the 'And.' How about Ladies of the Club?"

Laney leans back to daydream as she stares out the front windows. "I can see it. Painted fancy and in, oh…" She looks down. "Purple? Yes. Isn't purple supposed be royal? I think that's it." She bounces up from her chair. "Okay, on to whatever I'm needed for next door. Have y'all voted? It was quite the thrill to see my name on that ballot. I'm kind of glad I dropped out too late to take it off. I took a picture of it so I can show my grandkids one day." She's putting her coat on as she talks, then heads for the front door. "Y'all coming for the opening tonight? It'll be a celebration too. Now that the Conner family is a major economic force in town, between the club and AC's, hosting a party for the new mayor is just what we do! See y'all there!"

And she's gone. Shannon shakes her head and moves back to her worktable. "Never thought I'd say it, but I'm glad the old Laney's back. Her being all sad and confused is just not natural."

"So what do y'all think about her idea? Think it'll work?" I put away the notebook with name ideas and then walk back out to the middle of the shop.

Bonnie is working in her decorator office this morning, and as she heads back that way she yells to us, "Sounds interesting."

Shannon agrees.

Danny, however, who is leaning on the corner of Shannon's worktable, frowns. "I'm not so sure it'll work."

He has our attention. "Why not, sweetie?" Shannon asks.

His big, brown eyes and shaking head remind me of a cow. A sad cow. "Just seems to me Miss Laney does better with men than with women. I mean, I could see her running a club for men. Yeah, that'd for sure be a hit."

Hmm, the boy may be right. Laney does bring to mind Belle Watling from *Gone with the Wind*. But none of us are letting her open a club for men.

Chapter 41

"Smallest voting turnout in years," Jed Taylor says in his "been there, done that" voice. Which comes in handy as a high school principal. He's rocking back and forth with a cocktail in one hand and shrimp on a skewer in his other.

Griffin nods but adds, "Well, that's because most times we don't even need a vote. You always ran unopposed."

Jed winks at him as he points his empty skewer and chews. "Right you are. So, where is Mrs. Mayor? Figured she'd be here by now."

Laney swirls by with a glass of champagne. "She'll be here any moment. Be sure and grab a glass of bubbly so we can toast her arrival. Then we'll toast my new business."

I smile at my friend, who is still decked out in her purple suit, but with more makeup now that it's nighttime. I believe her hair also has a few more curls and inches of height to it. Plus, she's removed the silk scarf that hid her ample cleavage from daytime views. "That's very generous of you, Laney, letting Missus have her celebration first."

She leans in toward me. "Well, Alex pointed out that Peter is paying for the champagne. He didn't really give me a choice."

Alex calls for our attention from near the door. "Everyone, Mrs. Mayor will be arriving shortly. The waitstaff is circulating with trays of champagne and also sparkling cider. We'll be holding a toast when they arrive."

Jed reaches for a tray of glasses, leaving his cocktail behind at the same time that he snags a tall flute with lots of bubbles floating up to the top. "I bet she went down to the county courthouse for the close of the polls. We were one of a handful of towns with special elections. Not as exciting as some of the big election nights, but still, we won't get lost in the big-dog races." He stretches, looking outside. "Oh, there's a news van from down in Atlanta. There must really not be anything going on if they're here."

Angie comes by with a tray of appetizers. "These are bleu cheese–stuffed meatballs and candied bacon lollipops. Both are delicious." While we make our choices—but really, what choice is there? We all took one of each—she says, "Delaney got the news crew here. She's amazing with all her contacts. She hoped she could get them if we did our soft opening on election night."

"Where is Delaney?" I ask. "I haven't seen her."

The young woman shrugs. "She's around. Been here all day." She rolls her eyes. "Her and Mom both." Angie's goth phase seems to be over. Matter of fact, if I didn't know better I'd think her mother might've done her makeup.

"Everything is so nice." I move a little closer. "How is your mom? Driving you crazy?"

She looks at me and bites her lip, adding a little shrug. "Surprisingly not. Alex says she has more energy and is more efficient than a lot of the restaurant managers in New York. I guess it feels overbearing being around it every day, but here she's actually been a big help." Then she laughs. "Don't tell her I said that!"

"Promise."

The crowd moves toward the front of the restaurant. A few people have sat at the tables, but most of us are milling around, eating and drinking and talking. Outside the news team has turned on the camera lights, and Alex is posted beside the front door to open it for our new mayor. I'm happy for Missus. She's always wanted to be mayor, and there's no doubt she cares for Chancey. And, on the selfish side, maybe she'll be so busy she'll forget her plan to make Shannon's life, and mine due to proximity, a living nightmare.

Suddenly we're pushed back for the camera operator and reporter to come inside. They flip on their bright lights and move in. The reporter does an interview with Alex, which he handles so well. He calls for Angie to come stand beside him, and they look like a young, successful couple. I'm so proud of them. Laney and Shaw are to the side beaming, and Laney even has tears in her eyes. Alex is tall, and so he notices Peter at the door over everyone's heads. "Here are the real stars of the evening," he says. He moves past the cameraman to open the door. Peter holds it for his mother, and as she steps inside we all begin clapping. There's even some whooping and hollering. The camera and reporter both swing to them, and it's then that I realize Peter looks perturbed and Missus looks downright angry.

As the room settles a bit, the reporter's voice is loud and clear. "With your race too close to call, what do you have to say to your constituents who've gathered here to celebrate with you?"

Missus narrows her eyes and spews hellfire. "Laney Conner is a big old farce. She never dropped out. She just knew she couldn't win fair and square, so she wanted the sympathy vote." Then she flings out her hand, pointing at the Conners. "Look at her. Does she look like someone who didn't plan on being on television tonight?"

"Hey," Shaw says. "It's our daughter's opening night. What are you talking about?"

Peter puts his arm around his mother. "Don't worry. She officially withdrew. You're going to be mayor." He says even louder, for the camera, "Just a little hiccup. Now, where's that champagne?" He puts on a big smile and practically drags his mother on into the restaurant.

Laney catches my eye and mouths, "What in the world?"

I turn to find Susan heading for me, asking, "Did you vote for Laney? I did."

I groan. "Jackson and I both did. Didn't want her to feel bad if she didn't get any votes."

Griffin and Jed both sadly nod at us.

I quietly ask our little group, which has leaned closer, "So, what does it mean? She did file the paperwork to withdraw, right?" We all shrug at each other, and suddenly my meatball isn't settling in too well with the champagne. Lowering my voice even further, I say, "None of us wanted her to be mayor, right?" There's no hesitation. Everyone shakes their heads no.

"Hey, y'all! What do you think about that?" Laney is bearing down on us, and we jump back from our huddle. "Y'all voted for me? I mean, I knew I voted for me, but I just never knew y'all wanted me so bad. So, Griffin, Jed, do y'all think I can withdraw my withdrawal?"

"I knew it!" Missus screeches, and everyone swings to face her. Taking a step toward us, she fires at Laney, "I knew this was your plan all along." Then the champagne from her glass is flying across the room. Honestly it looks like it is in slow motion, liquid suspended in midair making its way to Laney. The target rears back, and the champagne hits her bare chest, then flows down her cleavage just like it's a funnel. Only a few drops hang on her purple lapels, but the rest of the drink? Gone. Lost in the regions of, well, you know. Gone.

Laney gasps, and with her wide eyes and glossy lips forming the perfect O, she looks like she's doing a promo shot for a racy video.

Yes, the camera got it all.

Looks like Laney's going viral.

CHAPTER 42

"I couldn't get Missus to come over here this morning," Delaney tells me under her breath. She and I are standing near the front windows inside AC's, waiting for Laney's interview with the same reporter from last night to begin. Angie is in school, but Alex is standing near us, ready to be called on.

Laney grins at us and waves. Then as the camera lights flash on, she adopts a serious look.

"We're back at AC's Restaurant in Chancey to follow up on a political story from yesterday's elections. Laney Conner was named the winner of the popular vote last night, but she had withdrawn earlier, so she will not be the new mayor. Ms. Conner, do you regret your decision to withdraw? Why did you withdraw from the mayoral race?"

"No. I don't regret my decision at all. I realized I wasn't the best person for the job and, well"—she gives the reporter a tiny, wicked smile—"I don't have the time to be mayor. My daughter and her partner, Alex Carrera—Alex, come sit here by me— they've opened this lovely, new restaurant and I want to help them. Plus, I'm opening a completely new business here on Main Street in Chancey very soon!"

Laney promotes Ladies of the Club, Alex promotes AC's, and Delaney nods as they repeat the lines she wrote down for them. Then the reporter turns to politics and the champagne toss. "While it was surely an exciting night, it got a little out of hand, wouldn't you say? Let's take a look." She lowers her microphone. "Mr. Carrera, you can go now. We'll just finish up with Mrs. Conner after we show the clip."

Alex stands. "Thanks. Come have dinner soon. We'd love to have you and a friend as our guests anytime." With a wave for the two at the table and another for us, he heads to the kitchen.

The reporter lifts her microphone and makes a motion at her cameraman. Laney demurely smiles at the reporter, who clears her throat and begins to wrap things up. "So I have to ask: Was the champagne cold?"

They laugh and Laney sighs. Today she's wearing a lavender sweater with a high neck. Two ropes of pearls and a dainty gold necklace add to her chaste, innocent look. "It was a tad cold now that you mention it. But, you see, we here in Chancey live life to the fullest. We are passionate people who love where we live. Our mayor—congratulations, Missus," she says, looking straight into the camera, "was just expressing her passion for our town." She smiles, dips her head, and bats her eyes better than Scarlett O'Hara ever hoped to. "Besides, when an election evening ends with champagne being thrown, can it be a bad thing?"

Delaney chuckles and lays a hand on my arm. "I might've written the line, but you can't teach what she knows."

"Thank God because she'd have schools all over the country."

"True. True." Her hand tightens on my arm. "So, can you talk for a minute? Here or Ruby's? Anywhere is good with me."

"Then let's go to Ruby's. I haven't been there since last week, and I wanted to check in on how the pie thing is going. Plus, I'm hungry."

I leave Delaney to chat with the reporter while I go on to get us a table. Laney was already heading back to the kitchen to go over some things with Alex, she explained with an air kiss and a wave at me. Life couldn't get better for Laney Conner. She beat Missus and doesn't have to do the job. She's already calling herself "the real mayor." You can imagine how that'll go over with Missus. But Mrs. Mayor will have to grin and bear it. She did throw champagne at her rival, and her rival has the gall to be forgiving and sweet. Oh, it's hard to be on the short end of Southern rules of etiquette.

"Good morning, Carolina," Libby calls as I walk in the door. "That color looks good on you! I had a blast up at your place this weekend. Coffee coming!"

I can't get a word in before she's back behind the counter, so I nod to some folks, mostly the men at the front table, and pick a booth. My jacket is an old but rarely worn one I found in my closet this morning. I'd forgotten about it, but it's perfect for this time of year when the weather can be so unpredictable. It's dark-pink, light wool without a lining. No need to take it off as it's not bulky, especially since I only have a thin mock turtleneck on underneath. I relax and take a calming breath. I'm surprised, but the weekend did rejuvenate me. And despite my fears, I wasn't left with a destroyed house. Everyone pitched in to clean on Sunday afternoon. My stomach muscles hurt from so much laughing. Or maybe it was the yoga stretching? Oh, I hadn't thought about that possibility. Maybe I actually worked out?

Libby arrives with her newly filled coffee pot. "I hear Laney's opening a club or some such right down the street. Cathy's already all over wanting to have a corner for her Sexy Belle stuff." She throws up a hand. "Not like before. That whole nasty shop filled with that nasty stuff. No, just the tasteful things. And what about Laney beating Missus!" She laughs and sets the pot on the table. "Me and Ruby have been hee-hawing about that all morning!"

"You can go ahead and fill this cup too. There's Delaney." Libby looks around, then fills the cup I'd turned over as I admit, "I don't think you and Ruby are alone in your laughter. Just hope Missus finds it funny sooner rather than later."

Delaney slides in across me. "Well, don't hold your breath for that. She was still spewing fire this morning."

"Hey, Miss Delaney. How are Missus and Peter? Still playing high and mighty?" She sets the pot down on the table again, this time with a bit of a bang. "You know you're too good a person to get mixed up with them two?"

"Oh, Libby, that's sweet of you to say. So, what are the muffin choices this morning?"

Libby screws her mouth up in frustration at Delaney's failure to heed her warning, then picks up her pot. "Apple cinnamon. Banana with and without nuts. White chocolate and citrus, but it's more citrus than sweet, and our meat one is sausage. No cheese or anything, just sausage. I think Ruby forgot the cheese." She takes a step away from our table, but then leans back. "To tell the truth, she's burning the candle at both ends with this pie thing." She gives us a look that says we didn't hear it from her, and walks away.

Delaney unwinds her scarf. "Ruby's not the only one forgetting things. She didn't take our muffin order."

"She'll either remember in a minute and ask or just bring us what she thinks we wanted. Either way we'll be good. I've decided whatever I get at Ruby's is what the Lord wanted me to have anyway."

"So the wedding," Delaney says. "Any questions?"

My mouth opens, but I only blink for a moment. "I guess, but I don't know enough to even know what to ask. First, what should I wear?"

She grins. "I thought you might be wondering. Oh, Libby?"

Libby stops in the center of the aisle, looks at us, and frowns. "I didn't get your order, did I?"

Delaney answers, "Banana nut for me."

"Same for me," I add.

She gives us a quick nod. "Carry on."

Delaney leans back. "Here's what I'm thinking. Unless you want something new, I've seen pictures of Anna and Will's wedding, and the dress you wore would be perfect."

"Oh, I love that dress. And the jacket keeps it from looking too summery." Not meaning to, I'd fulfilled the old adage for the mother of the groom: show up, shut up, and wear beige. Although I would call it more of a taupe than beige. It was perfect for the wedding and outdoor reception because it had a cute little cutwork jacket with three-quarter-length sleeves made of gauze. The skirt was trimmed in the same gauze, which gave it a soft touch. The fabric didn't wrinkle, but it didn't look like polyester. All in all, I've been looking for somewhere else to wear it, and here's my opportunity.

"I agree. My dress is ivory, and the accent colors being dusty rose and sage, your flowers will go perfect with your dress. Peter is wearing a black suit, as is the friend who'll be standing up with him."

Libby shows up with our muffins and sits them down before refilling our coffee cups. "You ladies need anything else?" She gives us each a quick glance, then focuses on Delaney. "Miss Delaney, I'm real sorry for what I said earlier. None of God's creatures are beyond redemption, and I shouldn't say such things about, well, your family-to-be. God might be using you to bring them around."

I begin to laugh and try to catch Delaney's eyes, which I'm sure will be lit up in amusement, so I'm surprised to find they're not. She's looking thoughtfully at Libby, and then she gives her a little nod. "You might be right. You just might be right."

Libby pats her hand, gives her an understanding nod in return, and moves on.

Delaney pulls her muffin apart and takes a bite, but she doesn't make light at all of what Libby said, so I don't either.

"Okay, so my mother-of-the-groom dress it is. Oh, wait, so who is standing up with Peter? I hadn't even thought of that."

She puts another piece in her mouth and waves that hand a bit as she chews. "Just an old friend of our family. Peter said he didn't know who to choose and let me decide."

"Seems like that's how he's doing everything. Delaney, Libby is right to a degree. I know you're just humoring her, but this isn't a good situation you're getting into. Stay here in Chancey if you want to so badly. You don't have to marry Peter, at least not this fast."

Her shoulders drop, and her voice hardens. "I know what I'm doing." She shakes herself, takes a deep breath, and then works up a smile for me. "Carolina. Just be my friend. Okay?"

"Okay." We focus on our muffins and coffee for a minute. "Anything else I can do? You sure you don't want a bridal luncheon? Or need help with the reception at the depot? I'd really like to help. Missus has agreed to hold off on the shower as you asked her to, but I'd be more than willing to put one together. Even a small one."

"I know, and I appreciate it, but honestly, we really don't need another shower, and my mother is perfect at all the rest. Well, at hiring people to do everything perfectly. Her friends own all kinds of frou-frou businesses that specialize in throwing expensive gatherings." She reaches out and pats my hand. "I know! Let's do a girls' lunch with the ladies who went to Laney's that night sometime after we return from our honeymoon." She pulls her hand back and looks down at the table. "Until the wedding I'm actually not going to be in town much. I'm moving my photography studio to Canton. Well, my assistants are doing the moving, but I need to be there to oversee it. Plus, I've moved out of my apartment and am living at home with my parents until the wedding." She's been talking quickly, but hesitates for a moment. Still focusing on the table, she rushes on. "This will allow Peter to tidy up some loose ends here." Then she raises her eyes to me. "Like Phoenix."

I gasp. "You do know."

"Of course I know. Unless I was in a coma, how could I not know?" Taking another deep breath she pulls herself together, licks her bottom lip, then continues. "Do you remember when the police came to talk to Phoenix at my engagement party on New Year's Eve?"

"Yeah, I do remember now that you mention it. What about it?"

She shrugs, then focuses her energy in my direction. "Nothing that anyone has to ever hear about. Hopefully. Phoenix has been presented with her options. She knows what she should do. Me being away for a few days should facilitate that. Now, I need to go." She grabs her scarf and purse, and moves out to the end of the bench. Her smile is back. "I truly appreciate all you're doing. We'll talk soon. I'll take care of the check." She jumps up and heads to the counter while I take my last sip of coffee and replay her comments about Phoenix.

Funny, but they sound more like they came from a mafia boss than a Southern belle.

Chapter 43

"So you weren't invited on my sister's shopping extravaganza either," Susan says, coming in the front doors of Blooming Books on Wednesday around noon.

I'm leaning over the front window, refilling spots where we sold the books right out of the display. Seeing as we're mostly a used bookstore, we don't usually have more than one copy of most books, but this display has been more popular than most. The cozy mystery covers are bright, full of interesting details, and have inventive names, like Diane Mott Davidson's *Dying for Chocolate* and *The Main Corpse* and those in Denise Swanson's Scumble River series like *Murder of a Small-Town Honey* and *Murder of a Barbie and Ken*. People keep coming in and claiming them right from the front window, which leaves me with holes in the display and few books on the shelves. I might have to institute a buy-back program, where we buy back books we believe we can sell again. It just always seemed like a lot of work.

Bonnie comes up with the creative ideas for the window and gets it started, but now with her decorating business she doesn't have time to keep it stocked and straightened up. I keep picking up duties as everyone around me finds more interesting things to do. Like Laney's extended shopping trip for a whole new wardrobe means I'm in charge of Crossings. Luckily we don't have any guests.

"Nope. She actually said I would 'only slow her down.'" I turn in time to see Susan fall onto the couch, then bounce up to sit on the edge. I give her a bit of side-eye. "You're full of energy today."

"Yes, I am. What are you doing for lunch? Want to take a ride?"

"Where to? Danny and Shannon are upstairs, but they'll be down before long. I really shouldn't go out to eat for lunch today. I brought an apple and some cheese from home. I was kind of planning on getting down to Ruby's for pie." I sit down as I frown. "But I had a muffin earlier. When Ruby opened the pie thing I kinda made myself promise I would never ever have pie and muffins in the same day."

Susan laughs. "That is a good rule of thumb. Okay, so since you're not having pie, just a ride in the country." She bounces up, and the chatter goes with her. "I'm going to look at the flowers in the cooler to take some to Mother. Her birthday is Friday. Laney better be back in town for our family dinner. She wasn't sure how long she'd be gone."

I take advantage of my seat and lean back into the cozy couch cushions. Susan chats with another woman who is also looking at the flowers in the cooler. Turning to look outside I decide an afternoon ride is a good idea. I did tell Kimmy I'd see her at Ruby's since she's starting her new job, but I'll see her tomorrow—though wait, she's not working there on Thursdays, and Ruby's Pies isn't open on Fridays. Okay. I'll see her on Monday. Besides, a sunny, halfway-warm day in January is too good to pass up sitting inside. I propel myself forward and up. "You know, Susan, a ride sounds good after all."

While I get freshened up, eat my apple, make a list of things for Danny to do, and put on my jacket, Susan decides on an arrangement, marks it "sold," and then slides it to the back of the cooler.

Shannon had moseyed on downstairs and behind the counter, where she and Susan are talking as I approach them. "Here's a to-do list for Danny. I'm going to go to lunch with Susan."

My partner scowls at me. "Danny's busy right now."

"Okay. But he is working this afternoon, right?"

"I said he was busy right now. I didn't say he wasn't working."

This is the old angry Shannon from when we first started working together. "Do you want me to not go?"

"Did I say that? Go. Have fun. I'm fine here." She slams the cash drawer closed and picks up her phone.

"Shannon. Look at me." Susan has moved to the door, and I take her place at the counter. Sometimes I forget how young Shannon is, and that she's pregnant. "Is everything okay?"

With an exasperated sigh, she looks at me. "Everything is fine. I know what I'm doing. Danny is just busy with something, and he'll—" She stops and looks back to where we hear him jogging down the stairs. "There he comes now."

He half runs to the front. "No good, babe. Have to call later." He comes to stand beside me, also facing Shannon. "Hey, Carolina." He glances at my jacket. "You just get here?"

"No. I've been here with you all morning."

"I meant from lunch." Then he laughs and hits the counter. "Oh, crazy me. You can't have been at lunch 'cause we were at lunch. Hey, is that for me?"

He's pointing at the list in my hand, which has his name in big letters at the top. "Yeah, it is. So you're good if I go to lunch?" I look from him back to my partner. My partner who looks like she could cry. "Seriously, Shannon. I'm good staying here."

She shakes her head and turns away. "No. Go. Danny and I are fine here. Go."

Danny doesn't look back at me. He's studying the list in his hand. I bend around the end of the counter to grab my purse. "Okay. I won't be long."

Susan pulls open the door and then follows me through it. On the sidewalk she points me across the street to her car and says, "Well, that was interesting. How are the two lovebirds? Ever get around to a real wedding?"

"Who knows? They have so many moving parts right now I just try to stay out of their way." I angle away from her to my side of her car and try to not think about Shannon. I have a feeling Danny is now trying to track down if he actually did have a vasectomy. I know that doesn't seem like something a man wouldn't be sure of, but you haven't worked with Danny Kinnock as much as I have.

We pass the Piggly Wiggly, the high school, and the road that turns down to the ballparks. The blacktop narrows a bit, and we're almost to the trashy little cinderblock bar, Dew Drop In, when Susan slows down. She makes a left-hand turn and drives down a little country road, but then with a right turn, we go into a grouping of homes. I look around as she drives through. "Isn't this Summerfield? Where Athena Markum lives?"

"Yeah, I just wanted to come in the back way to make sure the coast is clear."

"The coast is clear? Who are we hiding from?"

She doesn't answer but pulls into a driveway. "Coming in the back way I can see if anyone's here, but coming in the front I can't see until I'm right in front of the house." She turns off the car and lets out a little squeal. "Let's go inside!"

Before I can get any more information, she's out of the car, so I join her. The house is under construction but looks almost finished. The yard is only dirt, and there are still stickers on the newly installed windows. "I don't think I've been out here during the day. One of Bryan's friends lives here and I've dropped him off, but only in the evening. That house over there, I think."

"Yeah, that's the Pipers. Don't you love this front porch?"

"I do." It's wide and made of that plastic stuff that looks like wood and never rots. I think it's made from recycled milk jugs.

"Come inside. Look how open this floor plan is."

I follow her in the front door, which she entered like she owns the place. For all I know she does. The room is large and wide open. I know the houses here in Summerfield are energy conscious and efficient, but also feature luxury amenities. The tall windows, beautiful floors, and the spacious kitchen we gravitate to next all feel streamlined but expensive, with top-notch quality and attention to detail. "So, whose is this that we have to sneak in to see it?"

"Mine."

I whip around to where she's standing beside a bank of windows in the dining room. "You bought this?"

"No. Not me. Griffin." She turns and waves a hand out at the deck. "Look at that view. Griffin knows how I like a view, but even more…" She rushes over to open the French doors leading out to the large deck. "Look out here."

I meet her at the railing, and she's practically giddy. "Isn't that the perfect place for my garden?" The yard is flat before meandering gently down to a lake in the distance.

"It is. But again, why are we sneaking around?"

She sighs and turns around to lean back and face me. "Rachel told me about it, not Griffin. She said he wants to move back to town and he's buying this house."

"But you said it's yours."

"Okay, that's not quite true, but it won't be long, right? Why else would he be moving back to town? Things are really going well with us. I bet he wants to surprise me. We're working on not being the same old people we were before."

When I don't say anything she clouds up. "What? It's true. Leslie is coming home this weekend, and we're doing family stuff all day on Saturday. Rachel, too, before she leaves town."

"That's great. But I don't want to see you get your hopes all up and then…"

"I'm not. Griffin has already asked me to go to Peter and Delaney's wedding with him, and that's Valentine's weekend." Her giddiness is back. "You don't ask someone to a Valentine's wedding without having romantic feelings!"

"But that also doesn't mean he's buying this house for you."

"Of course not. I was joking. It's not for me as much as it is for us. Our family." She looks at her watch. "Come on. We should leave. Workers will be back from lunch soon." She starts inside, but I hold on to her arm.

"Wait. I'm really, really happy for you. For Griffin too. It's a beautiful house."

"I know. Thanks."

I follow her back through the open floor plan, which mimics the new, spread-out subdivision I can see through the front windows. There are a few large trees near the entrance, but it's obvious the land was used for farming before Summerfield was developed. All the landscaping around the houses is new, and it's true that it would be right up Susan's alley to fill this lot with flowers and vegetables and trees, to make this a home. That was one big problem they had; she never felt at home in the huge house up in Laurel Cove.

She pulls the front door shut behind us. "This feels like I belong here."

I grin at her. "You know? That's just what I was thinking."

She wraps an arm around mine, and we step off the low

porch onto the red-clay-stained sidewalk. "Don't worry. Griffin and I finally know what we're doing."

"Good. Like I said, I'm really happy for you."

She pats my arm before releasing it, and we each go to our side of the car. I keep my sigh to myself as I slide into my seat.

Being surrounded by so many people who keep saying they know what they're doing should ease my mind, shouldn't it?

Yeah—well, it doesn't.

CHAPTER 44

"I brought cake," Laney says as she bumps open the door to the mayor's office with her hip.

Missus's face tightens, and then she releases the grimace through sheer determination and smiles. "Wonderful. We were so afraid you were going to miss my swearing in."

Laney doesn't even look at me to shoot an insincere smirk. We all know Missus hurried the ceremony hoping Laney would still be on her shopping trip on Friday afternoon. I'd like to think Laney's lack of a smirk says she's maturing, but yeah, she's not. I still get her texts.

"Miss this? Oh, never. I'm so proud of you, and we are going to do such great things together. We, as in Chancey, not you and me. This job is one hundred percent yours. I won't hear of anyone saying anything else. I just am not listening. Not listening even one little bit."

See? Told you she's the same old Laney.

She looks around as if surprised to see how small the office is, sits the cake on a folding chair beside the door, and then pulls the leather satchel off her shoulder. "There are plates and napkins and forks in here. Now, how about one more itsy-bitsy picture with me congratulating the real winner?" She sounds completely sincere when she says "real," which makes it stand out more than a big ol' guffaw.

This is when I'm real glad the bakery provides those little plastic spatulas for cutting cakes. A real knife could be dangerous in this situation. I wait for them to squeeze together and take the picture. Yep, I'm now taking pictures. Delaney, true to her word, is not around. Charles is on deadline and said he couldn't in good conscience lend credibility to Missus being given actual power in town. Kimmy is too tired from her new pie gig, and so now I'm taking official pictures for the paper because what else do I have to do?

However, in her last text Laney said she was bringing cake, and there was nothing else on my schedule where I would possibly get a piece of bakery cake.

Laney looks great in a cranberry sweater and matching pants. She's cutting cake and laughing as she hands out the pieces.

Missus is fuming, but she's also sitting in the big chair. The mayor's chair. Even though it's Friday afternoon I can tell she's itching to throw us all out so she can get to work.

"Can I take a picture of you behind the desk? You look good there." I motion everyone out of the shot, and Missus lifts her chin. The chair is still large, but she fills it just fine. Her ego takes up any extra space. "Got it."

Peter steps up behind her. "How about one of with me and my mother?"

"Sure." I hold up my phone. Yes, I'm using my phone; that's how official I am. Concentrating on the picture I say, "So Delaney couldn't be here for the big day?"

"She's busy. Lots going on with the wedding coming up and her moving everything," he says, his smile never moving. Then he looks up. "Ah, there's Anna and Francie."

"I'm sorry I'm so late. Did I miss everything? I'm so sorry." Anna steps into the crowded space with her arms full and that harried look mothers develop overnight. Peter and I reach her at the same time.

He takes the baby carrier off her arm and sits it on the nearest chair. "There's our girl." He winks at Anna. "Both our girls. Let's get a picture of you and Granmissus."

"Oh no. I look awful. Just Francie."

"Here." I grab my purse. "Let's brush your hair, and I've got powder and lipstick." I hand her my purse and push her toward another folding chair. "We'll get a couple of the mayor with her great-granddaughter while you get ready."

Missus holds her arms out for Francie, and Peter hands her over. Francie is such a contented baby, and she makes the transfer without a fuss. I snap a couple of quick pics and check to see if they're any good. The tenderness on Peter's face catches me. That's the Peter I got to know when I moved here, when he was unsure of what he wanted. When he was my friend and just wanted to be happy. Staring at the image I realize it wasn't that long ago that he looked like this. When he was with Shannon and wasn't trying to be important and bossy and—

"Carolina? Are you wool-gathering again?" Missus scolds me. "We're ready."

"Sure. Sorry." Peter has stepped away, and the mayor is ready. Francie sees me, and I think she recognizes me because she's frowning. No, she's not frowning at me; she's frowning because she wants me. Of course.

"Okay. Anna, you can step up there now," I say.

She's taken off her coat and has on the cherry red dress she wore to announce her engagement to Will. We get pictures of the three, and then Peter joins in. Finally we're done, and I can hold my granddaughter.

She's better than cake.

"We might get snow this weekend," Laney says as she pulls

up in front of Blooming Books to drop me off since I'd walked over to the city building. "Slim chance, but still it would be nice."

"What? Did you buy a new snow outfit you're dying to show off?"

"No, I'm just tired, and it would be nice to be home with my family. Well, except for AC's grand opening."

I open the car door. "Well, I don't want any snow. Our guests this weekend all want to hike and be outside. They should be there soon, so I'm heading home shortly to check them in."

I get out and walk in front of her SUV. She waves at me from her window and yells, "Love the Valentine's display!"

"Thanks!" I yell back and then go to see what she's talking about as she pulls away.

Looks like Bonnie had more time than she thought she would this afternoon. Pink and red fills the window with a wonderful collection of romance books, old and new, racy and classics. There are cut-out hearts and kids' valentines, as well as candy, both chocolate and the pastel hearts with messages stamped on them. There are even hearts hanging from the ceiling with fishing wire. It's wonderful. Bonnie has outdone herself.

"So apparently Bonnie's gotten us ready for Valentine's!" I announce as I enter the store. "The window looks fantastic, doesn't it?"

Danny is standing at the counter, and his smile turns to confusion before the door closes behind me. "But Miss Bonnie's not here."

"Oh. The window."

"I did it. It was a lot of fun."

I head straight to the window. "You did all this? By yourself?"

The tall, young man comes to stand beside me, his hands stuck in the back pockets of his corduroy pants. "You like it?"

"Yeah. It's great." I turn to look up at him. "It's really great." I look around the rest of the shop. "So, uh, you think you'd like to do the rest of the shop?"

"Can I? Shannon wasn't sure if you'd be happy, so she made me wait until you got back."

Who am I to stop him? "Of course you can."

He flings his long, skinny arms around me. "Thanks. I'll get started right now." He releases me and hurries to the worktable, chattering as he goes. "I went to the Pig and got some construction paper and stuff. Shannon is upstairs. She'll be right down."

"Okay. I need to go on home since we have guests arriving. Is she sick? Should we check on her before I leave? Or I guess it's late enough we could go ahead and close. It is Friday."

He laughs as he picks up a piece of pink paper in one hand and scissors in the other. "Oh, Miss Carolina, she's just sick because she's pregnant. Alison was sick all the time with our girls." He relaxes his hand and rests it on the table with a sigh. "Hate to say it, but looks like Shannon's going to have a girl, too, since she's sick all the time. You know, I was hoping to have a boy this time. Having a son would be fun, wouldn't it? We could name him Danny Junior." His head springs up. "Hey, we could name a girl Danny, right? Danielle and call her Danny. Perfect. You have a good night, Carolina. Wait'll Shannon hears I've got us a name."

I nod as I walk to the door, turn over the closed sign, and step onto the sidewalk, pulling the door closed behind me. Yeah, just wait until Shannon hears. And Missus. And Peter.

Getting snowed in is sounding better and better all the time.

CHAPTER 45

"What a perfect weekend we had! The hiking was wonderful, but then inviting us to the restaurant's grand opening last night? So special!" the thirtysomething woman exclaims. Her husband and the other couple had already said some variation of the same things several times.

"You did have perfect weather since the snow never materialized." The panic of Friday night resulted in the Pig selling out of bread and milk, but Saturday arrived bright and sunny. Like many other households in the area, French toast featured prominently on our weekend breakfast menus.

"Sledding would've been fun, since you got the sleds and everything," the other young woman says as she pulls on the door. "Looks like the guys have the car loaded. Thanks again, Mrs. Jessup. We'll be back, I'm sure."

I step onto the porch to wave goodbye and get a breath of the brisk, sunny air. Same story, different day, with the snow—or lack of snow. Now the temps are cold but heading up for the next week or so. Some winters are like this in the South. We just don't get enough snow to speak of. Then, other years, snowstorms come in one right after the other. I even ordered sleds off the internet in the fall because our back hill would be perfect for sledding. With a shiver I dart back inside the warm house.

The warm, *empty* house.

After church we had another meal of French toast, this time with bacon instead of sausage. Jackson and Bryan went downtown to meet Colt and finish up Peter's office remodel. Savannah headed out shopping with Jenna and some of the girls for dorm supplies. Why she's going shopping for dorm supplies, don't ask me. I asked and was treated to a look of confusion from my second-born along with, "Mom? I'm a senior. You know that, right?"

All these people having babies have no idea. No idea at all.

While our guests packed, I scurried around the house getting it put back in order. I had a plan in mind. A plan involving a cup of hot chocolate, a book, and a quiet house.

As I settle into the sunshine-flooded chair beside the front window, watch steam rise off my cup, and open my book, I can't help but congratulate myself.

I love when a plan comes together.

"It's family meal night, or something like that," Jackson explains as he sets his work boots to the side of the couch, then pulls on his casual shoes. Despite his explaining, I still don't understand what we're doing. I just know I don't have to cook. He called around four this afternoon, when I'd had two blissful hours of reading, and maybe a little nodding off, and said AC's is doing a special thing on Sunday nights and everyone was going.

I'm dressed and ready to go even though I don't know what the "thing" is or who all "everyone" includes. I take our coats off the rack and hand him his. "How did the work on Peter's office go?"

"Great. It's all done. He seemed happy with it although he barely gave it a look."

"Maybe he's missing Delaney. She's not been around at all that I know of. She wasn't even at church this morning."

"Could be," he says with a shrug and no additional information, then yells up the stairs. "Bryan! Come on!"

Bryan pounds down the stairs. "Zoe says she's ready."

My eyebrows jump. "Zoe's coming?"

Bryan jerks open the front door. "Dad said she could." Then he's gone, out in the cold without so much as a coat. I grab his from where he'd dropped it when they came home earlier. At least it'll be in the car.

Jackson shrugs into his coat. "Is that okay? Figured since Savannah and Will are never around he might as well bring a friend. He really worked hard this afternoon."

Switching on the lamp so we don't have to walk into a dark living room later, I shake my head at him. "No, no problem at all. Just didn't know. So, did you text Savannah?"

I guess there was an edge to my voice because he frowns at me from where he holds the door open. "No. I take it you didn't either? I just assumed she had other plans."

"She was out dorm shopping with the girls this afternoon." On the porch I wait while he locks the door.

"Really? So she's thinking she'll have a dorm room?"

"Please. Like I would know something about that. I mean, I asked. Got my head bit off."

On the steps Jackson stops and hollers at his son. "Want to start the car?"

With a whoop, the jacketless boy heads our way. He grabs the keys from his dad, his coat from me, barely pausing in his trajectory. We take our time walking to the car and enjoy the mild evening. "So it's family style, you said?"

Jackson puts an arm around my shoulders and squeezes.

"Why don't we just wait and see? You know I don't know anything more than I did the first twelve times you asked."

I chuckle and lean into him. "Oh well. Hope springs eternal."

"Welcome back to AC's," Alex greets us, and he leads us to a table in the center of the room.

It's round and seats ten, and I hesitate. "We don't want to take your largest table. There are only four of us."

Jackson gives me a quizzical look. "I told you we were eating with Colt and Griffin. Didn't I?"

"No," is all I say as I sit in the chair Alex pulls out for me.

My husband doesn't take the clue I so graciously offered him that fewer words at this point would be better. "But I told you it was family style? You know that would have to mean a bunch of people, right?"

Alex must have felt the warning. He chuckles, then rushes on. "It won't always mean a lot of people, but tonight is different. It's something we're trying, and I know I didn't explain it very well, but on Sunday evenings, from five until seven, we're going to do family-style meals. Each week there will be one featured dish. Tonight is what I grew up calling 'kitchen sink pasta'—everything but the kitchen sink is in the sauce!" He winks at the alarm on Zoe's face. "You'll like it, I promise. Tonight is veggies and chicken in red sauce with two different kinds of pasta and bread. Speaking of which…"

One of the servers puts two bread baskets on our table as Alex moves toward the door. "And here are some more of your table." Susan comes bouncing in with Grant and Susie Mae in front of her. They are followed by Griffin.

She pushes the kids toward the side of the table where Bryan and Zoe are, but Susie Mae stops on the other side of me. "Can I sit beside you, Miss Carolina?"

"Sure. Your mom can sit on my other side. Jackson can sit over there by your dad."

Jackson has his hands on the seat next to me, which I've just selected for Susan, and he looks down at me. "But I thought…"

This time I don't have to say anything. He gets the message in my look.

Susan pulls Griffin's sleeve to sit beside her, and Jackson gets shuffled on down to a spot beside the last two open chairs, but when I see Colt coming in our direction behind Alex, I feel bad. Colt will end up beside an empty chair. Poor guy, he's already having a rough time. He shouldn't—but then I realize he's grinning from ear to ear. He moves to the side, and I realize there's a woman on the crook of his arm. Not just any woman—Phoenix. She leans in to him, pressing her chest against his arm, and whispers into his ear. His smile is slow, but there's no missing its message. Then he says it out loud in a delighted, husky voice, "Later, honey."

He helps her into her chair, rubbing his hands over her arms and waist, and well, I quit looking, and I shift to talk to Susan.

"You see this?" I whisper. "They're back together?"

But I'm the only one who looked away. Susan is staring at Griffin, who is staring at Phoenix and Colt's little display. My dining sidekick nods, then turns her face to me, though her eyes stay locked on the reunited couple. "What do you think of me getting a boob job?"

CHAPTER 46

"Well, this is just great!" I growl to myself as I watch the slow—very slow—train engines crawl in front of me. My brain was in overdrive trying to leave the house this morning, so I completely missed the blowing of the train horn, and now I'm stuck at the end of my driveway. This is the slowest train in history. And the longest.

I can't even call Laney like I planned to because it's also the loudest. But at least I'm warm and alone.

Laney and Shaw weren't at AC's last night because, according to Susan, the Conners were doing their own version of family night. Jenna was not supposed to go shopping for dorm things without her mother, so Laney had a meltdown. It's an emotional time when your first leaves for college, but then when your other first has also recently left home to move in with her boyfriend, and on top of all that you are dealing with those first-year post-pregnancy hormones? Not a good mix of firsts.

On her way to AC's Susan took them a casserole from her freezer, put it in the oven, dropped off a container of Mayfield's strawberry cheesecake ice cream, and left them watching Laney's favorite movie, *The Sound of Music*. Laney had gone to bed by the time we left AC's last night, so I was going to fill her in this morning.

But my morning has been hectic. Mostly the usual Monday morning stuff when it feels like Friday was at least two months ago and anything needed for school is only a distant memory. Fixing lunches is something none of us remember ever having to do apparently, and laundry… isn't laundry usually done on Sunday afternoon? But I had a book to finish, so…

My darling daughter's mood has gone from annoying to foul to putrid. We are going to have to have a come-to-Jesus meeting soon. I just keep hoping Jesus will meet with her without me and fix her. Just fix her.

Train cars covered in graffiti crawl by me, and I have plenty of time to try and decipher the cryptic writing and pictures. A couple of the angry-looking ones would describe my youngest's opinion of last night. Apparently Zoe Kendricks had never met Grant Lyles. Okay, we all know she's met him, knows him well. But last night? There was a halo of golden light shining around him and angels were singing. At least that was the look in Zoe's eye. She gazed at him with her head tipped just so. She laughed at everything he said. Even worse was the confusion on Bryan's face. He couldn't figure out what was going on.

However, he was sitting beside Susie Mae, and she filled him in. "Yeah, apparently Grant is Mr. Popular up at Darien Academy. You should see all the girls that just happen to stop by Dad's house. They all look like that."

Yep. That cleared up Bryan's confusion. And broke his sweet little heart.

I didn't want to give Zoe a ride home, but Jackson said we had to.

I didn't want to make Bryan go to school, but Jackson said we had to.

Like I said. It's been a rough morning. For everyone.

Finally, the caboose. Okay, okay. There are no cabooses on freight trains anymore. If you want all the details on why that is, you know who to call.

I don't know why, and I don't care.

"Hey there," Patty calls from her spot on the couch when I come in the back door of Blooming Books. "Andy dropped me off when he brought you that load of books back there."

"Did you make this pot of coffee?" There's no sign of Shannon having been down yet.

"Yep." Patty beams. "I'm feeling a lot better, and the doctor says I can have coffee in moderation. Plus, you know I only like it with a bunch of cream. Don't worry, I brought a whole, big container of it. Butterfinger flavor!"

"Do you need any more?" I ask, but she shakes her head and takes a deep sniff of her coffee wannabe. With my cup, sans Butterfinger creamer, I walk over and sit across from her. "You seem awfully chipper this morning."

"Like I said, I'm feeling a whole lot better. Plus, well, I helped in the nursery at Andy's daddy's church yesterday. I've always been afraid to touch a baby, but I got put on the schedule, and Andy said I had to do it. That his momma puts a lot of time into making the schedule and he'd heard what she says about the women that try and get off of it."

I can't help but chuckle and lift my cup in salute to Andy's advice. Church nursery schedules are not to be messed with. Or questioned.

"Those babies liked me, Carolina. They really liked me, and I liked them. They are so sweet and soft and, oh, they smell so good. And guess what?" Her face is fully serious as she stares at me.

"What?" I reply dutifully.

"I changed diapers. Even did a messy one. And I was good at it. Them babies didn't even cry. The real nursery lady, the one they pay? Well, she said I was a natural." Patty's eyes shine. I've never seen her this excited, even during her wedding. She shakes her head and reverently whispers, "Now I can't wait to have my baby. My very own baby." She moves her empty hand to her stomach and looks down. Her voice sinks even lower. "I can't wait to see you."

My eyes fill, and I settle back and relax. "I always knew you'd be a wonderful mother. Your baby is so lucky. Have you been thinking about names?"

She sighs, and the seriousness is back with her flattened eyebrows. "No. I've been so scared I haven't thought of one good thing about having a baby. Not one. But that's over. I'm going to find out if it's a girl or a boy, and then I'm decorating that nursery from the ground up." She looks around and whispers again. "I know Momma hired Miss Bonnie to do it, but I'm doing it. Well, me and Andy."

"Good for you. So I don't guess Shannon's been down?"

"No. Andy let us in with the key Momma gave us. Now that I'm feeling better I don't think I'll be coming over here as much, you know?" She studies me for a minute. "I believe in miracles now. Do you believe in miracles?"

"I suppose so. I don't guess I've ever really thought about it. But, yeah, why not. So, why do you now believe in them?"

"I know you'd think miracles would happen up in the church service, but nope. I was down in the basement just scared to death to walk into that nursery. Scared to death, I tell you. I was sweating, and my stomach was going between being in knots to falling plum down to my feet. Andy had to go upstairs to do the Bible reading, so he just kind of pushed me in the door and left. I thought I was gonna pass out. There was a baby crying, and the nursery lady picked it up, but then a little boy, Joshua was his name, well, he's just started walking and he fell, so she handed me that baby to take care of him. That crying baby!" Her eyes are so wide they look like they might pop out. "My knees barely made it to the nearest rocking chair, and I fell into it. Holding that baby! Well, I felt like crying myself, but I just pulled it closer and started rocking, and you won't believe it, but she stopped crying. Just stopped crying and snuggled into me." She takes a big breath and blows it out, still as serious as a heart attack.

But I can't help smiling. "Yeah, when you finally get a baby to stop crying, it sure does seem miraculous."

She frowns even more. "No, that's not the miracle. It's that everything inside of me lit up like a light was thrown on. And here's the miracle. All that fear, all that scaredness? Well it just, poof! Disappeared. Gone just like that." She nods, lifts her hand off her stomach, and points skyward. "God did that. My fear was big. Real big and real, well, you know—real. But it went away in a flash. And this morning? It's still gone. A miracle."

We sit in the quiet, and I can feel it. Her spirit is completely different. Her face, even the way she's moving her hands, is calm. Confident.

She looks past me. "I hear Shannon coming down the stairs. She moves a lot slower than Danny. Have you noticed sometimes it's like he's jumping down them stairs?" She giggles, and I do, too, as I nod.

She calls out, "Good morning, Shannon. I'm just sitting here telling Carolina about my miracle. About God answering my prayers."

Shannon approaches us, then stops beside my chair. "Well, I'm glad God's listening to you because he sure isn't listening to me." Her sigh comes from the tips of her toes.

Hmm. Sounds like Danny heard back from his doctor.

CHAPTER 47

"I can't do lunch at AC's until Friday," Laney says before even saying hello. "And don't say that I'm avoiding Angie. Because I am not!"

"I didn't say you were. I didn't even mention lunch."

"Oh." She pauses and takes a breath. "You didn't. Sorry. Just feeling a tad defensive and I'm not used to that."

"No. You are most definitely not used to that. What's going on?" I'm leaning on the counter, talking to Laney on the phone while we're in between customers. It's been the first chance I've had to actually place my call to her.

"Just trying to make everybody happy. I know now why I never ascribed to that bit of Southern womanhood. Susan can have it. I want Jenna's last months at home to be perfect, but I want to support Angie too. Then there's Cayden, he's got some kind of rash I need to get him to the doctor for today. As for Shaw, well, he's not happy either, but I think those two glasses of wine I had last night took off my edge long enough for me to help him take off his edge, if you know what I mean."

"Laney." I roll my eyes and grin. "Angie knows you support her. You were great at the opening, both openings, and we'll do lunch there soon. Friday, or even next week, sounds great to me, and I can call Susan for you. Take care of Cayden's rash and

Jenna. Besides, Jenna is nowhere near leaving; you have plenty of time to shop with her."

"Unless she gets everything she needs before I even get the chance," she says with a sniffle. "Sorry. So tell me quick, Colt and Phoenix are back together?"

"Apparently. They were all over each other." I can hear her talking to Cayden and putting stuff together on her end, so I decide not to fill her in on Susan and Griffin. "Listen, you sound busy. I'll let you go. Call me when you get back from the doctor." I'm not through talking before Cayden is crying so loud that all she can do is say, "Bye," and hang up.

My phone buzzes with a call, and I assume Laney's redialed me. "Hey. What do you need?"

"Pie."

"Susan?"

"I don't care if you ate enough doughnuts to float a battle-ship this morning. I need pie, and I'm heading to Ruby's right now. Meet me there." Then she hangs up.

Pie it is.

"I have a meeting this afternoon with a new sponsor for the park, so I can't have alcohol." Susan is seated in a booth and halfway through a piece of creamy chocolate pie by the time I get to Ruby's. Kimmy has already spotted me and is headed my way with a pot of coffee, her ponytail swinging behind her.

"Welcome! It's about time you came in. I've been looking for you! Coffee?"

"Sure." I don't get the word fully out.

"Pies today are chocolate there like Susan is devouring. We always have pecan 'cause it keeps so well, and the fruit pie today is cherry. Three pies a day. That's what we're starting out with. I think that's plenty, don't you?"

Her torrent of words stops abruptly, and I'm left staring at her. "Uh, yeah. You sure are full of energy."

"Dream come true, running a restaurant like this. What can I get you? I have other customers."

"Chocolate—"

"And a piece of pecan to try," Susan interrupts her. At the same time she brushes Kimmy away with a flick of her hand. Kimmy and her ponytail swish away, and Susan doesn't even look up. "Dream, schream. She's drinking Red Bull. I saw her down the last can. So, what was up with Phoenix last night?"

"You mean that she's back with Colt apparently?"

"I mean all her flirting with Griffin." Susan shoves a big bite of pie in and stares at me as she chews.

"Oh. That." While one half of the table watched Zoe fall in love with Grant, the other half watched Phoenix put on a clinic in doing lap dances in a family restaurant. Even though she wasn't actually sitting in Colt's lap, she might as well have been. Jackson appeared embarrassed and very interested in his pasta and phone. Griffin, however, was taking it all in. He might as well have been sticking dollar bills in the plunging neck of Phoenix's tight, silky wrap dress. But I don't need to mention that. "I don't think it was directed at Griffin. I think she was focused on Colt."

"Oh, puh-leese. She wants my husband. It was obvious. She was just using Colt. And doing that in front of my children!" She growls and finishes off her piece of pie, scraping her plate.

I sure am missing Laney. She'd have no fear in reminding Susan how she and Silas have acted. Or that she's the one who put her husband on the market. But, as we all know, I'm no Laney. "No, really. I think she's into Colt." Lowering my voice I add, "She and Peter are done, I get the feeling." I lean back. "Oh, Kimmy. That looks great."

"Give me that," Susan says as she grabs the plate of pecan pie.

"Don't take my hand off! Here ya go, Carolina." She sets my plate down and then rests her elbows on the table near me. "So, what happened last night at that dinner thing y'all went to? Zoe came home in a trance."

That takes the shine off my piece of pie. "Oh, she was pretty infatuated with Grant, Susan's son."

Kimmy blinks at me. "But I thought she and Bryan were, you know, an item?"

"Well, I think Zoe's made her feelings pretty clear that she only wants to be friends. Bryan's just been holding out hope." I shrug and pick up my fork. "He'll get over it."

She stands up, but slides a sly look at Susan. "Not sure how I feel about her being interested in that Lyles boy."

Susan stops mid-chew. "What? Why not?"

Kimmy takes a moment to think while studying Susan. Finally she shrugs, then pulls a card out of her pocket. "Watching you and that ex of yours has not been pretty lately. Y'all might need a little family counseling. Here's the card for our church's counseling service. The way you and Mr. Lyles run around town looking for action, well, let's just say I don't need that around my house. Enjoy your pie, ladies."

Susan lifts her napkin to her mouth and spits out the piece of pie she'd just put in it, wads up the napkin, and puts it beside her plate. "Kimmy Kendricks thinks Griffin is running around town looking for action?" She looks down and puts her hand on her stomach. "I think I'm going to be sick," she says as she scrambles out of the booth and dashes to the bathroom.

So having pie at Ruby's is pretty much like having muffins there—ya gotta look past the drama and just keep eating.

CHAPTER 48

Jackson comes in the French doors to the kitchen, an empty platter in one hand. "Yep. I think we've broken winter's back!"

"Honey, you'll jinx us. It's only the beginning of February," I lament as I carefully take the platter from him to put in the sink. There's blood on it from the stack of steaks he carried out to the grill, and I don't want that dribbled across the floor and counter.

"But it's like spring out there. The willow is getting ready to put out leaves, and the daffodils are up good. Those potatoes smell awesome."

"It's Savannah's favorite, the twice-baked ones, but in a dish. Doing them individually in the potato skins is too much work for this many people. You better not burn those steaks."

"Nope. Just washing my hands and headed right back out there. Bring out a glass of wine if you've got a minute. I've still got my beer."

I look around the kitchen. "Good idea." The table is set, the salad ready and in the fridge, and Anna and Will are taking a walk out on the train bridge with Savannah and Ricky. We paid for a babysitter for Francie so the new parents could relax and come over for the celebration dinner: Savannah has chosen where she's going to college! What a relief.

"Oh, it does smell wonderful out here." I walk to the deck

railing, and he's right. The willow branches look softer, and the daffodil buds are begging to show some yellow as they prepare to open. "But it's only February," I say out loud to keep myself grounded. However, I still take a deep breath. Underneath the steak I can smell the soft ground, the tree sap moving, the daffodils and everything else unfurling.

Jackson comes to stand beside me and offers his beer for a toast with my glass of red wine. "To Savannah. To us."

"Hard to believe, isn't it?"

"Very. But I think she's done a good job figuring things out. It's been a trial for us all, but she has to do things her way."

"Who would've imagined working at Andy's Place would end up like this for her?" I say, turning around to face him as he goes to the grill.

"I'm flipping the steaks, so tell the kids to come on in."

I give him a kiss on his cheek and walk back inside, leaving the door open to freshen up the kitchen. The four from the bridge are entering the front door at the same time.

Will says, "We got a whiff of the steaks and thought we better come on in. What can we do to help?"

Savannah assumes her royal stance, head held high, nose even higher. "I'll just take my seat since we are celebrating me."

Anna curtsies. "Of course, milady." Then she drops her *Downton Abbey* accent. "Where's Bryan?"

Savannah and I roll eyes, and the queen for the day says, "Upstairs moping. He thinks he's in love with Zoe Kendricks, and she's got the hots bad for Grant. It's not helping that he's left Darien Academy and is back at Chancey High."

I startle and come close to dropping the big salad bowl. "What? Grant isn't going to Darien anymore?"

Savannah takes the bowl from me while giving me a mocking shocked look. "You mean Susan hasn't told you?" Then she smiles and turns to whisk the salad to the table. "He only came back yesterday, and since it was Friday he only got his schedule and picked up books."

Ricky has pulled the oven mitts on, so I move out of his way, thinking back to when I last talked to Susan. It's been a very busy week at the store, especially since Bonnie has been working full time to finish decorating Phoenix's apartment and Peter's office. Shannon has been getting ready for Valentine's and dealing with her morning sickness.

Away from the store has been crazy too. Poor Cayden was diagnosed with hand, foot, and mouth disease, which is common but very contagious, so Laney's been nursing him at home all week. "Monday," I say out loud as I let the oven door close and turn it off. "Monday Susan and I had pie at Ruby's." I study the table to see if we have everything, but in reality I'm thinking back over the week. "No. I haven't talked to Susan since Monday. She got sick at Ruby's, and I texted to make sure she was okay later. She was, and that was it. But still, I can't believe she didn't tell me about Grant."

"What about Grant?" Bryan asks from behind me. He looks like he's the one who's been sick all week. And I guess in a way he has been. Poor kid.

I ruffle his hair. "I didn't know he was going to move to Chancey High. Did you?"

"Duh, Mom. Of course I knew," he drawls as he melts into his seat like his bones have turned to jelly.

"Hey," Jackson says as he comes into the dining room with the full platter. "Don't talk to your mom like that. And sit up before you fall out of the chair. Steaks are done!"

We get situated and say a blessing. Then Jackson holds up his iced tea and encourages the rest of us to lift our drinks. "To Savannah and the University of North Georgia!"

We all take our sips and then begin passing and dishing out food while Savannah looks around and sighs. A happy, contented sigh. "I'm even more excited since we went on the official tour. I'd been over there with Jill since her older sister goes there, but after yesterday it feels real. And isn't Dahlonega the cutest little town ever?"

Another reason the week flew by: Jackson, Savannah, and I took a tour of the university over in the small mountain town of Dahlonega yesterday (less than an hour away from Chancey) after we were informed it was Savannah's destination. UNG is one of several Georgia universities she'd applied to and received online acceptances for. Jackson and I were open to anywhere in the state, but there would be no out-of-state tuition from us. She had kept most of her acceptances to herself, saying she didn't want to have to talk about it all. Not exactly surprising knowing her majesty, but still exasperating. This past week she informed us that she has decided to major in digital marketing, which is what she's been doing on a small scale at Andy's Place. She said she'd decided the theater was more a hobby for her than a career.

Holding up her plate for a helping of potatoes, she goes into great detail about the computer lab and the marketing department, then continues talking between bites. It's like all that silence on the future has built up and the dam is bursting. Jackson and I keep smiling at each other across the table and silently congratulating ourselves on this amazing young woman we would have gladly given to a pack of wolves if they'd only shown up and asked any time in the last month. But it was all worth it.

Bryan isn't feeling the magic. And because misery loves company, he spouts, "Well, Ricky, what about that ring you were getting for Savannah?"

Around the table the only one looking confused is Savannah. Jackson and I meet eyes again, with gritted teeth this time. Anna shakes her head in tiny, quick movements at her husband, but he shakes his back at her and gives her that look of "Don't worry, I know what I'm doing." Will leans his folded arms on the table and focuses on Ricky, who is seated directly across from him. "Looks like we all know. I mean, you talked to Bryan, and he talked to me, and of course I told my wife." Then he raises an eyebrow at me. "You and Dad don't seem surprised."

"Laney wanted to give us a heads-up," I explain, then frown at our youngest. "But, Bryan…" Then I don't know what to say.

Savannah fills the silence. "A ring? And why does everyone know about, uh, *it*? Ricky?"

He laughs and picks his napkin up off his lap. Then he puts it on the table, looks sweetly at Savannah, and pushes back his seat, leaning to the side as if he's getting something out of his pants pocket preparing to, well, you know. However, as I start to throw my fork at him, he laughs and moves forward, pulling his chair back up to the table.

"I'm just joking." He looks at Savannah. "Yeah, I had plans to get you a promise ring, you know, so if you'd gone off far away we'd be, you know, committed." He rolls his eyes wide. "Believe me I know how those college guys are. But no need now, since you're going to be around here. You'll still be working some at Andy's, and I can be over at the college in no time at all, so I figure we're all good. Besides, I can use the money for a down payment on a new truck."

He chuckles and puts his napkin back on his lap. "Y'all should've seen your faces when you thought I was going to propose!" He grins at us all and then puts a big piece of steak in his mouth.

Which might not have been the best idea, since the young woman to his right is clouding up like a fast-moving hurricane in the Gulf Stream. "Like a leash? You thought you'd give me a crummy little promise ring so I'd be tied to you if I strayed out of your backyard?"

Yeah, he's rethinking that mouth full of meat. "No, uh-huh.

I mean…" He's chewing and trying to swallow, but it's too late. She's standing up and tugging at his chair.

"Get out. This is supposed to be a celebration. You don't belong here."

Ricky looks around the table for support or help, but he's like one of those political appointees: he only serves here at the pleasure of Savannah.

And she's no longer pleased.

CHAPTER 49

"Whew," Bonnie exclaims. She drops onto the chair beside me in the back of Blooming Books, where I'm checking in this Monday's morning haul. She looks tired, but contented and happy. "I'm glad that is all done! No decorating jobs until after the wedding Saturday. I'm all yours this week."

"Great, but I don't know what I'm supposed to be doing for the wedding, if anything. Delaney has still not been seen anywhere near Chancey. She answers my texts, but just barely. She keeps saying, 'Everything is good.'"

"Well, Peter was anxious to get his law practice up and running before going away next week on their honeymoon. Seems to me he'd just wait until they get back, but he said he had too many clients lining up to wait." Bonnie stands up as we hear the door to Shannon and Danny's apartment open above us.

I lay down the book in my hands. "Do you believe him? I mean, what clients could he already have?"

She leans closer and whispers, "I'm thinking they're friends of Delaney's father. I heard Peter on the phone talking to Mr. LaMotte several times."

I keep my "oh really" expression silent as Shannon approaches, saying, "Will you be done back here soon? I need that table to start laying out things for my Valentine's orders. It's going to be another crazy week." Bonnie takes the bossy tone to be a sign it's a good time to go open up the shop. She waves as she walks away.

"Yep. I came in early to get this done and get out of your way." I keep my tone calm, concerned. "How are you feeling?"

"Okay, I guess. Tired but apparently that's to be expected." She sighs and sits in the chair Bonnie vacated. She lifts her chin. "Danny will be down soon. He'll be a big help doing deliveries this week." She runs her fingernail along the table and follows it with her eyes. "Um, everything with us, me and Danny, is good."

After a pause I quietly ask, "Peter?"

She shakes her head, keeping her focus on her finger. "No. I'm leaving it all alone. Danny is good with how things are. I'm good with how things are."

"But I told you what Missus said. I don't think she'll leave things alone."

Shannon looks at me. "If Peter isn't interested there's nothing she can do."

"But Peter doesn't know."

She scoffs and looks around. "He's not stupid. He doesn't want to know. He's not interested, and I'm going to go on with my life. Look how happy Patty is now. I want that." She stares at me and rubs her stomach. "Me and my baby deserve it. Danny deserves it. He already loves this baby, and he loves me." She stands up. "Peter and Delaney can have their happy ever after, and I'll have mine." She slowly walks to her worktable, and I watch her as she goes.

That's another reason things were so busy in the shop last week. Sure, we had a lot of customers, but in between them we had interminable counseling sessions.

Danny had to have it beat into his head that his vasectomy had not failed, even after he was tested at the doctor. Shannon then had to have it beat into her head that he still wanted to be with her and wanted to be the baby's daddy. I tried beating it into both of their heads that Peter should be brought up to speed, but as you can see, I failed.

So, okay. We're moving on.

"I can't believe we are in Chancey!" Beau says as we are shown to our lunch table in AC's. "Last week they had some hiccups with service, but that's to be expected with a new place. I'm ready to overlook pretty much anything to keep them open."

"Can I get you ladies something to drink? You're waiting on two more, right?" The waitress is one of Savannah's friends, and she looks nervous.

"I'll take an unsweet tea, Katie. Are you enjoying working here?" I ask.

"Yes, ma'am. It's my first day and I'm only doing a quick learning shift with permission from school. It's already been busy. I hope I'm doing everything okay. What can I get you, Miss Beau?"

"Sweet tea will be great. We're waiting for Laney and Susan, but if they're not here soon we'll need to go ahead and order. I have Janice Wenton coming in for a perm at two."

"Yes, ma'am. I'll be right back."

Beau has on a bright-pink, long-sleeve T-shirt with tight-legged black jeans. She has a colorful knitted scarf tied around her neck, and with her short red hair she looks like she could be heading off to college in the fall. She leans forward. "Okay, before they get here, what in the world is Grant doing at Chancey High?"

I open my mouth at the same time I see Susan come hurrying toward us, so I close it and shrug.

Susan pulls out the chair on my right. "Sorry I'm late. Where's Laney? She's coming, right?"

"As far as I know," I answer. "So glad Cayden is better and they could all be at church yesterday."

Susan shrugs off her black wool blazer and lets it rest on the back of her chair. "Did y'all order? I know what I'm getting. We came to the family dinner last night. It was jambalaya since Mardi Gras is next week, and it was fabulous. He said he'd have plenty for lunch today. I highly recommend it."

Beau closes her menu. "I'm sold. So I was just asking Carolina: Why is Grant going to Chancey High?"

Susan stares at her like she's thinking, then grins. "Why not? It's a good school, and all his friends are there."

Now this causes me to stare at her, but she won't look at me. Then she exclaims, "There's Laney. Laney, here we are!" She waves her hand like we're not right in the line of traffic; it's just not that big of a place.

Laney has on another of her new outfits: a long sweater tunic, big jewelry, leggings, or at least pants that are tight enough to be leggings, and short boots. This tunic has a big cowl neck and is red. With her hair teased and styled to frame her face, which is fully made up, complete with lipstick matching her sweater, she looks like a million bucks. I think the week at home with Cayden might have been just what she needed to recharge and get ready for her next chapter.

She waves Katie ahead of her, then slips around to the side to sit down. She beams up at Katie as she sits our drinks down. "Unsweet tea for me. Susan, you want sweet?"

Susan nods, and Laney dismisses Katie with another big smile and a wave. Beau interjects. "Wait, I want to order. Jambalaya with cornbread." Susan and I both agree, and Laney frowns. "I'm not ready to order yet. What do you suggest?"

Sweet Katie looks like Laney just asked her if she could dance on the table. She stammers. "Me? Oh, I don't know. I haven't eaten here yet." Then she catches her breath. "Oh, what they told us to suggest, um, let's see. Uh, the flatbread pizza and, um, a salad? Oh, Miss Laney, I forgot. I'll come right back."

Laney grabs the girl's arm. "Sweetie, no worries. Just bring me the flatbread pizza and a side salad. You're doing fine."

Katie heads off and Laney sighs. "They've been so busy they are having to hire new people already. Katie is one of Angie's classmates who can work a couple of afternoons. I guess she's in that work study program. We called it DECA, I think, but anyway it looks like the kids have a success on their hands."

Beau squeezes her lemon into her drink. "Hallelujah. Finally a decent place to eat in Chancey. So, Susan, back to Grant being at Chancey High."

I get busy putting a packet of artificial sweetener into my tea, stirring it, tasting it. Anything but looking at Susan. For some reason she doesn't want to talk about Griffin's move off the mountain. We only talked for a minute at church yesterday, but it sounded pretty matter of fact. I'm not sure why she's hesitating now. She seems nervous.

Apparently Laney is thinking the same thing watching her sister stumble and explain without really explaining anything at all. She prods. "I thought Griffin was just tired of the big house up there and wanted to be closer to you and Susie Mae and, well, us? His family."

"Of course. Of course. Beau, maybe you don't know, but he's bought a house in Summerfield."

One of Beau's perfectly waxed eyebrows arches dramatically. "Summerfield? Oh!"

Susan coughs and looks down at her lap. Laney and I look at each other. Something's going on, and we don't have a clue.

"Here's your drinks," I say, and the conversation lags while Katie sits them down. Then when it continues to lag, even after she leaves, I say, "It's a beautiful house."

Laney nods. "Yes. I love the clean, open layout." She winks at her sister. "And it's got the perfect spot for a huge garden."

Susan smiles, but it fades fast. "So that's the story. Griffin is moving down, and Grant's going to school here."

Beau is quiet, and it's really not the good kind of quiet. I'm not sure how long Laney will be able to resist asking what's going on, but there's no need to worry. She has a new project to talk about. "Girls, you are not going to believe how absolutely fabulous Ladies of the Club is going to be. Everything, absolutely everything, is just going perfectly. Vendors are coming out of the woodwork, so I'm getting to pick and choose. Missus is eating out of my hand because of this mayor thing, so every single little permit or license is like finding pine straw in Georgia. Easy peasy, puddin' and pie!"

Our food comes, and it is delicious. Just enough spice in the rich jambalaya. Hot cornbread with plenty of creamy butter. Our food gives three of us something to do while Laney talks. Usually Beau will give her a run for her money, and that is how Beau was when she and I got here, but now? She's not said two words since Susan told her Griffin's new house is in Summerfield. I could leave when she does and find out what she's not saying, but...

Something tells me I'm not sure I want to know.

Chapter 50

"I cannot stand one more minute of that woman, all those women, in my house!" Missus announces when I open the front door of our house late Monday night. Then she points to her car. "Bryan or Jackson need to get my luggage." She stares me into opening the door wider and moving out of her way. "About time you answered the door. I thought I might have to sleep out there. Where do you want me?" she demands, marching toward the B&B rooms. "I know they're all open, but I can only hope at least one of them you've had time to clean."

She'd texted me asking if we had a room open, but that was all. No response as to who it was for or when they'd check in or which one she'd prefer when I asked, since all three indeed are open.

"Well, uh, the, um, Chessie is ready. You like that one, right?" I ask, following her down the hall.

"You know me, Carolina. I'm not picky. Anywhere away from that woman and her friends." We enter the cozy Chessie room, all in cream, soft gray, and misty blue. "Did you tell Jackson to get my luggage?"

"Not yet. What's going on?"

She looks around the room and then takes off her tailored raincoat with its thick, plaid lining and hands it to me. I walk to the closet to hang it up while she sits in the chair beside the bed. "Thank you, Carolina. I am simply exhausted." She studies her hands. "Camille LaMotte has always seemed a perfectly lovely human being. I never associated with her much as I was always on the more practical side of things. The business side of things. I identify more with Delaney's father, Thompson. He's very easy to talk to. He is a man of action, and he gets things done." She sighs and leans her head back, closing her eyes. "But then I guess you could say the same for Camille. She is most certainly getting things done."

I ease myself to sit on the edge of the bed. "Things for the wedding, I assume?"

"She is clearing every stick of furniture out of my house. Well, the ground floor. I've been so graciously allowed to keep my rooms intact." She raises her head and opens her eyes. "However, the woman is a nightmare, and I might kill her if I stay in that house. Thank God I have the mayor's office to go to during the day!" She stands and looks around. "Where is Jackson with my luggage?"

"He's not here, but he'll bring in your things when he gets home." I also stand. "So, how long will you be here?"

"I have no idea. At least until Friday. Did you know they've also wrested control of the rehearsal dinner out of my hands? As in to say there isn't going to be one. Not needed, Camille, or someone, decided. So we've had no shower, no bridal luncheon, no rehearsal dinner." She strides in front of me toward the hall door. "Fine! Let's keep to our lanes until we all meet at the altar and become one big, happy family!"

I follow her out of the room and down the hall. Now that she mentions it, it is kind of weird the way this week is going. Delaney and Peter are both busy, but not with the wedding. That's under Delaney's mother's complete purview. I thought we might have guests staying here this weekend, but no. Of course, I assume most of the guests for the reception will be coming from the Atlanta suburbs, so maybe it's too close to spend the night. "Why is she emptying your house of furniture?" I ask as we walk into the kitchen. "I thought the wedding was very small, just a few family members?"

She turns to face me. "Do you want the answer I keep getting?" She takes on a deep, slow Southern accent, all old Atlanta money, dropped jaw and rounded mouth: "It's my only child's wedding. It must be just as I've always imagined despite her and her father."

"Seriously? That's completely weird."

Missus drops to sit in one of the kitchen chairs. "I must admit, Carolina. It's weird even for rich people."

Jackson and Bryan carry in Missus's luggage when they come back from Bryan's basketball practice. They also let Peter in the door.

Okay, it's not like I wouldn't have let him in the door, but well, if I'd known he was out there, I can't say if I would've opened the door exactly. Anyway, we have another Bedwell on-site. One who is just as confused as the original one, but more accepting.

"Mother, let's just ride it out. You know this is going to be a wonderful thing for all of us."

Jackson and I mouth at each other, "Thing?"

The four of us are seated in the living room. Peter has not come to move in also, thank goodness. But when he came home to find out his mother had moved out, he knew where to find her.

Missus sniffs. "It's not like I have any choice in any matter of importance any longer."

Jackson laughs. "You're the mayor."

She skewers him with both her eyes and her voice. "Importance to my family. The town is in good hands."

Peter rises slowly. "Mother, there's nothing else to talk about. I had a long day at the office. You know I have the same sort of challenges there as you do at the house, and I'm dealing with them. I'm going home. This time next week I'll be in Turks and Caicos, the LaMottes will be back home, and you'll have your house all to yourself. Now, I'm going home." He thinks for a moment. "Honestly, this is probably the best place for you to be right now. Thanks, Carolina and Jackson. Just send me Mother's bill."

She bristles. "I can pay my own bill."

He wearily turns to her. "But can you?" They stare at each other, and then he heads to the door but says to Jackson as he passes him, "I'll take care of it. All bills should come to me from now on."

Missus doesn't say anything. Then she angrily stands and rushes out of the room. We all stare after her until we hear the door to the Chessie room slam shut.

"Thanks again. Mother is still getting used to how things are now that Dad is gone. I'm really glad she won the mayoral race so she has something to do other than try to boss me around." Peter opens the door and steps onto the porch.

We step outside behind him, and I ask, "How's Delaney doing?"

"Fine. She's busy. We just both want to get this wedding over with." He chuckles before he steps down the three steps. "I guess everyone can see that. We're just ready to get on with our lives. Our new lives as one family."

We wave and watch him get in his car, and then we bustle back into the warmth and light of the house. Jackson pulls me into a hug, and we stay like that for a long moment. Then in my ear he says, "There's not enough money in the world."

He is so right.

CHAPTER 51

Everyone in Chancey agrees with Peter by Valentine's Day morning: we all just want this wedding to be over with.

There's not been a parking space available on the square all week. Luxury cars, moving trucks, and delivery vans have come and gone and stayed, stayed, stayed! By Thursday no one not affiliated with the wedding was coming downtown, so much so that Ruby closed. Closed! She took Thursday and Friday off and headed out of town for a long weekend to visit Jewel in Florida. We stayed open because we are a florist and it is Valentine's week. AC's is catering the reception at the depot, so they've been very busy. They had customers because all these people had to eat somewhere and, after all, the groom is a part owner. I didn't really sell many books, but I did enjoy watching all the hubbub, and we put up signs blocking off our spots behind the shop, so there was no problem parking for us.

But finally, the big day is here, and I'm headed up the front steps of Missus's house with Anna and Will. Jackson wasn't actually invited to the ceremony—I know, strange, right?—but that was fine by him, so he's at our house taking care of Francie.

Something else extremely strange? I've not seen Delaney this whole week. I've not even met her mother, though Missus says that is not a loss. Missus has been busy every day as Madam Mayor, and in the evenings she's kept to her room. She's been very quiet, and I'm not complaining. But like I said, we are all so very glad this will all be over today.

Anna whispers, "They repainted the porch. All of it, the trim, the ceiling. Wonder how long these flowers will last out here. It's only going to get colder." There are baskets of dusty-pink heirloom roses, sage-green eucalyptus in bunches or sprays, and then cream-colored baby's breath in bunches with the roses, the eucalyptus, and alone. It looks lovely with the matching paint scheme of the porch. Yep, the salmon and mint green are gone. The porch now coordinates with the wedding flowers. Things like this have made me be very sweet to Missus this week. Well, pretty sweet.

It's been one jaw-dropping story after another. As Laney reminded me, Peter is now in control of everything, and he's given carte blanche to Camille LaMotte. I can't wait to meet her, which should be happening very soon.

"Welcome to the Bedwell home," a gentleman in a black tuxedo greets us as he opens the door. "May I take your coats?"

Anna steps farther into the entrance hall as another gentleman helps her take her coat off. He takes hers and mine, and walks off to our left while she says to the man who spoke to us, "Hello. I'm Anna Jessup. Um, Peter's niece."

He bows to her just a little. "Of course, Mrs. Jessup, and this is your husband and mother-in-law." He turns to me. "Mrs. Jessup, if you'll wait right here I will take your son and daughter-in-law to their seats and come take you to Miss LaMotte. She's waiting for you."

"Oh, I didn't know…" I start to explain, but he's walking away. Missus was right. The house looks empty except for flowers, which match the few couches and chairs scattered around the room: dusty pink, sage green, and cream. I'm glad my dress is a darker taupe or I might get lost in the sheer fabric draped on the walls. Every wall is covered, and it looks not exactly good, but not bad. More like a hotel banquet hall. But I don't believe I'll share that opinion with Mrs. Camille LaMotte. I can't see into the living room where the gentleman took Anna and Will, so I don't know who else is here. So far all I've seen are young men in black tuxes. There's low chatter coming from the living room. Wonder how many were invited to the ceremony? I know there are over a hundred coming to the reception, and even with snow forecasted, no one is missing that.

"This way, Mrs. Jessup," the man says as he approaches me. He holds out his arm for me to take his elbow, so I do. We walk down past the dining room, and he knocks on a door that I believe was F.M.'s library. When the door opens, sure enough there are books, but I don't believe this is Missus's furniture. It definitely is not the furniture F.M. would have in his library. It's all white wicker with dusty pink cushions. Even here the smell of old roses and spicy eucalyptus prevails. The man hands me into the room and then closes the door behind me.

"Oh, Carolina. I'm so glad you're here," Delaney says as she hurries across the room to me.

"Did you want me to come earlier? I could've."

"No. No, everything is perfect. I'm just so ready to walk down the aisle."

I reach out to her. "This dress is incredible." Her ivory dress is fitted with net sleeves and a net overlay. Intricate pearl and silver beading covers the bodice and accents the sleeves. The neckline is low, but covered with the netting and lighter beadwork. She swirls to show me the back where the beading accents a floor-length train, gathered at her waist where the plunging back comes to a point. Her hair is softly pulled back from her face and gathered in the back, where curls and waves fall. She turns back to me and smiles. Her makeup is done, and she looks so excited. Finally. It's good to be reminded this is a good day. A happy day.

She holds her arms out. "You can see I let Mother have her way. This dress cost as much as a car, and you saw what she's done to the house. I almost fainted when I got here this morning and saw it all. I can't imagine what it cost, but she's happy and"—she pauses her blur of words for a sharp laugh to leap out—"it's a dream come true. Absolutely a dream come true in so many ways." She whirls around again, and I catch her when she stumbles a bit.

"Delaney? Are you okay?" She seems almost feverish, and some of what I took to be a professional makeup job is actually her cheeks being flushed. "Here, sit down."

We sit on the couch with her clasping my hands. "Hasn't Mother gone completely overboard with decorating? It's atrocious, and I doubt Missus will ever forgive me, but..." She shrugs. "It won't matter in just a few minutes. Nothing else will matter. Oh, Carolina, you have no idea."

I laugh. "You're right. I don't. Can I get you anything? Some water? Or maybe a Xanax?"

"Not today. I can't believe I pulled it off." She grabs me in a hug. "I'm just so happy."

Another knock on the door causes her to pull away. "Come in."

A tall, heavyset man steps inside as we stand. "It's time. Oh, this must be Miss Carolina. Thompson LaMotte. Thank you for all you've done. You've made my daughter a very happy person." He strides across the room and takes my hand in his. "Camille and I look forward to getting more familiar with Chancey and everything about it. This day has been a long time coming."

Delaney crosses past us to the door, then turns back to us. "Is he out there?"

Her father nods and smiles at me. "Miss Carolina, your escort down the aisle awaits, and then we'll follow you."

I take a deep breath. "It's crazy, but I'm nervous. I guess not having a rehearsal, I'm just a little off-kilter."

He laughs and pats my hand. "It's a very short, simple ceremony. Gregory will walk you down the aisle, which is only a few yards to where the minister is standing beside the front windows. You'll simply step to the left, and he'll step to the right to stand beside Peter. Then Delaney and I will enter, and the rest will flow from there. Afterward, you and Gregory will follow the newlyweds back down the aisle, and it will all be a done deal."

I nod, but the way he said "done deal" causes goose bumps to sprout on my arms. Something is just not right. The father of the bride laying all this out for me? Wouldn't you think there would be a wedding coordinator or one of her mother's friends to do that? He motions me to the door, and as it opens Delaney comes up beside me and says under her breath, "He's right out there."

"Yes, Peter's right out there, and soon you'll be standing beside him." A peal of laughter makes me jerk my head around to look at her.

She shakes her head and waves a hand in front of her face. "Ignore me. I'm just excited. Now go. Go."

Mr. LaMotte opens the door, and I step out.

"Gregory, this is Mrs. Jessup. Oh, and here are your flowers." He hands me a beautiful, large bouquet, really large enough to be the bridal bouquet. I smell it and then look up as Delaney's father goes back into the room.

A young man comes toward me, and all the joy and excitement I just left behind me is nowhere to be found. Gregory looks terrified. I hold my hand out to him. "You can call me Carolina. Nice to meet you."

He nods and offers me his elbow. He's a nice-looking young man. Younger than I thought. I think he's younger than Will, but then again, Delaney only said he was a friend of the family, so I didn't really know what to expect.

"We have to wait for the music to change," he says, so we stand near the bottom of the staircase where we can't be seen.

"Do they have live music?" I whisper.

He shrugs. "I don't know. Sounds like it. I just got here a minute ago."

"Me too. Kind of weird, don't you think?" As I say that, the music stops, and Gregory tenses.

"Weird doesn't even begin to describe it. Here we go."

"What?" But then we are moving, and I face straight ahead. There are way fewer guests than I ever imagined in the room. Anna and Will are seated beside Missus, and that's all on that side. Peter stands in front of them. On the other side are only two women. One is wearing a corsage, so I assume she is Camille LaMotte. She doesn't look that scary. I feel a tug on my arm, and I realize Gregory is trying to disengage. We are already at the front. I give him a smile and step away. I get in place and look across to smile at Will, who gives me a little salute and a wink. He's getting to be so much like his dad.

Then the music, which is apparently not live but still really nice, changes in tempo, and the minister motions for everyone—all eight of us—to stand. As I turn to look at Delaney coming down the aisle, I see that Anna has taken Missus's arm and that Missus hasn't turned at all to watch the bride walking toward the front. Anna is whispering in her grandmother's ear, and then I see that Peter has noticed his mother is staring at him. I guess the emotion has finally gotten to Missus. I pull my attention away from them as Delaney nears. Do I take her bouquet now? No one mentioned that, but isn't that normal? Or do I take it during the ceremony?

When they arrive at the altar, there's no asking about who is giving Delaney's hand by the minister, which makes sense; they are grown adults. Mr. LaMotte kisses his daughter's cheek, pulls away from her, and sits down alongside his wife. The four of us in the wedding party turn to face the minister, and he begins. He goes straight for the official ceremony. No welcome, nothing flowery, just the facts, ma'am. Then he has Peter and Delaney face each other for their vows, and at that point she hands me her flowers. I take them and look up to see Peter's face. He looks nervous, but no more than you'd expect. Delaney's hand is shaking in his, so he squeezes it, then smiles at her. Behind Peter I look up to meet my counterpart's eyes and give the young man a smile. But he's staring at Delaney much like Peter is. No, *exactly* as Peter is, and I gasp.

Gregory is Peter's son, or I'm a dusty-pink heirloom rose with a eucalyptus chaser.

Chapter 52

"The minister said, 'I now present to you Mr. and Mrs. Peter Bedwell,' and Delaney stepped in front of Peter and said, 'Peter, I now present to you Gregory Duvall, your son.'" I'm talking furiously fast into my phone as Jackson and I are driving to the depot for the reception. I'd already called Susan and told her the news, and now I have Laney on the phone. I would never survive living in Chancey if I let them show up to the reception ignorant of this.

Laney exclaims, "I'm not waiting on the babysitter to show up. We're coming now even if we have to bring Cayden with us! I'll see you soon."

Dropping my phone into the cup holder, I lay my head back against my seat and close my eyes. "I feel like I've been talking nonstop since I left Missus's house. Poor Missus. She was completely blindsided. I mean, so was Peter, but she just couldn't believe it. She thought she and Mr. LaMotte had put together this wedding. She felt all in control—of course not about the house and moving up to our place, but about putting Peter and Delaney together. Come to find out, she was as much of a pawn as Peter."

"But why didn't Delaney just tell Peter?" Jackson is slowly driving down our hill, and the late afternoon sky is heavy. It feels like snow, but hopefully most of it won't come until later.

He shakes his head again. "Even years ago, but especially once they got back together?"

I take a deep breath. I can't remember what I've told who, so I just go back to the beginning. "She explained to us all right there after the ceremony that she gave Gregory up as a baby to be raised by her aunt who had been a nun. She was the other woman there beside Camille; she's Mr. LaMotte's sister. She left the convent and raised him over in South Carolina as her son; Duvall is her middle name, an old family name. So she dropped LaMotte and took Duvall for her and Gregory's last name. Delaney and Peter had broken up when she found out he was cheating on her. She left school, never telling him she was pregnant. Gregory knew Mrs. Duvall wasn't his real mother, and I guess had suspected Delaney wasn't his cousin but his mother. Then when he turned eighteen they told him the truth. But he wanted to know who his father was. Delaney told us she'd sworn to herself and her parents that she'd never risk Peter taking him away. She said they decided the best way to make sure of that was for her to marry him. She assured everyone she loved Peter and they were now going to be a happy family."

Jackson scoffs as he drives past Blooming Books. In the lights we can see that the snow has begun. "That's just crazy."

"Except I believe she's truly still in love with Peter. This is seriously a dream come true for her."

"But if she loves him why didn't she tell him the truth after they were engaged?"

"This is where I think her father comes into play. He knew all about the way F.M. had the Bedwell money distributed and decided this was the best way. Plus, I don't think he's a nice man. I think he liked pulling one over on Missus and his new son-in-law. It was kind of creepy how much he enjoyed the whole thing. He is very much a man used to being in control."

We pull into the parking lot, and the snow is really coming down. Jackson looks out his window and says, "I think we should check the weather forecast before we go in. I do not want to get stuck down in town if the roads get icy."

My phone chimes, and I look at it. "Oh, that's Laney. They aren't coming. Their babysitter's parents won't let her drive with the snow coming, and Shaw is concerned about the roads out where they are anyway."

We sit in the warm car watching the snow and trying to get up the desire to go inside to the craziness we know awaits. There's a knock on Jackson's window.

Griffin and Susan are outside the window, and Griffin yells, "Y'all coming in?"

We look at each other and shrug. "For a little while will be okay," I say to my reluctant husband.

We get out of the car, and Susan gets close to me as the guys walk on ahead. "Okay, that was the craziest thing I've ever heard. How did Peter take it?"

"Pretty good. Gregory seems like a nice kid. Goes to Elon and is majoring in pre-law. If you're going to get handed a kid, that's not a bad way to start. Gregory only found out last night who his dad is and knew he'd meet him today. Explains why he was so terrified-looking when I met him."

Susan looks around and then, tugging on my coat sleeve, pulls me back farther from the guys. With her head close to mine she asks, "So, what did Beau have to say the other day after lunch?"

"Beau? Nothing, why? She left before we did, and I haven't talked to her."

She doesn't say anything, so I ask again, "Why?"

"She just seemed awfully interested that Griffin's new house is in Summerfield."

"Oh, yeah, you're right; she did." I slow us down before we get to the steps. "Do you know why?"

She shakes her shoulders and sniffs. "Not really. Just rumors. Did Laney text you that they aren't coming? I don't know how long we're going to stay. Griffin says we need to put in an appearance since several board members of Mountain Power will be here. But I don't think we'll be here long."

I nudge her and grin. "Well, Griffin doesn't have to go all the way up the mountain if the roads get bad. He could stay with you, right?"

She stops walking altogether and turns to me. Her eyes are shiny, and she shakes her head. "He just wants to be friends."

I'm truly surprised. I already had them in the *back together* category in my head. "Oh, Susan. I'm sorry, but that's not a bad place to start. Y'all have a lot of history. He'll figure things out." She shrugs and moves on up the stairs ahead of me. I don't understand why she's acting like there's no hope. However, she doesn't have a lot of patience, and in her mind they were already back together and living in their dream home.

Jackson waits at the door to go inside with me. He holds it open for Susan to enter behind Griffin.

Instead of keeping the door open for me, though, he pushes it closed and pulls me to the side of the porch. This front corner looks down the train tracks, and we stand there, wrapped up together, our faces turned into the dark. I finally lean back to look up at him. "Are you okay?"

He grips his tongue between his lips for a moment, staring into the dark. "Griffin is seeing someone. He says you know her."

"What? I know her? Who is it?"

He frowns. "Athena? I got the idea she's younger than us."

"Athena Markum? Yeah, she is definitely younger than us." I slap my mouth. "She lives in Summerfield."

"Yep. That's the one. He wants us to have dinner with them next weekend."

I back away. "Not happening. Ever. What a jerk!"

"Hey, don't be mad at me. I'm as shocked as you."

I move back into his arms, and then we walk to the doors. Inside we can see Peter and his son. "Wow," Jackson says. "They really do look alike. But, you know, they look happy."

Missus is sitting beside them with Delaney's arm around her. I chuckle. "Missus still looks shocked, but she really didn't handle it too badly."

"Well, she had a baby she gave away that ended with Anna, so she knows things can turn out okay."

I nod. "That's right. I'd almost forgotten about all that. These people that want everything to be perfect seem to be the very ones hiding a lot of mess." The long table of food looks good and the bar well-stocked, but as I look around the room I know where I want to be. "This snow is pretty scary, and we do live on top of a big, big hill."

Jackson laughs and tightens his arm around me. "I can make us a fire, we have those little marshmallows for hot chocolate, and you do know all the words to 'Let it Snow.'"

With my hands grasping the lapels of his coat, I pull him around to face me. "One more condition, buddy: Did you buy me a big, red heart box of candy?"

He slowly shakes his head, then grins and nods. "Of course I did." His eyes droop into a sappy, lovesick look. "Carolina Jessup, will you be my valentine?"

"The chocolate tips the scales. Sure thing, Mr. Jessup. Now let's go home and leave these people to figure out their own lives." My voice goes all sultry as I pull him with me away from the door. "We have chocolate to deal with."

Following me down the steps, he gooses me, and I yelp as I dart out into the falling snow laughing. He's right behind me, and I let him catch me for a kiss in the swirling flakes. He wraps me up and mutters into my hair, "And little marshmallows, Mrs. Jessup. Don't forget the marshmallows."

Sign up for my newsletter and check out all my books at
www.kaydewshostak.com

I love being friends with readers on Facebook.

Thank you for your reviews on Amazon!

The tenth book in the Chancey series will be coming next year, but the fourth in the The Southern Beach Mysteries series releases later this year.

Books by Kay Shostak

The Chancey Books

Next Stop, Chancey
Chancey Family Lies
Derailed in Chancey
Chancey Jobs
Kids Are Chancey
A Chancey Detour
Secrets Are Chancey
Chancey Presents

Florida Books

Backwater, Florida
Wish You Were Here

Southern Beach Mysteries

The Manatee Did It
The Sea Turtle Did It
The Shrimp Did It
The Shark Did It (Coming Late 2021)

CPSIA information can be obtained
at www.ICGtesting.com
Printed in the USA
FSHW021154280421
80747FS

9 781735 099132